St. Martin's Paperbacks Titles By
Christine Warren

BIG BAD WOLF

YOU'RE SO VEIN

ONE BITE WITH A STRANGER

WALK ON THE WILD SIDE

HOWL AT THE MOON

THE DEMON YOU KNOW

SHE'S NO FAERIE PRINCESS

WOLF AT THE DOOR

Anthologies

HUNTRESS

NO REST FOR THE WITCHES

THE DEMON YOU KNOW

A NOVEL OF THE OTHERS

Christine Warren

St. Martin's Paperbacks

THE DEMON YOU KNOW

Copyright © 2007 by Christine Warren.

All rights reserved.

For information address St. Martin's Press, 175 Fifth Avenue, New York, NY 10010.

ISBN: 978-0-312-36589-9

Printed in the United States of America

St. Martin's Paperbacks edition / May 2007

St. Martin's Paperbacks are published by St. Martin's Press, 175 Fifth Avenue, New York, NY 10010.

10 9 8 7 6 5

To my best girlfriends.
Delicate flowers, each and every one.

PROLOGUE

*t*he demon called Rule shifted restlessly in the plush leather club chair in the library of Vircolac and struggled not to look as impatient as he felt. Judging by the grin on Rafael De Santos's face, he was failing miserably.

"Believe me," the Felix said, swirling a brandy snifter in one elegant hand, "it's not that I don't sympathize with your predicament. I do. Completely. It's just that after the past six weeks it is so refreshing to be listening to someone *else's* problems for a change."

"Your problems were of your own making. Had you truly wished to remain hidden from the humans, I am sure you could have found a way."

Rule knew the accusation was unfair, but he wasn't in the mood to play fair. He wasn't in the mood to play at all. Not after relating the story he'd just spent the better part of an hour telling to his host in the mortal world.

It was one thing to fight a war when your focus was on surviving from day to day, on doing what had to be done. It was quite another to hear yourself explain it to an outsider in all its hideousness. And Rule hadn't been feeling exactly chipper to begin with.

He'd just spent close to a year tracking down a reliable informant to keep him apprised of the activities of the fiend Uzkiel. Five days ago, the informant had disappeared along with Rule's best chance of discovering exactly how said fiend planned to launch a full-scale war against the rest of the Below and the Watch, the demon police force that kept its kind in check. Rule felt entitled to his bad attitude.

De Santos shook his head. "I wish it had been that simple. But progress is unavoidable, my friend. Especially the kind we most wish to avoid."

"How comforting you are," Rule muttered.

"Ah, but you didn't come here for comfort, did you?" As head of the Council of Others, De Santos had a special talent for perception. Or maybe he had risen to head of the Council because of that perception. Either way, it was a quality Rule recognized and grudgingly respected. "We have not seen you Above in the past year, in spite of our reassurances that you would always be welcome among us. Your assistance in the matter of Dionnu and his minions will not be forgotten anytime soon."

Rule shrugged off the thanks. He hadn't helped defeat the Faerie king out of the goodness of his heart, so he didn't need praise for it. It had been just another part of his job. "I have been busy with my own concerns Below. You and the Lupines seemed to have your situation well in hand."

"So, what is it that has finally brought you back to us?"

Draining his own brandy without so much as a blink, Rule debated for a moment how best to tell the other man his news without causing undue alarm. Too bad there wasn't such a way.

"I . . . seem to be missing a fiend."

Unlike many Others, who tended to be a temperamental lot—shape-shifters especially—De Santos had earned a reputation during his life for his eerie calm in even the most stressful situations. For that reason, he didn't leap to his feet and shout his demand for an explanation, as much as Rule guessed he must be wanting to. Instead, he carefully crossed one ankle over the opposite knee and raised a dark eyebrow. "I beg your pardon?"

The steel beneath the polite question made it impossible for Rule to mistake that calm for disinterest. The Felix was not happy with this news. Rule had not expected him to be. The last time fiends had been set loose in Manhattan, people had died, humans and Others alike. It had not made the head of the Council a happy werejaguar.

"Not one you need to be terribly concerned with," Rule clarified before he had another battle on his hands. "It is a minor fiend with few powers and fewer brain cells. Not terribly evil and not terribly ambitious. It only concerns me because I have been using it to gather information on the activities of the fiends I *am* worried about. We have reason to believe a sect of fiends may be planning some kind of attack on

Infernium, so I can't afford to lose the information this small fiend has been able to supply me."

De Santos looked only vaguely reassured, not that he likely cared all that much whether the largest of the cities Below stood or fell. "And you think that this fiend might have come up Above? I thought you were going to make sure that didn't happen after the last time."

The demon gave his host a bland stare. "And how easy do you find it securing your own borders? Mundane or magical."

"Point taken. Still, I'm not sure how much I'll be able to help you in locating this fiend. Manhattan is a large place, figuratively speaking, and if the creature has a brain in its head, I would think it would be keeping a low profile and staying out of places where it might run into one of my people."

"Like I said, it is not very smart."

De Santos smiled. "Ah, yes. Well, certainly I will keep my eyes and ears open and let you know if I hear anything. But if I were you, I would not wait by my telephone, as it were."

"I do not plan to," Rule said, setting aside his empty glass and pushing to his feet. "I had mostly intended to visit you as a courtesy, since I had entered your territory uninvited, but I decided it could not hurt to apprise you of the situation just in case some information happened to knock on your front door and present itself to you."

The Felix rose as well and offered his hand. "You would be the first to know, my friend. But what are your plans in the meantime?"

Rule shrugged and let his hand drop to the hilt of the sword he'd set beside his chair during their meeting. "I'll do what a soldier of the Watch is trained to do. Find the fiend and eliminate it, before it has the chance to do the same to anyone else."

CHAPTER ONE

Abby Baker crouched in her hiding place between two parked cars and cursed the day she was born.

Well, okay, she didn't curse the day she was born. She didn't curse at all. Good Catholic girls like her didn't do things like that. Not even when their current situations practically begged for a nice, juicy expletive.

Considering that her main preoccupation of the moment had to do with staying alive and uninjured, getting upset with her own nativity wouldn't have made a lot of sense. Instead, she chewed on the remains of her right thumbnail and tried to decide who needed a good divine intervention more just now, her or Terry.

To be honest, if Abby had been ready to take up cursing, it would make more sense for her to curse the day Terry Freeman had been born, since he was the one who'd gotten her into this mess. Or to curse the day she'd been stupid enough to agree to accompany him into the middle of a riot.

A swell in the volume of the chaos surrounding

her had her peering out from behind a dented fender and into a normally quiet street in the Garment District. The glow of a burning vacant building made it no struggle to see what was going on, but Abby wasn't certain she could count that as a good thing. The fire department said they had the blaze contained, so it wasn't in danger of spreading, but that was about the only danger that had been contained in a five-block radius.

Angry figures with angry voices filled the streets from about two blocks behind Abby to the small neighborhood square two blocks ahead. They were protesting the same thing people had been protesting all over the country for the last six weeks: the unbelievable, surreal, and highly disturbing knowledge that the things that go bump in the night were also going bump in the day. Quite possibly in the apartment next door.

It was too freaky to be real, except for the fact that it was, and the entire world had seen the video footage to prove it. Less than two months ago, an international press conference carried live on all the major American networks, CNN, MSNBC, FOX News, the BBC, Al Jazeera, and Television Borneo, for all Abby knew, had revealed that vampires, witches, faeries, werewolves, werecats, werebears, and were-everythings didn't just exist, they voted. And on top of that, they had been secretly negotiating for the past two years to secure their civil rights with the human governments of the world.

It had been the real-life equivalent of Orson Welles's *War of the Worlds* broadcast, and nothing

on earth had been the same since. In fact, after all of
this, news of an alien invasion would likely make
the average New Yorker yawn and roll his eyes.

Maybe her mother hadn't been exaggerating when
she called her daughter's defection from their small
town upstate to the big, bad city "Abby's descent into
the fiery pit." Even if it had been meant as a joke.

At the moment, it hit uncomfortably close to home.

Right now, the neighborhood around her did look
a bit like some distorted version of hell. Or at least
of a war zone. Abby wouldn't have been a bit surprised to see a tank rolling down 7th Avenue tonight.
In fact, she might even have welcomed it. Soldiers
were supposed to help the civilian victims in armed
conflicts, weren't they?

The average protester on the streets around her
may have started out armed with nothing more dangerous than poster board and a loud mouth—which
was more than dangerous enough, thanks—but as
night had descended on the city, tempers had short-
ened and Abby thought she spied more than one
makeshift weapon in the crowd. The whole situation
had degenerated into a seething mass of blunt-force
trauma just waiting to happen.

Abby's free hand rose to finger the small gold and
garnet cross she wore around her neck, and she wondered for the millionth time in the last ten minutes
how on earth she'd gotten herself into this situation.

*C'mon, Abby. This is my big break; I can feel it.
You gotta help me.*

Terry's wheedling voice echoed in her head and
answered her unvoiced question.

Terry Wayne Freeman had been the instrument of her downfall, not because he was a tool of Satan, precisely; Terry was just really good at wheedling. The youngest of five kids growing up in Harlem with parents who worked around the clock to support them, he had developed a formidable charm against which even the strongest soul became powerless. He'd even put himself through his last two years of journalism classes at CUNY by running a three-card monte stand near Times Square.

Abby liked to delude herself that it wasn't the wheedling that got her, though; it was the begging.

Abby, please. Gus says I can take the old backup van and equipment if I can find someone to help me operate it. It's all like ten years out-of-date, but what the hell. Once he sees the tapes, it's not gonna matter. This is my chance. I'm sure of it.

His big brown eyes had pleaded with her, and he'd squeezed her hand like she was the source of all salvation. Sheesh, did she have "sucker" tattooed on her forehead, or what?

Please, Ab. You gotta help me. I'll owe you so big, I'll be doing you favors on the other side of the pearly gates. I swear it. If you'll just please, please, please help me out here.

She was supposed to say no to that?

"Though I have all faith, so that I could remove mountains, and have not charity, I am nothing."

Was this really the right moment for a recitation of her grandmother's favorite passage from Corinthians? The "charity" Abby had felt toward a twenty-year-old kid with a Cronkite complex had landed her so close to those pearly gates he'd mentioned, she figured she could have given Saint Peter some fashion tips.

She must have been high on fumes from her correction fluid when she'd agreed to help Terry out. For pity's sake, she was a junior researcher. A glorified gofer! She had no business being in the same room as a TV camera, let alone pretending to operate one. She must have lost her mind.

Abby Baker had always been the boring one, the girl voted Most Likely to Be Forgotten. The kind who gave the old-fashioned term "wallflower" a new lease on life. It wasn't that people disliked her; they just tended to . . . overlook her. Part of that had been due to the painful shyness she'd carried with her all through her school days, but part of it was just because she was infinitely overlookable. She had plain features, plain brown hair, and a plain, if slightly well-padded, body. The only unusual thing about her was her mismatched eyes, one blue and one brown, and those tended to make people too uncomfortable for them to dig much past the rest of her plain brown wrapper.

Eventually, in college she'd learned to force herself past the shyness. She had friends, but they tended to be nearly as quiet as she was. None of them lived in the fast lane. Heck, she didn't think any of them had even made it to the highway; they tended to stick to the pedestrian walkways.

So why in heaven's name had her life chosen this moment to start getting interesting?

A tattoo of racing footsteps had Abby ducking back between the parked cars. She knew hiding wasn't helping her out of the situation those correction fluid fumes had landed her in, but that didn't mean she was ready to give up the strategy. Or to, you know, stop quaking in fear.

She watched as several sets of boots ran past and groaned when she saw the military fatigues tucked into the tops of them. Apparently, the mayor had made good on his threat to call out the National Guard if the protesters got out of hand again. She couldn't fault the decision, only the timing of it. He should have gotten the situation in hand weeks ago, instead of letting it build to the flash point like this.

She added it to the list of the politician's sins. Since the press had uncovered the fact that the mayor had known about the plan for a massive worldwide supernatural revelation at least a week before the general populace, the list had grown to epic proportions. Abby thought it might have been a good idea for him to have a plan in place from the beginning, just in case the public didn't deal well with the news of the millennium.

That was just a theory, since she wasn't actually a politician or anything, but she didn't think it sounded unreasonable.

The only thing that sounded unreasonable to her at the moment was spending the rest of the night crouched in the gutter between a couple of old clunkers. Not only did she feel ridiculous, but her legs had begun to cramp up on her too. Terry was still nowhere to be seen, but that didn't mean she couldn't find a way back to the news van and into her apartment in the quiet of Greenwich Village on her own. She was a big girl, twenty-seven, smart, single, and perfectly able to take care of herself. She could even do it without indulging in a self-pity party.

Probably.

Venturing another glance out into the street, Abby grimaced. The sight of the crowds of protesters and the sound of soldiers shouting as they tried to regain order failed to reassure her of her safety.

She looked around a nearly bald tire and scanned the rows of parked vehicles for her getaway car. The van she and Terry had driven here sat at the curb about half a block away, waiting for the perfect escape, taunting her with its nearness. Fifty feet away and it may as well have been fifty miles. At least three dozen very unhappy protesters, some of them brandishing their signposts like clubs, stood between her and it. Since she couldn't get to the stupid thing, she felt rather inclined to resent its existence.

Somewhere in the neighborhood a wolf howled, and a moment later the sound of sirens added a distinctive wail to the established pandemonium.

Abby grimaced. Just the trifecta they needed to round out the evening: police, ambulances, and a werewolf.

Abby still couldn't get used to thinking the *w* word like that, with no hesitation and no "and Lon Chaney Jr. as" thoughts anywhere in sight. But considering it had only been six weeks since the Unveiling announcement, as it was being called, she figured she could cut herself a little slack.

It wasn't every day that the whole fabric of a

girl's reality shifted to admit the entire cast of the Sci-Fi Channel's October lineup. Thank God. Everything still had a bit of a surreal quality to it, as if this were all some sort of dream of a collective consciousness and in a while everyone would wake up and forget about vampires until Hollywood released a new John Carpenter movie or Anne Rice published a new book.

It was only when things like a bit of cinder blew onto Abby's skin and singed her that she admitted this whole thing wasn't a dream and she could end up spending the night in a jail cell with the anti-Other protesters if she didn't get her butt in gear and into that van in the next ninety seconds.

Muttering the Hail Mary under her breath, Abby yanked hard on the remains of her courage and duck-walked to the edge of her hiding place to survey the current situation.

The main body of the crowd was still in the square about a block and a half up, but since the protest had devolved into chaos a couple of hours ago, rioters had been moving closer and closer to her concealment. She could hear groups of them chanting slogans the KKK would have been ashamed of, which was precisely the thing the crowd needed to shift the mood from tense to ugly. She felt the shift as clearly as if someone had just flipped off a light switch and plunged the neighborhood into darkness.

Now might be the time to make a break for it.

"Hey, freak! Where do you think you're going?"

The question, issued in a sneering shout, was definitely as unattractive as the new mood of the crowd, but what concerned Abby was that it sounded as if it had come from right next to her hidey-hole.

Mouthing another prayer and wishing she'd worn her rosary to work that morning, she braced the palms of her hands against the gritty pavement and peeked into the street.

She craned her head to the side until she could see the designer sneakers and baggy, beat-up blue jeans of the young man who had just spoken. Her gaze traveled up the jeans and over the muscular, tattooed arms that looked as if they'd been drawn on by a three-year-old with ADD and a morbid imagination. The hoodlum wore a basketball jersey at least three sizes too big, and if she hadn't seen the patchy stubble covering his acne-marked face, she would have pegged him as too young to grow a beard. Revising her estimate of his chronological age upward and his emotional age downward, she pegged him as old enough to know better but clearly too stupid to care.

He had been leaning against the car to Abby's left, but he and his two identically aggressive yet empty-headed companions pushed away from it. Like a wall of muscle and menace, they shifted their stances to loom over a slim teenager with wide brown eyes and two stubby little horns peeking out from among his mud-colored curls.

Sweet Lord.

Abby's stomach twisted in time with her conscience. The kid wasn't human. You'd think an Other would know better than to go wandering through this neighborhood tonight. Just because Terry hadn't gotten a chance to file a story about the demonstrations before he ran screaming into the night didn't mean the news outlets wouldn't have mentioned them. And that meant walking into the middle of one of those riots without even trying to blend in with the human crowd came close to suicidal—not to mention idiotic. What, the kid didn't own a baseball cap?

"I-I'm sorry?" the Other stammered, looking confused.

"You should be." Hoodlum number one's friends snickered at his witticism and egged him on. "Little unnatural freak like you ought to apologize for breathing the same air as us humans."

The three thugs took a menacing step forward, and Abby winced. The Other just stood there, wide-eyed and vulnerable, like a brain-damaged gazelle in a pack of hyenas. Why didn't he run or turn into a werewildebeest or cast a spell or something? If he wasn't going to be human, shouldn't he at least know how to defend himself against them? Or against, you know, anything? It's not like Abby would have taken a stroll through a gathering of werewolves without a silver bullet or two on hand.

"Pardon me?"

"Yeah, you should apologize." The ringleader bared his teeth and flexed his tattoos as he turned to sneer at his friends. "I think Goat Boy is starting to get the idea."

The other two stooges began to sidle around the sides of the Other, penning him between them and the line of parked cars.

"I wonder what else we could teach him?" thug number two said.

"How 'bout a lesson?" thug number three growled, just before he took the first swing.

Stifling a surprisingly girlish squeak, Abby fumbled with her pockets, searching for her cell phone. She wasn't quite sure what she was going to tell the emergency services operator—"Yes, I know the police are already on the scene, but could you just send them two blocks down, please? Tell them to look for a beige Dodge Dart and an orange Chevelle with an idiot on a cell phone hunkered down between them"?—but she couldn't just sit there and watch three jerks kick the crap out of someone half their size.

The kid might not be human, but he was still a person, right? That's what all the press conferences and news releases and public-service announcements the Others had been airing for the past few weeks had been saying anyway, and Abby liked to think she kept an open mind.

She patted herself down, searching from pocket to pocket, until her stomach took a sharp dive straight into her tennis shoes.

She'd left her cell phone in the van.

She remembered now. Terry had borrowed it to call the station and beg Gus one more time for a real cameraman, not that it had done him any good. Then, instead of handing it back to her, he'd set it down on the center console while he gave her a crash course in operating the clunky old video cam. She should have dropped the darned thing on his head and caught the first subway back to her apartment. As it was, she'd dropped it anyway when Terry had taken off, and she'd been too busy looking for a place to hide to worry what happened to it.

Torn between Good Samaritanism and self-preservation, Abby eyed the distance between her and the van, then looked back at the violence blocking her way, tempted to write this whole thing off as a clear example of the principle of every man for himself.

She'd almost done it, too, when she saw the third hoodlum land a punch to the Other's kidney that had the kid staggering backward with a pained cry. That's when her conscience kicked into overdrive and her common sense went on a three-week cruise to Bimini. Maybe her brother had been right when he told her she'd spent too many weekends in Sunday school. . . .

Her legs protested as she slowly rose from her concealing crouch into a slightly more upright crouch that she hoped would not gain her any unwanted attention. She had no plans to stick her face in the way of any of those flying fists, but if she could sneak past them, she could make a run for the van, call 911, and be back in her apartment without a pit stop in jail *or* the hospital.

Keeping her head down and her back against the Chevelle, Abby crossed her fingers and slowly, an inch at a time, began to ease past the commotion. She made it about three and a half feet before another wolf's howl—this one sounding a lot closer than last time—sliced through the air and had all four brawlers turning toward the source of the sound.

Unfortunately, it turned out that the source was a couple dozen yards behind Abby.

She froze like a deer in headlights. She probably looked like one, too, halted in midstep with her eyes wide open and focused on the danger barreling toward her at top speed. While she watched, the hoodlums saw her, shouted something foul, and looked fully intent on making her rethink that trip to the emergency room.

They didn't even manage a step forward. Something rumbled, deep and threatening, behind Abby, something that had the three hoodlums raising their gazes above her head and turning whiter than bedsheets.

The Other, though, never got past staring at Abby. His brown eyes locked with her mismatched ones and widened. She saw his lips move, but a third howl made it impossible to hear what he said. By the time the cry had faded, all she could hear was more of that low, menacing growl and the disgusting, if unoriginal, epithets spat out by the thugs.

"They're freakin' werewolves!" thug three screamed, his voice suddenly high-pitched and girlish.

"Dude, run!" yelled number one, leaving the last remaining attacker to half-throw, half-shove the Other in Abby's direction before taking off like Satan and all the hounds of hell were following close behind.

Abby saw the whole thing happen, almost like a frame-by-frame analysis. She saw when the hoodlum grabbed the other by his shirt collar, half-lifted him off the ground, and started to pitch him toward her, but she couldn't move fast enough. The startled Other went airborne and slammed into her, knocking her back to the pavement and driving the air out of her lungs. Just before her head bounced twice on the unforgiving asphalt, the Other caught her eyes again and—for some disturbing reason—smiled.

Great, Abby thought. I just risked my neck for a horny lunatic.

CHAPTER TWO

hoever had coined the phrase "hell on earth" had known whereof he spoke. As far as Rule could see, the situation here made the Below look like a summer vacation spot.

Tahiti, the French Riviera, the Underworld. Package deals available.

Dark eyes narrowed, Rule scanned the crowded Manhattan street, trying to sense the presence of anything unusual. He could feel the fragile pulse of humanity, the earthy richness of shape-shifters, the sparking energy of magic users, and beneath it all he scented just the faintest whiff of fiend.

If anyone was to recognize that particular odor, it would be Rule. Fiends and demons had lived side by side in the Below for millennia now, evolving into separate races the denizens of the world Above neither recognized nor understood.

While humans used the term "demon" to refer to the warped and twisted beings of evil they depicted in their stories and films, in reality the demons were simply supernatural beings who had once upon a time served as the messengers for all living races.

What the humans called demons the demons themselves more properly classified as "fiends," creatures of pure and voracious evil.

Since the end of the Fae–Demon Wars when the defeated had been banished to live in the Below, demons and fiends had struggled to master that world for their own ends. While the demons' ends involved an orderly and organized society, the fiends focused more on gaining and hoarding power until they could use it as a springboard to grant them permanent entrance into the human world. It had been this way for so long that no one could remember the first demon who had placed himself in the path of the fiends who wanted the freedom to come and go from the earthly plane as they wished, snacking on the human hearts that grew there in abundance. Rule only knew that he and the others like him descended from a long line of demon warriors whose job it was to keep the fiends in line and stop them from wreaking havoc on the vulnerable humans.

A week ago, that had seemed a hell of a lot easier.

Of course, a week ago, Rule had been leading a Watch troop of warriors like himself in an elaborate and highly effective surveillance operation. For months they had monitored a small but ambitious fiend lord who seemed to be making plans to start a war in the Below. Unhappy with the restraints against murder, mayhem, and torture placed on him by his demonic rulers, Uzkiel had gathered to him an army of like-minded and violent fiends who believed that by destroying the ruling parliament of demons, they would be free to take over the Below and turn the Underworld into a true vision of hell. Rule intended to keep that from happening, and his surveillance team, with the help of a minor fiend-turned-snitch, had been doing a damned fine job meeting that goal.

But that was last week, before one of Rule's lieutenants had been killed, Uzkiel and his ringleaders had gone into hiding, and Rule's snitch had disappeared. Now Rule didn't even need a handbasket to get to hell; he'd already arrived and unpacked.

Ironically, hell looked a lot like the Garment District.

Judging by the signs on the cross streets and the tour of Manhattan that the Council of Others had given him the last time he'd been here, this *was* the Garment District. This time, however, the streets he vaguely remembered overflowed with loud, unruly human demonstrators and frustrated, angry Other counter-protesters.

Rule had advised the Others from the beginning that revealing themselves to the humans was a bad idea. He'd foreseen a future a lot like this, although in his imagination there had been more weapons and a lot more blood. As far as he could tell, the Others were getting off lightly for rocking the boat of the world in which they lived. From what he remembered of humans, they tended to react first by killing anything they didn't understand.

Sometimes he wondered why folk like him went so far out of their way to protect the contrary things.

Impatient, Rule glanced once more through the

crowd, his gaze skimming past the humans and Others around him.

The human world was not his favorite vacation spot, but then, he wasn't currently on vacation. He had come Above because he'd gotten a lead that told him his missing snitch might be hiding out up here. It wasn't a bad plan for the informant, considering that few fiends managed to make their way to the surface without being stopped by Rule or one of the other demon hunters like him. The only way for fiends to get into the human world was to be invited, which usually meant answering the call of a summoner and exchanging services to him for the chance to see things Above. That naturally tended to limit the number of fiends or demons in the Above at any given time. On the surface, the snitch would have to spend a lot less time looking over his shoulder for the minions of the fiends he had betrayed.

The trouble materialized when Rule looked below the surface. Those limits on the travel of fiends into the human plane should have kept his snitch out of it, especially, Rule imagined, since a summoner would not have any reason to call on that particular and extremely minor entity. The fiend had to have found another way into the Above, which was something Rule intended to ask it about just as soon as he got his hands on it.

Rule just hoped the snitch was counting on the limits to keep away both its pursuers and a demon hunter determined to bring it back Below.

Not many on their home plane realized that Rule

had been issued a standing invitation to the human world in thanks for his assistance with a problem the Others had been having last year before their Unveiling. As long as the snitch didn't know about it, it wouldn't be expecting Rule to have followed it to Manhattan. That might be the only advantage the demon got.

Stifling a growl, Rule started forward again, keeping to the shadows of the buildings lining the street and walking deeper into the crowd of anti-Other protesters. He knew there was a fiend here and hoped like hell it was his snitch. Rule needed to find the little shit before one of the fiend assassins who'd been sent after it did. The information the snitch provided had kept the Below out of a war for months now, and Rule wasn't inclined to let one break out now.

The problem was finding the fiend in the sea of bodies around him. The fire currently burning in a vacant building down the street filled the air with the scent of flame and ash, obscuring the fiend's natural charred aroma. It wouldn't be impossible to track it by scent, but Rule didn't want to rely on just one sense.

His gaze scanned the crowd, looking for anything unusual. He had no idea what the fiend looked like at the moment, which wasn't helping, but if it was in this crowd, then it would be blending in. It had probably hitched a ride in some unsuspecting human's body, taking possession of a portable hiding place as it moved through the crowd. That meant Rule would have to use a more refined sense than his usual five to locate the snitch.

Or maybe not.

Feeling his spine stiffen, Rule honed in on a small knot of humans standing in the street a little more than a block away. The humans themselves didn't interest the demon, but the figure that walked briskly past them, hands shoved in pockets and chin tucked to chest, did. On top of the young man's curly head, two small, blunted horns poked out from a mess of brown curls, and around him Rule picked up a thin haze of smoke and magic.

Score.

Shrugging his shoulders under the long coat he wore to conceal the armament he carried, Rule locked his gaze on the young Other and strode forward. Time to catch a fiend.

CHAPTER THREE

Something was seriously wrong.

Rule saw the young, horned Other surrounded by the three human thugs and stepped up his pace. Only his demonically keen vision let him see the group standing nearly three blocks away from him, but the distance didn't affect his instincts. Those were on high alert. The itch on the back of his neck and the faint whiff of sulfur in his nostrils told him that the Other was someone he didn't want to lose track of, and that included seeing him beaten to death on a darkened street corner.

If this was Rule's lucky night, the kid was currently playing flophouse to his missing demon; and if not, then the Other had at least bumped into someone with a bad attitude and ties to the Below. At this point, even that slim lead made Rule's nipples hard. There were times when a demon had to take his thrills where he found them.

The small group stood too far away for Rule to hear what they were saying, but judging by the look on the kid's face and the flexing of the thugs' muscles, whatever the topic of conversation, it wasn't making anyone very happy. Not Rule, not when he saw thugs number two and three start to ease their way around the Other's sides, circling him like a buffet table. And especially not when a small, tentative stir of movement between two parked cars next to the brewing altercation caught Rule's eye.

He couldn't put his finger on why he noticed the tiny shift of light and shadow; there definitely wasn't anything about the figure who had caused the movement that should have drawn his attention. It was a human woman, and he didn't think he'd ever seen one that looked less interested in drawing anyone's attention.

She had hidden herself in the narrow space between two cars, and even from a distance, her small stature forced Rule to scan his gaze down toward her toes in order to determine whether or not she was anything more than a child. The curves visible beneath her faded sweatshirt and grungy jeans made that call for him. Still, she shouldn't have stood out.

Her hiding place pretty much sucked, but she looked like the type who didn't need to hide, since she already blended into the scenery. She had ash-brown hair and medium-fair skin and an average body that never should have held Rule's attention, but for some reason, he couldn't look away.

He had lived close to a thousand years and seen the sort of women who made the battle over Helen of Troy look like a schoolyard scuffle not worth the effort. He'd seen female shifters with the sort of feline grace that made being in heat a permanent state for any male, and witches who could steal a man's breath without ever casting a spell.

He couldn't even see this human woman's face, but he suspected if he had, it would have been as ordinary as the rest of her. The most interesting thing about her seemed to be the fact that she had gotten caught up in the middle of a riot in a city going mad. But when Rule looked at her, the itch on his neck intensified and crawled down his spine like an army of stinging insects.

Something about this situation was *very* not right.

A shift of muscle and menace yanked his attention back to the Other and his thuggish enemies. Rule's stride lengthened. His fingers itched with the need to reach for a weapon, but the sight of a six-foot, four-inch man striding down a Manhattan street in the middle of a riot brandishing the four-foot-long broadsword that the army of Watchers favored would probably have drawn the kind of attention he just didn't need. He wanted to get to the tense little group at the end of the next block without drawing any more of the riot along with him.

Unfortunately, the riot managed to get there before him. When the first blow struck, Rule bit out a curse and broke into a run. He knew that no matter how slowly a battle might seem to move when you were in the middle of one, in reality they tended to end in a matter of seconds. Not enough time to cover the distance still remaining between him and the fighting.

Between the parked cars at the side of the road,

Rule saw another flash of mouse brown, and he watched in horror as the woman rose to a crouching position as if she were insane enough to contemplate making a break for it. Which would be a really stupid thing to do.

Teeth grinding in frustration, he watched as the whole situation exploded in front of him, less than fifty yards away. The sound of a Lupine howling in the background just lent that special touch of black humor to the whole thing, as if someone had scripted it as part of a B-rated horror movie with barely a fraction of the class of an old Hammer flick. Didn't the werewolves and the . . . whatever kind of Other the kid was know better than to take an evening stroll in the middle of a crowd that would just as soon burn them at the stake as grant them the "equal rights" they were so determined to win for themselves?

Just as Rule had predicted, the fight between the Other and the thugs was quick and brutal. Aside from the whole three-on-one thing was the fact that the Other apparently had about as much combat training as your average Franciscan nun and even less idea of how to defend himself. He hit the ground in about two and a half seconds, but not before he hit the human woman and knocked her hard to the pavement.

That couldn't be good. Too many damned things could go wrong when a demon-touched Other came into close physical contact with an innocent human, most of which didn't even bear thinking about.

"Not good" took a sharp turn south when another

howl went echoing past Rule's ear in a blur of speed and musky earth. Lupines. Two of them, headed straight for the scene of Rule's best lead in a week. He did not need for werewolves in battle mode to get to it first.

Tucking his head down, he flattened his mouth into a line of annoyance and began to push his way determinedly through the dense crowd. If he wasn't cursed with atrocious luck, maybe he could reach them before anything else went wrong.

*t*he blow to the head didn't knock Abby unconscious; it just made her wish it had. She felt as if someone had cracked her skull open like a coconut and was now making a Thai stir-fry with the contents. She could almost swear she saw a ring of little songbirds chirping in a circle around her head. Or the remnants of it.

Cautiously, she lifted a hand to her hair, expecting to find it wet and matted with blood, but the only debris seemed to be sand and road grit. How she could have a head-on collision with the asphalt and not wind up bleeding baffled her, but she felt too much relief to quibble. Maybe her big brother was right about her hard head. Either that or God had been paying extra careful attention to her prayers tonight. Already the shock and pain of the initial blow seemed to be fading.

With a groan, she pushed herself into a sitting position and tried to shift her weight off the collection of pebbles currently digging into her hip. Panic raced through her.

"My legs! I can't move my legs!"

"I think that's probably because there's a body draped over them."

Abby choked off another scream and blinked up at an unfamiliar figure with curly brown hair and a dry smile. She'd never seen the woman before in her life, but she had the kind of face that always seemed familiar. She didn't look threatening, so Abby dropped her gaze back to the unconscious Other and felt herself go pale. "Body? Is he dead?"

A second woman, this one shorter and fairer, with a tousled shag haircut and a set of EMT overalls, crouched down beside Abby's knee and laid two fingers against the young man's neck. "Nope. Just unconscious."

Abby resumed breathing on an exhalation of relief. "Fabulous. I don't want to hurt him, but I'd really like to get him off of me. Now. I'm feeling a little less than safe not being able to run for my life at the moment."

The brunette just smiled. "I can't say I blame you. If I were in your shoes, I'd be beating a path out of this mess, too." She extended her hand expectantly. "My name is Samantha."

There was no way Abby could ignore that gesture without looking like a jerk, especially since no one else appeared to be going out of their way to help her out here, so she shook the woman's hand reluctantly. It felt calm and friendly and very warm.

"Abby."

"And I'm Carly," the blonde said. "I'm a paramedic. Before you go anywhere, you should let me give you a quick once-over. That was a pretty serious knock upside the head you just took."

"Yeah, I know." Unconsciously, Abby brought a hand back to her head and felt around for the crater she was pretty sure she ought to have there. She shook her head, amazed to find it wasn't even pounding. "But I don't think it was as bad as it looked. Honestly, I feel fine."

She wondered if she looked as surprised about that as she sounded.

Carly brushed Abby's hand away and probed carefully at the back of her skull. Then Carly frowned and probed a little less carefully. "I can't find a lump," she muttered to herself.

"That's what I mean. I'm fine. It was just one of those banana peel things—looks like a body cast waiting to happen, but everybody gets up and walks away afterward."

"Yeah, except those only happen in the movies," Carly said.

Samantha stepped closer to the other two women and leaned down toward them. If Abby had been forced to describe Samantha's expression, she would almost have called it wary, as opposed to worried.

"What do you mean?" the brunette asked. "There has to be a lump."

While Abby appreciated the concern these two strangers were showing for her well-being, enough was enough. She'd had a long, lousy day, complete with conning, desertion, and bodily injury, and now she wanted to go home, slip into a bubble bath, and pretend that none of this had ever happened.

"No, really," she told the women firmly. "I'm telling you, I'm fine. Not lumpy at all. Promise."

"No lumps, no cracks, no divots. But she smells pretty human." Carly held up an index finger and positioned it about a foot in front of Abby's nose. "Follow my finger with your eyes."

Jerking back, Abby frowned at her. "What do you mean, I 'smell' human? And I told you, there's nothing wrong with me—"

"Just making sure. Now follow my finger."

Abby recognized that tone of voice as the same one her brother used when he meant "shut up and do it anyway because I'm bigger and meaner and I won't go away until I win." Sighing, she completed the unnecessary task with obvious reluctance. "See? Nothing to worry about. Everything is completely normal. I'm fine. So now I think it's time for me to go home."

Past time, if you asked her.

Without waiting for permission or another examination, Abby leaned forward to push the unconscious body off her legs. The last thing she needed was for them to fall asleep and foil her plans for escape.

The Other was a skinny kid, but he had towered over her five-foot, two-inch frame, so she braced both hands against his torso and heaved with all her might. If she shifted him even a few inches, she should be able to drag her legs out from underneath him and free herself. Instead, the Other spun away from her shove as if he'd been shot from a cannon.

All three women watched, their gazes fixed on the figure's revolutions until he thudded to a stop against the tires of the SUV across the street.

For several seconds, no one said a word. Then Samantha turned toward Carly and frowned. "I thought you said she was human."

The paramedic shrugged. "She is. Smell her yourself."

Shocked and speechless though she might be from watching herself toss another person around like a Frisbee, Abby still couldn't completely ignore it when the brunette stepped close beside her, leaned over, and inhaled deeply. Scrambling to her feet, she crossed her arms protectively in front of her and felt a niggling of unease. "What the heck are you doing?"

Samantha ignored her, her brow furrowing as she took another whiff. "I don't know," she said, looking at Carly. "It's almost human, but there's something . . ." Another inhalation. ". . . something . . . odd."

"What do you mean, 'odd'?" Abby demanded, then gasped and took another step back. Fear clenched in her gut like a fist. She tried to brush it away, since no one had threatened her in any way, but her instincts ignored her. "What do you mean, 'human'?!"

"What kind of odd?" Carly demanded as if Abby hadn't spoken.

"Didn't you smell it?" Samantha was still talking to Carly, but her gaze was fixed firmly on Abby. Samantha seemed to be cataloging every feature, every detail, and frankly, it was making Abby nervous.

Carly shook her head and pushed herself to her feet. "No, but my allergies have been acting up lately. I can barely smell dinner."

"It's like . . . charcoal. Like something burnt."

Abby stepped nervously aside, not thrilled about the positioning of two strange women penning her in while they discussed the way she smelled. She also wasn't thrilled by the messages her newly-back-in-gear brain was translating from her instincts. She looked from Samantha to Carly and back again and swallowed hard. "Are you two . . . Others?"

"Lupines," Samantha said, softly, as if she were breaking some bad news. "Werewolves. We're both members of the Silverback Clan. That's the pack you might have heard about in the news recently. Our alpha was in on the negotiations before the Unveiling."

Was that whooshing sound Abby suddenly heard the sea, or was all of the blood really rushing out of her head?

She was talking to a couple of werewolves.

The knowledge threatened to stagger her. Her instincts shouted at her to

run!

hide!

Get away from the predators! Now!

Now! Now!! Now!!!

But Abby liked to think she didn't let her instincts rule her.

She was an intelligent woman not prone to snap decisions. Sure, there were certain things she'd always taken on faith—the existence of God, the possibility of miracles, how someone had figured out a way to make half-and-half fat free—but that didn't mean she was ignorant or bigoted. She really believed

it when she read that all men were created equal, and
the media kept explaining that werewolves—Lupines,
they called themselves—were not that different from
humans in character; some were good, some were
bad, and some fell in between.

So why wouldn't her heart stop beating at warp
speed?

These two had stopped to help her, not hurt her.
They had saved her from almost certain physical assault at the hands of the thugs, so they couldn't be evil.

Could they?

"Don't worry," Samantha said with a little laugh.
Her smile stayed in place, but Abby could see a little
of the warmth and vitality in it drain away. "We're
not going to bite you or anything."

Abby could feel herself blushing even as her instincts raised an immediate doubt. She felt like
she'd just hung a No Coloreds sign around her neck.
Humans only at this lunch counter. She wasn't really
like that, was she?

"Oh, I-I never thought," she stammered. "That is,
I . . . I just . . ."

Samantha shook her head. "It's okay. We realize
we take some getting used to for most humans, and
you haven't known about us long. But we honestly
aren't going to hurt you. We just wanted to make
sure you were okay."

Abby shifted her weight and tried to smile back.
"No, I'm sorry. I can only imagine what my face must
have looked like. It was rude. It's just . . . you're the
first were-Lupines I've met. Since the announcement,
anyway. I was a little surprised."

"We get that a lot." Carly shoved her hands in the pockets of her coveralls and raised an eyebrow. "So, now that you know what we are, why don't you tell us what you are?"

CHAPTER FOUR

A bby blinked. "Say huh?"

Samantha glared at her friend, then turned back to Abby with a reassuring smile. "Carly doesn't mean to be rude. She's just curious. We both thought you were human at first."

"I *am* human."

"Know many other human women with no muscle tone to speak of who can toss a grown man fifty feet by accident?" Carly looked torn between amusement and skepticism.

"I work out," Abby protested. If she called running back and forth to the deli all day for coffee for the reporters "working out."

If she'd thought her instincts were screaming at her two minutes ago, she didn't want to contemplate the bullhorn they'd suddenly seemed to discover.

"It's okay. We understand about anonymity." Samantha reached out and patted her hand. "There are lots of us who aren't ready to call attention to ourselves yet. We're not going to out you against your will."

Abby saw her vision distort. Or maybe that was the fabric of reality. "No, you don't understand. I have nothing to out. I'm human. I'm straight. I'm Catholic. I don't have anything to hide."

"Of course not," Carly agreed cheerfully. "You're just the human girl next door. Absolutely."

Abby started to nod emphatically but found herself stopping a millisecond later with Carly's wrist clenched in her hand and her body half turned away, as if deflecting a blow.

What the hell was happening to her?

The Lupine grinned. "Provided the girl next door has a black belt and superhuman strength, speed, and agility."

"Carly, you're scaring her." Samantha gently tugged the two of them apart. Her eyes, golden brown and filled with concern, searched Abby's face. "You honestly don't know what's going on, do you?"

"I don't even know what you're talking about," Abby protested. She took a step back, her head shaking almost involuntarily. "I'm human, and the only thing going on is a riot that I'd like very much to get away from now, so if you don't mind . . ."

Samantha sighed. "I bet you're feeling like you just entered *The Twilight Zone*."

Carly shook her head. "Sorry, sweetie. Rod Serling is dead. I'm afraid this is the real thing."

Okay. It was definitely past time for Abby to be leaving. Before the niggling sense of unease in the back of her mind became full-fledged panic.

"Look, um, thanks for your help and everything,"

she said, backing farther away, "but I've really got to get home. I, uh, I have to be at work. Tomorrow. Early tomorrow. In the morning. It was . . . n-nice to meet you—"

"Wait."

Samantha stepped forward, and Abby felt like slime when she flinched away from the Lupine. But that didn't stop Abby from flinching.

"I'm not going to hurt you," Samantha said, "but I don't think it's a good idea for you to go wandering off by yourself. Not right now. Not until we figure out what's going on."

"Nothing is going on!" Hysteria edged Abby's voice, but she couldn't seem to help it. She *was* hysterical. "I'm fine. I'm normal. And I'm going home."

Her hip banged into one of the parked cars, but when she tried to ease to the side she found that Carly had beaten her to it. The blond Lupine had moved so fast, Abby hadn't even seen her, but she now blocked the way between Abby and freedom.

"I'm sorry," Carly said, not sounding sorry at all. "We can't let you do that."

Abby laughed at that, one of the unfunniest things she'd ever heard. "What do you mean? I can do anything I want. I'm an adult, this is a free country, and I don't take orders."

Samantha's smile was sympathetic. "Carly just means that we don't think you should be alone right now. After all, it's obvious that something . . . unusual is going on."

"There's nothing unusual—"

Carly just raised an eyebrow and looked point-edly at the still-unconscious Other lying on the pavement more than fifty feet away.

Abby sucked in a deep breath and squared her shoulders. "It was just a fluke. An adrenaline rush."

"Sweetheart, you could *freebase* adrenaline and you wouldn't move that fast."

Samantha's voice broke in soothingly. The sort of tone people used with sleepy babies and rabid dogs. "I was thinking we could go see some friends of mine. They're a lot better at unraveling mysteries than we are. I'm sure they could help us figure out what's going on."

Abby had a sudden vision of standing in the middle of a room full of unfamiliar people, each of whom was leaning close and trying to sniff her. She shook her head vehemently. "No. That's not a good idea."

"We already promised not to hurt you," Carly said. "I'm not sure you'll get the same offer from them." She jerked her thumb in the direction of the crowd of protesters.

While the three women had been talking, the crowd had begun to drift closer to them, and they didn't sound any friendlier than they had an hour ago. By this point, Abby wasn't even sure they could distinguish friend from foe or frightened from furry. Still, there was no way she'd go wandering off with two werewolves she had just met and didn't know from Adam. She wouldn't have gone off with two humans she'd just met, let alone a couple of monsters. That was an invitation to serial killer victimhood if she'd ever heard one.

Even as she drew breath to launch another protest, the crowd's chanting grew louder. Abby could hear the undertones of hate and fear in their voices. Never a good mix.

"They've already seen you with us," Samantha pointed out, sounding more urgent. A few of the men at the edge of the crowd were looking in the women's direction and frowning when they saw the unconscious form lying on the side of the road. From where they stood they probably couldn't see the kid's horns, and the rest of him looked perfectly human.

Abby felt another surge of panic. Surely the crowd couldn't think *she* was Other. She searched frantically through her memory. Did the crowd know the two women with her were werewolves?

"But they don't know you're Lupine," she protested, not sure if she believed herself.

"They do now."

Impatience and irritation clear in her voice, Carly took a deep breath and shifted right in front of Abby's eyes. Abby's and the entire crowd's. One minute Carly was a short, moderately attractive blonde, and the next the air around her seemed to pulse and shiver and in her place stood a huge, rangy wolf with sandy-blond fur and challenging hazel eyes.

Beside her, Abby heard Samantha swear. "Oh, shit! *Run!*"

If Abby hadn't known better, she would almost

have thought Carly grinned at that a split second before all three of them took off down the street at a dead sprint with cries of "Werewolf!" echoing close behind them.

CHAPTER FIVE

For the second time in ten minutes, Abby felt like she had made a significant impact on asphalt. Or rather, that asphalt had made a significant impact on her. Only this time, she didn't have to fall down to do it. The hard, unyielding surface came to her. Vertically.

The mob's angry reaction to Carly's transformation was still echoing in Abby's eardrums, and her feet had barely gotten the message that her brain wanted them to get moving when she turned and took one step straight into a warm, muscular surface that felt a lot like a city sidewalk but smelled significantly better. Like wood smoke and August sunshine and dark, rich myrrh.

To her left, an angry growl accompanied the shifting of tawny fur as Carly took a threatening step toward the man in front of them. Was that a bad sign?

Raising her head enough to get a glimpse at a man's face, she found herself raising it even farther to manage one of the man-shaped mountain in front of her. She had a vague image of a firm jaw, sharp blades of nose and cheekbones, and fathomless, glittering black eyes before the world turned upside down and Abby found herself staring at a patch of pavement she was already way too familiar with. Then the pavement started to move, and she heard the growl behind her turn into a snarl.

Blinking in reaction, Abby felt the press of a broad shoulder digging into her stomach as she bounced across it on the enormous man's way down the street. Now two wolves followed along behind her, teeth bared and muscles bunching as they prepared to launch an attack on the back beneath her.

"I am taking her to Vircolac," a voice boomed from somewhere near her left hip, "and it will be a lot quicker if you wait to try and tear my throat out until we get there."

Quicker, maybe, said a voice in the back of Abby's head, *but a hell of a lot less safe.*

Abby couldn't disagree with the sentiment, but what she really wanted to know was where had the voice come from? And who did it belong to, because she was fairly certain she wasn't the one who had thought it.

Abby felt her stomach clench against her kidnapper-cum-rescuer's shoulder. What was going on?

When I said "less safe," the voice continued, *that was your cue to start kicking and screaming and hauling ass in another direction. I'll help, but you gotta get things started.*

"What?!"

Unless you plan to stop fighting me about who's

*in charge here, you gotta make the first move, sweet
cheeks. It ain't hard. Just put one foot in front of the
other. Directly into the jerk's kidneys.*

A dull buzzing began to fill Abby's head, but it
didn't drown out the fact that she was hearing voices.
Hearing *voices*!

"Wh-who are you?" she forced out.

"We can deal with pleasantries later," the man beneath her answered without the slightest hitch in his
stride. "Right now, it is far more important to get
you out of harm's way."

"I wasn't talking to you! Unless you were just
talking to me?"

God, please let him say yes. Please let him say
yes. . . .

"I never said a word. In case you hadn't noticed, I
am busy at the moment."

*Sorry, toots. That was me, not the caped crusader.
Now about this escape plan of ours—*

"There is no escape plan!" Abby squawked, pressing her hands against her captor's back and raising
her head to look around. Maybe she wasn't really
losing her mind. Maybe someone was running along
beside them and not rattling around inside her head
and making her believe her marbles had suddenly
gone missing.

Of course, if there was someone rattling around
inside her head, then she really had lost her mind.
Because that kind of thing just didn't happen.

"Good. I would advise against trying." The arm
clamped around Abby's thighs tightened a warning.
"Not only would an attempt meet with failure, but I

hazard a guess you would find little to recommend the company of our pursuers."

The behemoth still thought she was talking to him.

Figures he would. Sun demons like him are all a bunch of arrogant blighters.

"Demon? Did you say demon?"

"Keep your voice down, little one. Unless you would like to add to our already considerable entourage."

"What entourage?" Abby focused on the rapidly receding group of humans chasing them. She tried not to notice the speed with which the buildings on either side of them blurred past. She'd never been a great passenger, and she didn't think anyone would appreciate it if she lost her lunch down her captor's back. "We've nearly lost them."

Don't talk to him. You'll only encourage him.

"Does that mean if I stop talking to you, you'll shut up, too?"

Nah. I don't require encouragement.

"Clearly."

But I do need your cooperation if we're going to escape. Now listen—

Abby shook her head. "I'm not in the mood to listen. And on top of that, I took abnormal psych in college. I know what happens to people who start doing what the little voices in their heads tell them, and it's never good."

Who are you calling little?

"Argh!" Abby clenched her hands into fists and smacked them against the closest available surface, which happened to be the back of the man carrying her. "Would you just shut up and get out of my head?!"

The behemoth didn't even grunt. "I am not in your head, little one, but you can rest assured that as soon as we reach safety, you will be required to explain what you meant by that remark."

Oh, goodie, Abby thought.

Now aren't you sorry you didn't cooperate on the escape thing? the voice asked.

Arroooooooooo! Carly howled.

Abby looked over at Samantha, waiting for the last member of their group to give her opinion, but the Lupine just looked back at her with golden brown eyes and gave a terribly canine shrug.

"Some help you are," Abby muttered, and let herself collapse back against the shoulder beneath her. "When I get out of this, I'm going to find a pile of liver and teach you a helpful little command called 'sic 'im.' "

This time, Carly's howl sounded suspiciously like laughter.

CHAPTER SIX

*t*he fact that Abby ended up in the front hall of a private club in one of the old-money neighborhoods of the Upper East Side felt weird enough. Add to it the facts that the club happened to be owned, operated, and patronized completely by Others, and that she'd arrived in a fireman's carry over the shoulder of a man whose name she didn't know, and that they'd been trailed by two shaggy werewolves, and that Abby kept hearing the voice of someone who was definitely not her inside her head, and the sum total pushed things firmly into the realm of freaktacular.

Of course, how not to view the entirety of her current situation as freakish was beyond Abby's poor powers of self-delusion. She might have her doubts over the possibility of her being anything other than the human she'd been for all of the twenty-eight years of her life so far, but she couldn't deny that something very weird was going on.

It was like she'd become a character in a comic book when she wasn't looking. If she'd gotten caught up in some sort of radiation leak, she might have understood, but nothing remarkable had happened. One minute she'd been hiding, and the next she'd been on the pavement with super strength and speed and God knew what else, trying to figure out what in the name of all things holy was happening.

A gnawing ache settled in just below her breast-bone, but considering Abby still hung over a certain someone's shoulder, she couldn't even rub at it. All she could do was wait for the ax to fall. Or maybe the Others would use something different, like a . . . a . . . a magic butter knife or something.

Well, she supposed she could put up some kind of struggle, but it seemed pointless. As the mountain beneath her had pointed out earlier, someone would end up catching her, and that someone's mood would likely deteriorate as a result of the trouble of chasing Abby.

Besides which, there was that whole "paralyzed by fear" thing. Or "paralyzed by shock," at least. Either way, moving still seemed a wee bit beyond her.

When Samantha had suggested taking Abby to visit some of her "friends," Abby had envisioned a small apartment with an early hunting lodge decorating scheme, not the newly infamous and wholly mysterious Vircolac club.

In the short time since the Others had revealed themselves to the rest of the world, the club had become well-known. It served as the headquarters of the Council of Others, the group that apparently governed the city's Other population, and was owned by a Lupine named Graham Winters.

Winters had been in the news a lot, as both a representative of the Others who had negotiated the treaties and the head of Manhattan's local werewolf pack. Abby remembered seeing him on TV and thinking it was no wonder he was Lupine. No man that good-looking could possibly have been human.

There had been protesters outside the club, but that hadn't stopped her kidnapper and his canine accomplices. They had hustled her around the corner and down a small alley to a service entrance at the back of the grand old building. Samantha had shifted and entered a code on a keypad beside the heavy steel door. Seconds later, she'd ushered all of them inside before Abby could so much as open her mouth. Leading the way into a dark wood-paneled and marble-floored hall, Samantha had instructed the others to stay put and disappeared behind one of the several doors that lined the hall.

Abby watched from her head-down position over the man's shoulder by the simple method of shifting her upper body to the side and using a grip on her captor's waist to hold her in place. By looking around the man's torso she could get a fairly decent view of the hallway, even if everything was still upside down.

After a few minutes, the door had opened and Samantha had reappeared, dressed in a loose-fitting sweat suit and balancing another bundle of clothes under her arms. She was following a petite blond woman with bouncing curls and big blue eyes.

Those eyes should have looked ingenuous and guileless, Abby thought, to complete the picture of angelic innocence the woman projected, but instead they were shrewd and thorough as they inspected Abby from head to toe. Or at least, all the visible parts of her.

Conscious of the grubby state of her clothes and what had to be the rat's nest of her hair and the way she and the remnants of her dignity hung over the shoulder of a giant, Abby fought not to squirm under the careful appraisal.

"I'm Tess De Santos," the blonde said as her gaze settled back on Abby's. Tess held out a slim hand decorated with brightly polished nails the color of fuchsia flowers. "Rule, you can put her down now. It's not like she's got much chance of getting away if she makes a break for it."

Abby felt herself swinging through the air and took a moment once her feet touched the floor to let the blood that had pooled in her head settle back where it belonged. And try to get her bearings.

Like that's gonna happen.

She shook the other woman's hand cautiously. "Uh, Abby. Baker."

The blond woman's hand felt different from Samantha's, cooler and softer, less vibrating with contained strength. Abby felt the hand tighten around hers, and her eyes widened. Her glance flicked back up to meet one of bright blue. Tess was staring at her as if she could see straight through her eyes and into her subconscious, something Abby wasn't sure she'd be comfortable having anyone do, let alone a stranger in a club populated by the kinds of beings who used to keep her from sleeping at night.

The blonde's mouth curved into a wry smile. "Don't worry, Abby. I promise, none of us is going to bite. Especially not me. I don't even have fangs."

Oh, my God. Could this woman read her mind?

Someone inside Abby's head snorted.

Tess laughed. "No, I'm not reading your mind, Abby. Just your face. And let me say, I hope like hell you don't play poker, hon."

Releasing Abby's hand, the woman turned to the man who had carried Abby in, the one she'd called Rule, and nodded. "There's something going on in there, all right, but I can't tell what it is without doing some sort of spell. It's not a surprise, though, given those eyes of hers."

Always self-conscious about the mismatched colors of her eyes, Abby squirmed. "What do you mean?"

"You have heterochromia—one blue eye, one brown eye."

"Um, I had noticed that."

Tess smiled. "It's not a criticism. Personally, I think you have beautiful eyes. But there are some superstitions out there that say having eyes like that makes a human either a witch, a psychic, or an open doorway for passing spirits in need of a body."

And let me tell you, sweet cheeks, I've never been happier to see a human with your condition in my life. And that's sayin' something.

Abby tried really, really hard to ignore that voice. The one inside her head. That didn't belong to her.

"What is going on is obvious," the man called Rule broke in. Abby looked up—way up—into his face and saw his fallen-angel features tighten into a frown. "She has had contact with a fiend. Enough contact that I strongly suspect it is still with her. The reason I brought her here is so that we can attempt to determine exactly what demon it is."

Abby blinked, because she really couldn't think of any other way to react. How did things keep getting weirder? "You people think I'm *possessed*?"

What? You thought this was a ventriloquist act?

"Well, I don't think you're psychic," Tess shrugged, "or you wouldn't look so shell-shocked at being here right now. And I know you're not a witch, because I am. Like they say, it takes one to know one. So that leaves us with the possibility that you really have been possessed by something that slipped in through your blue eye and set up shop in your unconscious."

"Because I have a blue eye?" Abby couldn't help herself. She knew she sounded so incredulous as to border on shrill, but who could blame her? "You have two blue eyes; does that mean you're doubly possessed?"

"Nope. Having two blue eyes is like having two brown eyes. Or two green eyes. Or two red eyes with yellow polka dots. Having two of anything is fine. And having mismatched eyes when you're Other isn't a big deal, because Others are already attuned to the supernatural. They *are* supernatural. But when a human is supposed to have two brown eyes and one of them turns out to be blue instead, it means something in that human is open to our world in a way that it isn't open in other humans."

Beside her, Rule shifted impatiently. "It is very kind of you to try and explain things to the girl and try to help her understand her situation, Tess, but can we perhaps hold the lessons later? After we have determined what exactly is inside of her?"

"Okay, once again, I was having a conversation with someone who is not you, so chill for a sec, wouldja?" Abby slapped a hand over her own mouth and felt her eyes widening until they threatened to bug out of her head. "Ahninteenat."

Rule turned to look at her with that inscrutable expression. "I beg your pardon?"

She parted her fingers just enough to make the repetition intelligible, but she didn't lower them. Maybe by keeping them in front of her mouth she could stop anything else horrifying from escaping her lips. "I said that I didn't mean that."

"Then why did you say it?"

She shook her head so fast she felt a little dizzy. "I didn't. I swear. I mean, well, I did, but I—it wasn't . . . I mean, it wasn't really me. Saying it. I don't think."

Rule frowned.

"I think what Abby is trying to say," Tess broke in, sounding drily amused, "is that I had a very valid point about the fact that she might be possessed by something. In this case, something with a bit of a smart mouth, it seems."

Abby peered at her over the tips of her fingers. "You realize that sounds vaguely insane, right?"

Tess arched an eyebrow. "Six weeks ago, didn't werewolves?"

The woman had a point, but that didn't mean Abby intended to give her credit for it. Not when she was having to struggle so hard not to schedule a fitting for her own little white coat with the buckles in the back. "And you can just tell this from looking at me?"

"Like I said, I'm a witch." Tess turned to Samantha and Carly. "So why don't you tell me everything that happened before you got here?"

Carly finished pulling on her own sweats and shrugged. "You want it unabridged or the *Reader's Digest* version?"

Was Abby the only one here who had been even slightly disconcerted by the fact that when both women had shifted back to their human forms they had been stark raving naked? Or who found it unusual to get dressed in the middle of a hallway with the same nonchalance as in a women's locker room?

Judging by the looks on everyone else's faces, Abby guessed she was.

Hey, don't go makin' waves. I gotta say, I been enjoying the scenery.

Swallowing against the urge to start babbling incoherently—and maybe drooling—Abby stepped in front of the werewolves and crossed her arms over her chest. "Look, I'm not entirely convinced that this whole thing isn't a nightmare I'm having after a bad batch of moo shu pork, but since I don't seem to be about to wake up, I'm at least going to dream myself into a starring role here. If you want to know what happened to me, why don't you try asking me?"

Tess shrugged. "No skin off my nose. I just thought you might still be a little shaken up by the whole thing. But by all means, be my guest and start spilling your guts."

Abby could have started off by telling Tess she wasn't feeling "a little" anything. She'd stopped feeling little a while ago. She was now thoroughly . . . whatever she was . . . and not seeing her way back anytime soon. But at least that voice in her head seemed to have quieted down for the time being.

Fortifying herself with a deep breath, Abby considered warning Tess to be careful what she wished for before she squared her shoulders and gave a summarized account of her day so far. It felt more like a week when she thought about it, but she was trying really hard not to do that.

She started, just like her trouble had, with Terry's frustrated ambition to be the next Peter Jennings and related the whole tale of their mission to cover the demonstration. She spoke of the escalating tension that had eventually led to Terry turning tail and running away at the first hint of a threat on his person, of her hiding place between the cars, and of her encounter with the thugs, the Other, and the werewolves and . . . accomplice . . . who had brought her here. By the time she finished, she felt like she'd lived the whole thing over again, and she had to stop herself from looking around for a hidden camera.

Rule had listened to the whole story almost as intently as Tess, but it was the woman who spoke first.

"Tell me again about the Other who ran into you."

"Was thrown into me," Abby corrected. She

shrugged. "I'm not sure how much I can tell you. It's not like I'm up on all the . . . er . . . varieties of Others out there. So far, all the stories I've worked on have been about vampires, Lupines, and witches."

"The big three," Tess agreed.

"Right. Well, anyway, it's not like I could identify this kid on sight. He looked pretty normal to me, if you discounted the horns on his forehead. Like your average college kid, really."

"What kind of horns did he have?"

Two months ago, that question would have had Abby searching for the nearest exit and the number of Bellevue's admitting department. Instead, she stood there and searched her recollection for the closest example she could summon. "I don't suppose you've seen *The Lion, the Witch and the Wardrobe*?"

"Of course I have! I loved that movie. Not as good as the book, of course, but it was Hollywood after all." The look on Abby's face must have been as confused as the reaction in her head, because Tess grinned and looked unrepentantly mischievous. "Just because we've seen—or been—real-life examples of the creatures in C. S. Lewis's imagination doesn't mean we can't appreciate his ability to tell a story."

"Oh." Abby blushed. "Well, in that case, the horns looked like he was Mr. Tumnus's long-lost cousin. From what I could tell, though, his legs bent the right way around."

"He didn't smell much like goat, either," Carly offered. "If he did have satyr blood, it couldn't have been more than half, if that."

Tess hummed. "And you said he smiled at you when he knocked you down?"

Abby nodded.

"Well, that must have been when the possesser changed places." Tess said it as if she were explaining how to make scrambled eggs.

"Possesser?"

"Sure. You are the possessed, in the throes of possession. Therefore, whatever is possessing you is the possesser."

"Possessed? You were serious about that? You think I'm possessed."

"What else would you call it when something is inside of you thinking things you wouldn't think and saying things you never meant to say?" Her shrewd blue eyes fixed on Abby's face steadily. "That *is* what's been happening. Isn't it?"

"But the Other didn't have heterochromia. His eyes were brown. Both of them."

"Yes, but he's part satyr. Like I said before, the situation only seems to apply to humans. With heterochromia, a human's psyche seems to be more like that of an Other, more open, which is what allows for the possession."

Abby looked frantically for some way to refute the other woman's conclusion, which felt a lot like looking around for a log to grab onto before heading over the edge of the waterfall. "No. I can't be. It's not possible." Her hand flew to her throat. "I'm wearing a cross and everything!"

"Abby, we're not talking about vampires here," Tess said, sounding very much as if she was trying not to laugh. "And even if we were, the cross thing is a myth. Others have nothing to do with religion. Christianity won't protect you from us any more than it will protect you from a crocodile."

Abby shook her head. Again. If people kept telling her things like this, she was going to deny herself into a concussion. "I didn't say anything about vampires, but demons are demons. They're the embodiment of evil. God's symbols *have* to have power over them."

Oh, sweet cheeks, who decided it was safe to let you go wandering the big bad world all alone? Were they nuts?

Rule opened his mouth, but Tess cut him off. "This is not the time, pal." She turned back to Abby. "Don't get our friend started on demons and the misconceptions we mortals have over their origin, history, society, and biochemistry. The lecture is like a five-hundred-part series. Suffice it to say, what you think you know about demons is quite likely a big load of bupkes. Besides, right now, we can't say exactly what it is that's possessing you."

Abby frowned. "So I'm not going to start spitting pea soup any minute now?"

Tess had the grace to look uncertain. "Well, no. I mean, that movie was about demonic possession. But we're still not sure that—"

"You mean I'd spit pea soup if it *was* a demon?" Her voice sounded high-pitched and uncomfortable, even to Abby. Heaven knew what it must sound like to anyone else in earshot. At the moment she didn't care. "I'm possessed by a demon?"

"We don't know that. It could be anything at this point."

"Then let's hurry up and figure it out!"

"It isn't a demon," Rule's voice rumbled out, providing a convenient and large target for Abby's glower.

"And how would you know that for certain? Are you some kind of expert on demonic possession?"

"Well, actually . . . ," Samantha said, pursing her lips and studying the polish on her toenails.

Tess didn't waste time with beating around the bush, which Abby was beginning to view as something of a trademark of hers. "Rule *is* a demon, Abby."

Surely a person's blood couldn't *really* freeze in her veins, right? That was just an expression.

Wasn't it?

Every muscle in Abby's body tensed against the instinct to take a step away from the towering male figure, but will is never a match for instinct. She sidled closer to Tess. "A what?"

"A demon. And you can stop looking like he's going to pull your heart out through your nose just to listen to the squicking. It turns out that's not actually a demon pastime after all."

At least that implied that Abby wasn't the only one in the room who'd ever thought it might be.

Nah, they're more inclined to honor you to death. Those guys have no idea how to have a good time.

The mountainous kidnapper didn't look anything like any demon Abby had ever envisioned. Not only did he not have ram's horns and goat's legs; he also didn't even give her the willies. At least, not the kind of willies she thought the embodiment of pure evil ought to. He did do strange things to her stomach, but she thought that had more to do with the fact that he happened to be one of the most gorgeous living beings she'd ever set eyes on. If he *was* living, that is.

He had the physique of a warrior, all muscles and sinew and dense, heavy bones. His face could have been carved in granite by an Italian master attempting to depict one of the archangels. Dark golden hair framed his head like a halo, and those fathomless black eyes made her want to do things she wasn't even sure were physically possible.

Heh-heh. Glad to feel you've got a pulse, sweet cheeks, but seriously, these thoughts of yours are making me see Rule in a new and deeply disturbing light. So you think you could cool it?

A demon couldn't do that to her. Could it?

Unless he was an incubus. Maybe all those medieval stories about innocent young virgins being seduced by man-shaped creatures in the dead of night weren't so far-fetched after all.

Oh, brother.

Tess tucked a stray curl behind her ear and sighed. "Now really doesn't strike me as the time to give you the *Cliffs Notes* history of demons and their kindred, so let me just assure you that Rule is one of the good guys and get back to the business at hand, which involves finding out if whatever is inside you is playing for the home team." She looked at Rule. "What's your take so far?"

The enormous man—*demon*!—frowned. "I am unable to say for certain unless I can make contact with it, but I can smell a hint of sulfur about her."

Abby saw Tess's eyes widen and her face blank. She took that as a bad sign. "Sulfur? I smell like sulfur? As in 'fire-and-brimstone' sulfur? Then it *is* a demon!"

"It's not a demon." Tess grimaced. "Maybe we can't put off that history lesson, after all. But if I could make a suggestion, I'd say we should have it someplace that isn't in the middle of a hallway. (A) because I'd like to sit down, and (B) because I have a feeling that before the class is dismissed, someone around here is going to need a very large drink."

"I don't drink," Abby murmured while the voice inside her head said, *Make mine a double.*

CHAPTER SEVEN

Rule leaned against the mantelpiece in the upstairs library and kept his eyes on the human
woman. She looked a bit like someone had
just hit her on the back of the head with a Louisville
Slugger, wide-eyed and dazed and more than a little
pale. Her mismatched eyes almost blended together
now, mostly because her pupils had dilated until
only the barest rim of iris could be seen at the edges
of the deep black pools.

The tickling in his chest irritated him. He would
have called it heartburn if acid reflux existed in terms
of his physiology, but he couldn't. Instead, he chose
to ignore it, along with the tingling at the base of his
spine that urged him to stand closer to her. Close
enough to touch that milk-pale, baby-smooth skin.

Rafael had joined his wife and the others when
they'd adjourned upstairs. He lounged in an armchair beside the fireplace, his expression intent and
serious as Tess and Samantha filled him in on the
origins of the current situation. He looked no more
thrilled about it than the rest of them.

"What, in the end, did you determine?" he asked

when the others fell silent. "Is the possession demonic?"

Rule stifled the urge to growl. "It's not demonic."

Rafael's lips quirked. "I apologize, my friend. Fiendish, is what I meant to ask."

Abby seemed to flinch at that, and Rule felt the strange urge to temper his instinctively blunt assurance. "It looks as if it could be. As I told your mate, I cannot be completely sure unless I am able to make contact with the being."

The Felix raised a dark brow. "You were waiting for a formal introduction?"

"No, but permission would make things easier." His gaze stayed on the woman. Her innocent features proved appallingly easy to read. She appeared ready to scream or to pass out. Neither of which would be very helpful at the moment. "It would make things easier for me, and more . . . comfortable for her if she invited me to look more closely."

The delicate jaw firmed, chin lifting as she drew in a breath. "*She* would need to know what exactly you meant by 'looking' first."

Rule watched her face and considered his response. It would be a lot easier to do this with her cooperation, but he wasn't sure that would be her first inclination when she heard what he had in mind.

"I would need to make contact with the presence in question," he ventured after a minute, "draw it to the forefront of your consciousness so that I could speak to it. Ask it some questions."

He saw how much that idea thrilled her. Her dark eyes flared, and she drew in a breath that shook.

"You mean I'd need to let it take over? Let myself really be possessed and go all Linda Blair?"

Mentally cursing the producers of that movie for all the trouble they'd caused his kind in recent years, Rule gave a curt nod. "For a few minutes."

"How do you know?"

"How do I know what?"

She scowled up at him, her arms crossed defensively over her chest. He tried not to let them draw his eyes to where they didn't belong. "How do you know it would only be for a few minutes? What if this demon decides it likes being in control and refuses to fade back into the background?"

"It's not a demon," he gritted out.

"Whatever. I'm the one who's being possessed by it, right? I think I should be able to pick my own terminology."

Tess stepped between them. "Yeah, let's not waste time arguing about that. We need to find out where we stand and do something about it. Before it becomes a moot point." She turned her blue eyes, hardened with determination, on Abby. "Look, I get that this whole thing is making you a little nervous. And I can't say I blame you, but if Rule says this is what has to happen, then I believe him."

Abby frowned at the other woman, but Rule thought he could see more than irritation in her fine features. Fear lurked there as well. "But what if the . . . the *thing* inside me decides it likes being the one in the driver's seat? What if it won't let me go?"

"That isn't going to happen," Rule announced,

his voice firm but softer now. "I promise. I will not allow it."

"And I believe that, too." Tess reached out and took one of the obviously unsure woman's pale hands between her own. "It will be okay, Abby. You can trust us."

That made Abby snort, a half-amused, half-resigned, wholly desperate sound. "At the moment, it doesn't look as if I have all that much choice."

No one said anything to correct that notion.

Her mouth tightened. "Fine." She backed herself up to the nearest armchair and sat, her fingers clenching on the upholstery. She raised her gaze and her eyebrows in Rule's direction. "Do we need to wait for the old priest, or are you going to handle this yourself?"

Rule bit back his retort. The whiteness of her clenched knuckles revealed the nerves concealed by her smart comments. In other circumstances, he'd have relished making her eat her words, but not just then. Stuffing down the inappropriate urges stirring at the back of his consciousness, he took a step forward and placed himself directly in front of her chair.

"No need," he rumbled. "This won't take long."

Her wide eyes followed every movement as he crouched down before her and reached into his pocket. He drew out a short silver chain from which dangled three small charms. Flipping one to the forefront, he palmed it before gently prying Abby's fingers from the chair arms and pressing her palm to his. He saw her flinch and her expression shift into the early stages of panic as the metal began to heat between them.

"Shh," he soothed, keeping her gaze locked to his, intentionally blocking out every trace of their fascinated audience. "It's all right. It'll be over in a minute. I promise."

A slight grimace twisted her mouth, and her breathing sped up, grew shallow. "I'll bet you . . . say that to all the girls," she hissed just before her pretty, mismatched eyes rolled back in her head and she collapsed, folding forward at the waist like a poorly balanced doll left unsupported on a shelf.

Mouth grim, Rule caught her shoulders in his hands and shifted her up to rest against the back of the chair. Her head lolled against the dark wing, and her breathing was fast and shallow, like an animal panting. The sharp smell of sulfur grew stronger.

"Um, are you sure she's supposed to do that?"

Rule ignored Tess's question and continued to grip Abby's hand in his. Her skin had gone deathly cold, clammy. It took on a sort of waxy grayness that added to the impression of lifelessness, but he figured Tess had been referring to the waves of movement undulating beneath Abby's skin. Up and down her arms, the flesh rippled as if something trapped beneath it were trying to get out.

Which was almost true.

"Show yourself," he growled, his eyes fixed on the young woman's sweat-beaded face. She seemed to flinch at the command. Her shoulders jerked unevenly backward, and her hand fought to free itself from his grip. He laced their fingers more tightly and held firm.

"Is she okay?" Samantha whispered, only to be shushed by the others.

Rule deepened his voice and repeated himself, his eyes narrowing. "Show yourself now as friend or fiend."

Abby jerked again as if she were trying to push through the back of her chair and get away from the harsh presence kneeling before her. That wasn't Abby trying to escape, though, and the knowledge stripped away Rule's last vestige of patience.

"I command that you show yourself!"

The screech nearly shattered his eardrums.

Abby's body flew toward him, the fingers of her free hand curled into claws, teeth bared in a furious snarl. Her eyes were open, but they'd rolled so far back into her head that only the whites were visible, giving her an unearthly, vacant look. He fought the urge to flinch away from the attack, but she never made contact. Bare centimeters away from him, she slammed to a halt, like a dog that had reached the end of its chain. With another screech, she collapsed back into the chair, forcefully enough that the heavy wooden frame groaned in protest.

"My God! She's gonna hurt herself. You have to stop this!" Out of the corner of his eye, Rule saw Samantha take a step forward to rush to Abby's aid. Tess caught Samantha at the shoulder, and Rafael rose from his chair to block the Lupine's path.

"Leave them be," Rafael said. "Rule knows better than we do."

Rule had to suppress a snort. He hoped like hell the Felix was right about that.

Tightening his grip on the young woman's hand, Rule leaned in closer until his breath brushed her skin and he could feel the unnatural waves of heat pouring off her.

"Speak," he said, his voice low and commanding. "Tell me what made you take what is not rightfully yours."

"Nnnnnnnnnnnnnnnnnn . . ."

The whine built in the back of her throat, a high, pathetic keening that set Rule's teeth on edge and made the hair at the nape of his neck bristle to attention.

"Nnnnnnnnnniiiiiii-I didn't mean to!"

It spat forth like a bullet from her lips in a voice too deep and too disturbing to be hers. Rule had to stifle the urge to duck.

"Rule, I swear to the *depths,* I didn't mean to. It wasn't my fault!"

"Oh, wow," he heard Carly breathe from somewhere behind him. "I don't think Abby lives here anymore."

She lived there all right, but at the moment there was someone else answering her doorbell. And judging by the first words out of its mouth, Rule had a sneaking suspicion he knew exactly who it was.

"Lou."

The figure who had been Abby leaned forward,

the whites of her eyes glittering eerily and emptily in the room's mellow light.

"Don't be mad, Rule. I swear I wasn't planning on messing with any humans. I swear it." Just like Abby had gone missing from her eyes, Rule couldn't hear her in the voice, either. The low, androgynous whine sounded nothing like the light, feminine, faintly panicked tone he'd heard before he called forth the fiend in her. "I was minding my own business when a bunch of humans decided to attack the Other kid I'd hitched a ride with. They were gonna be trouble, I could tell. So I dove into the nearest hiding place I could find. I didn't know she was gonna be a human!"

Rule didn't buy it. "You knew the woman was not Other, Lou. Even you are not stupid enough to make that mistake. The girl's humanity all but glows from her."

"But-but—"

"And even if you had not seen it, you sure as hell should have smelled it." Rule leaned farther forward, following the recoiling body until he pressed nearly nose-to-nose with it. The fiend tried to sink back into the chair, but it had only so far it could go. "She smells like cotton candy, Lou. Do you know many Other women who smell like human confectioneries?"

The bite of sulfur in the air suddenly sharpened, and Rule felt the fiend's rising discomfort. "I—I—I didn't stop to think, Rule. I was . . . too freaked out. I thought those thugs were gonna *kill* me!"

Rule snorted. "You are a fiend, Lou. You cannot die like that, and you and I both know it. Now tell me the truth."

Tess shifted behind them. "Rule, maybe you should back off a little. That position Abby's in right now is looking pretty uncomfortable."

With her back and limbs arched and twisted in ways only a human contortionist could probably think of, Rule figured Tess might be right. But at least Abby couldn't feel anything just then, and he needed to get some information before he let Lou slink back into the woman's subconscious.

"She will be fine. She will not even remember this when she wakes." Rule braced his hands on the arms of the chair to either side of Abby's body and poured on the menace. "Tell me what is going on, Lou. Why did you disappear? What are you doing Above?"

"I can't telllll youuuuuuuuuuuuuuuuu!"

The fingers on Rule's free hand itched to wrap around the fiend's neck. They even twitched on the arm of the chair, digging into the leather the way they longed to dig into Lou. But Rule couldn't move them. He saw too clearly that the only neck available belonged to Abby, no matter whose voice was coming from it just then. The sweet, warm scent of her reminded him with every breath that if he tried to hurt Lou, he'd end up hurting Abby by default.

Something deep inside him balked at the very idea.

Instead, he remained close, leaning in until the fiend had to feel his power seeping through the human skin that clothed it. "You do not have a choice,

Louamides," Rule growled. "I command you to tell me what you are running from."

The figure in the chair quivered like a whipped puppy, a long, humming whimper vibrating from somewhere inside like an alarm buzzer. Rule could hear the others in the room shifting restlessly behind him, but he ignored them. He knew this fiend, knew its name, knew its weaknesses. It would never be able to hold out against Rule, for which he was grateful. The sooner he got the information he needed, the sooner he could bring Abby back to the forefront of her own mind.

"Louamides Asgarumel, I command you to answer my questions!"

"*Uzkiel!*" the fiend wailed. "Uzkiel and his minions hunt for me. I had to get away from them. Uzkiel knows I have the *solus* spell, and he'll kill me to get it. He got suspicious about me. He knew someone in his company was passing you information and he guessed it was me. He sent me to fetch the spell as a test, but I didn't know what it was. If I give it to him, it'll kill me; and if I don't, *he'll* kill me. I had to hide. I knew being Above would make it harder for him to find me, so I hitched a ride on the first summoning I heard, and I've been here ever since. But I was laying low! I was staying in the Others. I wasn't making waves, I swear. If it hadn't been for those lousy riots, no one would ever have known I was here. I promise!"

Rule didn't think the figure had drawn breath during that entire speech. It spoke so fast, Rule was amazed it didn't trip on its borrowed tongue. When it finally skidded to a stop, Rule felt almost dizzy from the speed.

The uneasiness he felt came from something entirely different.

Behind him, Rafael stepped forward, casting a long shadow across Rule, the chair, and the panting, quaking fiend curled up inside Abby Baker's contorted form.

"Did any of that make sense to you?" the Felix asked softly.

Rule looked up into glittering green eyes and jerked his head once in affirmation. "Unfortunately, yes."

CHAPTER EIGHT

Abby struggled back to awareness through a layer of dense, sticky confusion, as if whatever was inside her had filled her head with warm caramel while she'd been someplace else. It wasn't painful, but it wasn't very pleasant, either. She forced her eyelids open against the weight that seemed to have them glued in place and frowned up at the circle of faces peering down on her.

"What happened?" she croaked, frown deepening. And why did she sound like Tom Waits after a bad case of laryngitis? "Did you find out what you wanted to know?"

She watched while Rafael De Santos switched his gaze from her face to Rule's and back again. "I think the answer to that may turn out to be rather subjective, my dear."

"What do you mean?"

"In his mysterious feline way," Tess said, "my husband is trying to say that we got answers to a bunch of questions and had time to hash them out while you were unconscious. But I'm not sure anyone actually likes those answers."

Abby felt her stomach clench. "So you were right. I really am possessed."

Carly nodded vigorously. "That's a big ten-four."

The clenching turned into something resembling what happened at a taffy pull. It pulled and twisted and folded and then started the process all over again. Abby's skin, too, felt different. Tight, buzzing. Over-sensitive, as if something had been crawling on it and the sensory memory still lingered behind.

Her hand went instinctively to her throat and grasped her cross. The warmth of the metal and stone, the familiar weight and shape of the necklace, comforted her, just like it always had.

She frowned. *Exactly* like it always had. It didn't burn or scar her. It didn't feel any different than it had on the first day she'd clasped it around her neck. Even that vague feeling of being watched she'd had earlier had settled down. Maybe this demonic possession thing was just a mistake.

"I wonder if it could have been a kind of hypnotic suggestion thing," she ventured, her voice hopeful in her own ears. "You know, I bought into the possession story, so when you all started asking me questions, my subconscious just filled in the answers it thought you wanted. After all, I'm wearing a cross. I should be protected from demons and vampires and all that stuff."

Even before she'd gotten the explanation out, Abby could see five heads shaking in firm unison.

"No such luck," Samantha said, looking genuinely sympathetic. "Remember what Tess said before about the whole 'bupkes' thing? I'm afraid it's really real. It's a possession."

Abby let her head thump back against the chair back. Actually, she didn't so much let it happen as she was unable to stop it. It was spinning so fast and so crazily, she figured she should be grateful it was still attached. She just couldn't decide if it spun because of the shock or the possession.

How on earth was *any* of this possible?

"A demon," she murmured, staring at the ceiling, her head shaking slowly. "I'm possessed by a demon."

"It is not a demon," the demon growled. "It is a fiend."

Abby tilted her head enough to look at the scowling man who stood at the foot of her chair. "So you've said. A number of times. You seem to like making that distinction."

"It's an important one where he comes from," Tess broke in as the muscle in the side of Rule's jaw jumped and clenched. "You see, most of what those of us who grew up in this reality have learned about demons is apparently wrong. What we call demons the demons call fiends. The demons themselves aren't inherently evil. Who knew?"

Abby blinked. "You're arguing semantics with me? This is my soul at stake!"

"Your soul is in no danger. At least not from me, nor from Louamides," Rule said.

"Louamides?"

"That is the name of the fiend."

"Whatever. You're a demon. Forgive me if I have

trouble taking your word for it." Abby glared at
Rule, and the tightening of her facial muscles felt
like a vise squeezing shut around her head. She mas-
saged a temple with her fingertips and let her eyes
close against the ache. "Look, this is all a little much
for me to take in at the moment. You might say it's
been a pretty eventful day."

The crawling sensation on her skin became less of
a memory and more of an actual real-time sensation.
Her eyes popped open and she glanced down at her
arms before her gaze settled on Tess, who seemed
one of the most reasonable of the apparent authority
figures in the group surrounding her. "How about you
do whatever it is you need to do to get this demon—
excuse me, to get this *fiend*—out of me, so I can go
home and go back to being a normal human being?"

Pushing herself out of her chair, she took a minute
to roll her shoulders against the tension that had
built up there. Nearly every muscle in her body felt
tense and stretched, but her shoulders and neck
seemed to carry the bulk of it. She needed a massage
that would stretch into the next century. It felt like
she'd been doing some kind of calisthenics while
she'd been unconscious.

Maybe she had been. She *hated* the feeling of
having done things and said things she couldn't remember. Even if it hadn't really been her doing and
saying them, it had been her body. She should have
remembered it.

The silence finally brought her stretch to an abrupt
stop with her arms above her head and her shoulders
somewhere up near her ears.

No one in the room said a word. They just stood there and looked at one another. Meaningfully.

The taffy pull resumed work in her stomach. In double time.

"What is it? What's wrong?" she demanded.

"It's not quite as simple as that, Abby." Tess exchanged glances with her husband and with Rule. Glances Abby's stomach interpreted as fuel for the taffy machine. "There's a lot to consider—"

"Fine. Consider it after I've been exorcised." Abby locked gazes with the witch and forced herself not to flinch or rub her hands over the creeping skin of her arms. "Right now, I want this thing out of me."

"Unfortunately, we have to think about more than—"

"I don't *care*! Get it *out of me*! If you can't do it, I'll find someone else who will!"

Her plan involved whirling on one dignified heel and stalking with perfect power and poise out the door of the club and into the door of the nearest Catholic church, but things didn't work out quite that way. Par for the course, really.

She managed about half a step before the demon stepped in front of her, blocking her path more effectively than a police barricade. She dodged to the side, but he moved faster and shot out a hand to grasp her upper arm.

"I cannot let you do that."

Her snort all but echoed in the sudden quiet of the room. "I don't remember asking permission." She tugged ineffectually at her arm, but Rule's grip only tightened.

"I noticed. But even had you done so, such permission would be denied."

Words Abby had never imagined thinking, let alone speaking, surged to the tip of her tongue, intending to tell him what he could do with his arrogant, dictatorial attitude. She knew they would earn her a mammoth amount of penance at her next confession, but oh how she imagined they'd be worth it.

"Abby, we're not trying to order you around. We're trying to protect you," Tess said, stepping forward and placing her hand over Rule's on the other woman's arm. "You didn't hear all the details of the situation. It's not safe for you to go wandering around the city on your own. Not while Lou is still with you."

"Fine. Point taken. Get whatever it is out of me, and I'll be perfectly safe."

Her pointed glare earned a matching scowl from Rule and a hasty exchange of uncomfortable glances among the room's other occupants.

"What?" she demanded.

"We cannot remove the fiend from you at the moment. It is impossible," Rule decreed.

Abby's stomach took another ride on the new roller coaster in her gut. "You mean, it's stuck?"

"I wouldn't have put it quite that way," Tess pursed her lips, "but I suppose it's not an inaccurate assessment. We tried to perform a sort of exorcism on you, and it didn't work."

Suddenly the sound of Abby's heartbeat seemed to be the loudest thing in the room. "You mean I'll have this thing inside me forever? For the rest of my life? Isn't there a way to pass it on to someone else, like it got passed on to me? There has to be a way."

She looked frantically around the room, her pleading gaze resting for a moment on Samantha, who made a noise of distress and stroked a hand down Abby's other arm.

"It's not permanent," the Lupine soothed. "In a few days, Tess will come up with a spell that will work in place of the exorcism and you can go right back to normal. But for now, we're going to have to focus on the other part of the situation."

The demon beside them snarled.

Tess shot Samantha a glare. "You're not helping, Sam."

Abby tried to wrap her mind around what she'd just heard and felt a headache coming on like a freight train. "What are you talking about? What situation? If you think there's a way to get rid of this fiend, you need to find it now! I want it out of me!"

A sharp jerk broke the demon's hold on her. Her eyes wide and nervous, she backed away from the others the Others!—until her knees bumped into the edge of an armchair. Samantha stared guiltily at the floor, while Tess watched Abby with her mouth compressed into a flat line. The demon had his dark, fathomless eyes fixed on her, his expression hard and uncompromising.

"Right now, you only need to concern yourself with one name. Uzkiel."

A shudder ran down her spine with such force, Abby felt her feet shift from the floor. The name meant nothing to her, but it must have meant something to whatever lurked inside her.

God, she hated having feelings that didn't belong to her!

"Who is Uzkiel?" she demanded, stuffing down the bile of fear that rose in her throat when she spoke the name.

Rule sighed. "This is not a simple story. Nor is it brief. You really should sit."

Abby took one look at the enveloping wing chair behind her and repressed a snort. Instead she stepped over to a plush ottoman—gritting her teeth when the wall of Others moved with her—and perched on the edge. At least the footstool didn't have a back. She could always jump off the other side if worse came to worst.

"OK, tell me what's going on."

Rule settled his imposing frame into a seat facing her and leaned forward, bracing his forearms on his thighs. "The first thing you must understand is that the human conception of what you call 'demons' is, as Tess told you earlier, very wrong. Demons have existed since long before your kind became aware of your God. In those days, we were called *daimon* and we were the messengers between the worlds."

"Between what worlds?"

"All of them. Surely you have realized by now that more exists in the universe than this single reality." He raised an eyebrow, but Abby just pursed her lips and nodded for him to continue. She had no earthly idea what she'd realized over the last few hours, let alone the last few weeks. "We carried news and messages between all living creatures, until the Fae declared war on us."

Tess dragged her husband to sit beside her on the sofa near Rule and made a rude noise. "You're lucky neither Fiona nor Luc is here to take exception to your POV, pal."

Abby had no idea who Tess was talking about, so she ignored her. "The Fae? You mean faeries?" She tried to imagine a squadron of fluttering little Tinkerbells attacking an army of figures like Rule and nearly laughed out loud.

"As I said, more exists than what you might think you know. In any event, the war between the Fae and my kind lasted nearly a thousand years," he continued. "Eventually, the treaties signed between us banished the demons to the Below where we have lived in exile ever since."

"I thought you said before that everything I knew about demons was 'bupkes'? That sounds a lot like the battle between Lucifer and God's angels to me."

Rafael gave a shout of laughter that echoed around the room. "My apologies," he chuckled when his wife hit him in the chest. "It was simply the idea of anyone mistaking the Fae for 'God's angels.' The idea is too amusing." He snickered. "You will understand when you meet Fiona. Trust me."

Abby had no intention of broadening her acquaintance in the Other world, but she held her tongue. She needed the information more than she needed to make a point right now.

Rule's mouth had curved into a half smile at Rafael's reaction to her opinion. "I am familiar with the story, but believe me, the reality was much different. The Fae are no angels, and before we descended to the Below, my kind were no devils."

"But they are now? I thought you all tried to tell me that demons aren't evil."

"We are not. We are not so different from humans: some good, some bad, and some mostly indifferent. But there are some among us who did not deal well with our exile." His dark eyes caught hers. "The world Below is very different from this one, with forces at work for both the light and the dark. Those trapped Below who have been warped by the dark are very similar to what humans have come to know as demons. We call them fiends. There are fiends who have given completely over to the dark, but you may rest assured that Louamides is not one of them. He is a minor entity. You will not find yourself burdened with the curses of evil. You are not damned and will not feel the ill of it."

This was all a little much for Abby to take in. "Splitting hairs?"

Rule's mouth tightened. "Merely attempting to avert the splitting of heads. Yours among them. My kind have assumed the duty of protecting ourselves and this world against the fiends by establishing the Watch. I am one of its officers. It is my job to ensure the fiends do not stir up trouble in the Below or in this world."

"Well, that seems to be going just swimmingly."

The demon looked like he wanted to strangle her. With exhaustion creeping rapidly up on her, Abby couldn't bring herself to care. There were plenty of witnesses. Maybe that would at least slow him down.

"We have heard rumors that the fiends have begun to plan an attack on the capital city of the Below, Infernium." He continued as if she hadn't spoken, but his tone was even grimmer than before. "I and several of my men formed a kind of . . . task force to prevent the rebellion. We drafted an informant in the company of the leader of the discontents. Louamides is the fiend who was assisting us and Uzkiel is the fiend whose plans we sought to foil."

"Louamides? One of you said that was what the thing inside me was called, didn't you? I'm being possessed by a fiendish stool pigeon?"

"An informant. A very important one that I have traveled from Below specifically to find."

"Great. Fine. You found him." Abby glared. "Now tell me why you can't get him out of me."

"For two important reasons. First, as you already know, the fiend appears trapped. And second, Uzkiel sent Louamides to find something for him, a very powerful bit of magic called the *solus* spell. When Lou realized that passing the spell to Uzkiel would mean not just his death, but the war we have all been trying to avoid, he fled. As long as Uzkiel is looking for him, he must stay hidden."

"Then he can darned well hide somewhere else!" Abby jumped to her feet, panic lending speed to her movements and about an octave to her voice. "This is your war, not mine! I don't want any part of it. Find someplace else to store your blasted informant and let me go home. Now!"

Tess got to her feet as well and sent the men back into their seats with an authoritative glare. When she turned back to Abby, Tess kept her voice calm and her expression soothing.

"We're not doing this to torture you, Abby," she said. "It's not our idea of a good time, either. And Rule isn't lying about the first spell I tried to get Lou out of you failing. Trust me, figuring out why that happened is going to be my top priority. But Rule's top priority has to take into account the fact that you were seen in public with Lou's last known host. Uzkiel has an army out looking for it, and we have reason to believe they've made their way into our world to look for you. If Lou was able to piggyback on another summoning to enter our world, we have to believe other fiends are capable of the same trick. We can't let them find you."

Abby set her jaw. "They won't have any reason to come after me once you find a way to get rid of the fiend they're looking for."

"And how are they supposed to know it's gone? Are you planning to take out a newspaper ad? It won't stop them from coming after you to find out for themselves." Tess's guileless blue eyes suddenly looked a great deal harder than they had a few minutes ago. "It also won't stop them from doing whatever they think they have to, or even just think would be fun, to get you to tell them where Lou has gone. We can't take that kind of chance."

"There are many chances we cannot afford to take right now." Rule's voice sounded firm and hard, as if his being adamant was likely to make a difference to Abby. "The spell Louamides carries gives Uzkiel too compelling a reason to continue to search for him, and I cannot allow it to be found. Until Tess can relocate it, you are the best hiding place I have."

"I'm not a hiding place; I'm a *person*! and there's no reason you can't find *another* person for the job. You've got seven million, nine hundred ninety-nine thousand, nine hundred and ninety-nine other choices."

"You wish to ask another person to go through what you have just gone through and more?" His tone and his expression matched in their utter blandness.

Abby's first instinctual answer to that question was a resounding, "*Yes!*" But something stopped her from saying it. Blast her conscience anyway. So instead, she pursed her lips and just glared. At everyone.

"I'm sure it sounds horribly selfish of us to ask this of you," Tess said, her mouth twisting in a self-deprecating smile, "and I'm fairly certain that it is horribly selfish, but it's not just about keeping Louamides in hiding. It's also about keeping you safe. This is more than a human can deal with, Abby. Not even one of us would want to deal with it on our own."

The room seemed to spin around Abby. She couldn't decide if she was about to faint or throw up or just break down and cry. If she had anything to say about it, she'd probably do all three just as soon as she got back to her apartment.

She took a deep, shaky breath. "Okay, I appreciate the fact that you're concerned about my safety.
That's very hum—" She caught herself and broke
off awkwardly. "That's very . . . kind of you. But
I'm a big girl. I can take care of myself, and frankly,
that's what I prefer to do."

Samantha turned her own set of puppy dog eyes
on Abby. How did she do that when the darned
things were blue instead of brown?

"You're not safe, Abby," the Lupine said, her
voice low and urgent. "You need protection, and
trust me, that kind of thing is our pack's specialty."

She frowned. If she needed protection, she'd call
her big brother. And his assault rifle, hand grenades,
and utility knife.

"No, really. I'll be fine. I've got good locks, a
building with a doorman, and if I need protection,
my brother can—"

Rafael and Rule looked at each other, heaved si-
multaneous and nearly silent sighs, and turned back
to her. She wasn't going to like this.

Hey, look. You're starting to pick up the signals,
she thought.

At least, she *thought* she thought it. Who knows
who might be in control of her inner voice at the
moment?

The Felix stood, the charming smile slipping
from his face, leaving behind a fine-bladed expression of arrogant command. "I had hoped you would
not put me in this position, Miss Baker, but I am
afraid I have no choice. We are no longer asking you
to put yourself in our care. We are ordering it. You

will stay here in the club under twenty-four-hour guard until we have found and dealt with Uzkiel."

Abby's jaw dropped to the Oriental carpet and bounced twice. She didn't know who said what came out of her mouth next, but whether it was her or the fiend possessing her, she wholeheartedly agreed with the sentiment.

"Over your dead body!"

CHAPTER NINE

t ess had been right. Poker was definitely not Abby Baker's game.

Rule saw the intent to move in her eyes before her muscles got the signal. When she shot out of her chair, he leaped in front of her, and when she bolted for the door, he got ahold of her arm before she could so much as twitch in that direction. Judging by the frantic strength she put into fighting his grip—obviously augmented by Lou's presence inside her, because, Rule figured, her left hook didn't usually threaten to crack ribs—it was a good thing he'd been paying attention or she'd have been hell on wheels to catch.

No pun intended.

"Let go of me!" she howled, writhing like a fish on a hook in his grip.

Cursing under his breath, Rule grabbed her by both arms and spun her around to press her back against his chest until his arms crossed in front of her like a straitjacket. The hold immobilized her upper body, but that didn't stop her from using her heels to try to dislocate his kneecaps. It was a good thing she was so bloody tiny or she'd probably have broken his nose with a vicious head butt. If she slammed her head into him any harder, something was bound to crack. Whether it would be his collarbone or her skull was up for debate.

Face set, he caught Rafe's gaze over the top of her tangled hair and jerked his chin toward the door. "I've got her. Take everybody else out. She may be feeling a little outnumbered just now."

"Outnumbered?! I'll show you outnumbered, you slime-sucking son of a syphilitic goat!" Her shrill scream made a greater impact than her epithets; it nearly burst his eardrum.

Rafe nodded. "If you need backup, you know where to find us."

If this had been a movie set, Abby's eyes would have been glowing with red-orange flames. As it was, smoke was nearly pouring out of her ears.

"You think I'm going to forget you were in on this just because you leave the room, you catnip-chewing cretin?! I'm going to get out of here and I'm going to make every *single one* of you *beg* my pardon!"

Tess winced and ducked as Abby's increasingly loud tirade became increasingly moist as well. "Um, I think that's our cue to exit, baby. Come on. Getting Gabriel into his bath and pajamas will seem like a cakewalk tonight."

"Actually, why don't you guys have a nice night out?" Carly suggested, pushing Samantha out the door ahead of her and glancing warily back over her shoulder at Rule and the still-swearing and struggling

Abby. "Sam and I can babysit. We'll make sure the kitten gets to bed shining like a new penny!"

A moment later, the library door clicked shut, leaving Rule alone with the Tasmanian devil–woman in his arms.

His biggest problem, he realized as a particularly violent motion sent her undulating against him like a belly dancer, wasn't that the human female seemed in no hurry to calm down; it was that his attention had fixed more firmly on the warm, soft weight of her in his arms than on the fact of her determination to do him great bodily harm.

She felt amazing. Her soft curves and silky skin had obviously been designed for loving, not fighting, and the incongruous strength she currently possessed only drew more attention to the plush welcome lying in wait beneath her snarling attack. The exertion had begun to speed her heart rate, dampen her skin, and make her breathing fast and ragged just like it would be if he had her beneath him, bare and begging. . . .

Shit.

Gritting his teeth and banishing the image from his mind, Rule moved quickly to separate their bodies. He had more important things to think about right now than his sudden and obsessive interest in a human woman who never should have made him look twice. From a distance, she looked like a mouse. Maybe if she'd stayed that way when he got closer, his libido would have been easier to control.

"Calm down," he hissed into her ear, thinking about what good advice that was. For both of them.

He saw his breath stir the baby-fine ash-brown hair at her ear and tried not to picture what the pale, plump lobe might taste like.

What the hell was wrong with him?

"I said, calm down," he repeated in a growl. "No one is going to hurt you. I swear it."

Her shriek rang with frustration. "No one is going to hurt me? What the hell is wrong with you? This is kidnapping! You think this is my idea of a good time?"

"I think nothing of the sort, but unfortunately, none of us have a choice in the matter just now."

"Oh, that's rich! No choice. Because, you know, you're under some kind of divine compulsion to grab me off the street, take me to your secret hideout, and keep me prisoner against my will."

The only compulsion Rule felt at the moment couldn't have been further from divine in origin, but he had no intention of discussing that with her.

He grunted when she landed another solid kick to his left knee. "You know exactly where you are; therefore, the 'hideout' is hardly secret. And I believe it would be better for all of us if you took Tess's suggestion and began to look at this as a form of protective custody. No one here means you any harm. In fact, it is quite the opposite."

She turned her head until her blue eye pinned him with a look of icy rage. "If you want to help me out, you'll let me go. I have friends and family to keep me safe."

"You're being ridiculous." Rule shifted his grip on her. "If we let you leave here, you would be dead within the hour, along with your friends and family. I guarantee it."

He saw her blink. It wasn't much as far as weakening went, but he would take what he could get just then. If she didn't calm down enough for him to let go of her soon, he was afraid he'd do something stupid. Like lick her. All over.

"And it is not only your life at stake," he reminded her. "If you die, Louamides becomes an open target, and if Uzkiel finds him, any chance we have of defeating Uzkiel dies as well."

Her compelling eyes narrowed. "Let me just tell you that reminding me of the thing that's currently *possessing me* is not going to put me in a very cooperative mood right now!"

Rule met her gaze squarely. "What if I remind you that if Uzkiel finds you and retrieves the *solus* spell from Louamides, your vision of Armageddon will look like a summer picnic in contrast to the hell those fiends will loose on the earth."

She heard that. He felt it in the way her struggles suddenly eased even as her muscles stiffened. He resisted the temptation to press the advantage and let the silence fill the space between them.

"You act like that should mean something to me." She sounded far from happy, but she was no longer shrieking at him. "I have no idea who this Uzkiel you keep mentioning is, or what the heck a '*solus*' spell is, or why you think I have any influence on the fate of the universe. I'm not even that important to my boss. Why should I be important to the fabric of the universe?"

"I am not an expert on why. My concern is with how. Or rather, how not, as in how not to bring about a bloody reign of fiendish tyranny."

"You paint an impressive picture; I'll give you that. But I still don't really understand how I'm the secret to the triumph of good over evil."

Rule slid his hands down to her wrists, ignoring the smooth glide of her skin beneath his hands. Gripping her wrists not tightly but securely, he turned her to face him.

Stars, but she was tiny. The top of her head didn't quite reach his shoulder, and the body that had fought so hard against him a few minutes ago looked delicate enough to break with a harsh word. She wasn't small or waiflike by any means, but she was so soft and so obviously human she may as well have been a baby bird.

"If you can remain calm for the next few moments, I will do my best to explain it all to you."

She shot him a dirty look that he was willing to take as agreement, but he didn't release his hold on her wrists. He used it to steer her the few steps to the sofa and urge her to take a seat. Settling beside her, he kept a wary eye on her. She might look like a baby bird, but she clearly had the temper of a rabid raptor.

"I gave you a brief summary of the difference between my kind and the fiends like Uzkiel," he began. "We are called sun demons because even after years of living Below, we still retain an affinity for light. We can gain power from it, unlike the fiends, who shrink at the light of a full moon. In the midday sun, they are powerless."

"Like vampires."

He sighed. Hadn't the Others managed to educate the human populace about anything since they Unveiled? Because he certainly didn't have time to give an abridged history of supernatural-kind.

"Like your popular mythology of vampires, yes. The vulnerability has given us a distinct advantage over the fiends and has allowed us to avert war for centuries. When the fiends first began to evolve, the rulers of the Below appointed the Watch as a sort of police force to keep them in line. We ensure that they do not get out of hand, because if they were to take over the Below, it would be only their first step."

"And the second step?"

His jaw flexed. "Above. Many Others theorize that fiends are the source of the demonology of human society, because they fit many of the stories of evil demons causing death and destruction for men. Fiends feed on the life force of other beings, and human hearts are one of their favorite snacks." He saw her swallow hard. "Light has always been one of our most formidable weapons."

Abby eyed him warily. "Why does that sound like you're saying it in the past tense?"

"Because our fear has always been that if the fiends were to find a way to make themselves immune to the effects of light, they would be invulnerable."

"But they haven't found it, have they?"

"They have been looking for a very long time, and before disappearing, Louamides was one of the fiends Uzkiel had assigned to the task."

She was shaking her head even before Rule completed the thought. Her eyes filled with mingled fear and denial, and he could only nod in return.

"The spell I mentioned before—the *solus* spell—has the power to harness the energy of light, even light as powerful as the sun, and render it into darkness. It would allow the fiends to create a permanent nightfall wherever they went. They would be free to conquer not just the Below, but the human world as well."

"How is that possible?" Abby felt her features draw together in a kind of baffled horror. "How can any person make that kind of magic?"

"Any person could not. The spell is only known to most of our kind as a legend, and the legend says it took the combined power of five of the most powerful Fae of the warring years working together for five full cycles of the sun to craft the spell."

"But why would the Fae create a spell that could only strengthen the demons in the middle of a war against them?"

Rule shook his head. "You forget, until the end of the war when the demons were banished below, the fiends did not exist. All our kind were demons and all of us could draw our strength from the sun. The *solus* spell was invented as a kind of Doomsday weapon. If the tide of battle turned against them, the Fae could cast it and rob our armies of the bulk of their power in one fell blast."

"Why didn't they?"

"Self-preservation. The Fae would enjoy a darkened world no more than we would have. They may not draw their power directly from the sun as we do, but they prefer it to darkness."

"What happened to the spell after the war?"

"That is what the fiends have wanted to know. It disappeared."

"And I just have the kind of luck to get involved just as it's been found again after how many years?"

"A few thousand."

A sort of sick comprehension dawned in her expression, and she braced her elbows on her legs, burying her face in her hands. "This can't be happening."

He caught the mumble and wished for a way to reassure her. Hell, he wished for a way to reassure *himself*. "Unfortunately, I'm afraid that it is. It's happening right now. And the only way I know to keep the situation from getting even worse is to keep Louamides safely out of Uzkiel's sight until the rest of the Watch can locate him and bring him under control."

Rule braced himself for more screaming, but it didn't materialize. Instead, Abby turned her brown and blue eyes on him and studied him in silence for several minutes.

Her expressions might be easy to read, but her eyes were fathomless. He could see the doubt, the fear, the frustration, even the anger on her face, but in her eyes all he saw was a warm, deep calmness that made him want to crawl inside her. It was a separate instinct from the one that wanted to *get* inside her through an entirely different route. That one he understood, not so much its cause but at least its intent. This one confused him. This wasn't lust but something . . . sweeter.

It made his scowl deepen.

Abby sighed. "Look, I'm trying—I'm *really* trying—to see your point. I promise. But maybe if you tried looking at this from my perspective instead of just trying to intimidate me into cooperating—"

"I am not trying to intimidate you." Forcing the tension from his expression, Rule leaned back to try to give her as much space as possible while still staying close enough to grab her if she tried to bolt. "I'm just trying to explain to you why I can't let you wander around the city alone. Not while Louamides is still with you."

She laughed, but he heard no amusement in the sound. "So, what? I'm supposed to just nod and smile and take up knitting until you solve a problem you've clearly been fighting for a lot longer than I've been caught up in it?" She shook her head. "I don't know what world you come from, but I'm from this one, and around here we have to do things like pay rent. And buy groceries. That requires that I 'wander around the city,' as you like to put it."

He leaped on the opportunity to reassure her. The fact that she was throwing this kind of obstacle in his way meant that she was weakening. Whether she'd begun to see reason or she'd just gone cross-eyed from exhaustion, Rule didn't care. It was the outcome that mattered.

"We all realize that this is inconvenient for you. We would never put your livelihood in jeopardy," he reassured her. "The Council will be more than happy to pay your rent and see to any other bills for as long as you are required to stay in hiding."

She cast him a sour look. "Unless 'the Council' plans to keep paying my bills for the rest of my life, I have to go to work. If I don't show up tomorrow, I'll lose my job."

"You cannot tell them you are ill? Do you not have vacation time?"

"Vacation is what you call a week spent lounging on the beach, or touring Napa Valley. Being locked in a nightclub with a bunch of inhuman strangers is not a vacation. Besides, if I want to take a vacation, I have to request the time in advance. I can't just stop showing up and call it a vacation."

"Who do you work for? I will speak to her."

"It's a he, and trust me, that scowl will work even less on him than it does on me."

Rule cursed and rose, shoving a hand through his hair and prowling toward the fireplace on the other side of the room. "I am trying to make this easy on you, but there is only so much I can do. I cannot let Uzkiel find you, and I cannot protect you if you are not kept somewhere safe."

He knew while his mouth was moving that he was asking for trouble. He glanced back at the sofa and saw Abby's eyes narrow and knew she was about to give it to him.

"Well, forgive me for making your life difficult," she said, pushing to her feet. "Here I am with my entire life turned upside down, my body invaded by something I didn't believe in two months ago, and my freedom snatched away from me by a walking mountain with an attitude problem. What do I think gives me the right to get upset about any of it? I'm just behaving like an absolute crybaby!"

He opened his mouth, but nothing got the chance to emerge.

"Let me repeat my suggestion that if I'm such a pain for you to have to deal with, I'd be more than happy to get out of your life just as soon as you *let me go!*"

She stalked toward him with each step, her eyes blazing and the fear in her expression transmuted clearly into rage. She poked a finger at him in time with the cadence of her speech until she issued her last command with the tip digging into his chest and her gaze spitting fire at him.

Rule broke.

He couldn't help it. He'd been fine while he sat next to her; he'd even been in control while he'd been touching her, trying to keep her from hurting someone, herself included. But the minute she touched *him*, the minute her fingertip came to rest on his chest and the warm, sweet scent of her breath rushed over his skin, the grip he had on his control shattered like cheap glass.

As he muttered a prayer and a curse in the same breath, his hands came up to sweep her arms away and drag her hard against him. He saw the look of shock and the quick shiver of fear before his last rein broke and his mouth slammed down over hers like an invading army.

And he knew his troops had hers hopelessly outnumbered.

◆ ◆ ◆

Abby knew she'd just taken a flying leap off the Cliffs of Insanity, but by the time she realized, it was too late to do anything except spread her arms and yell, "Banzai!"

One minute she'd been trying to have a reasonable conversation about the least reasonable thing that had ever happened to her, and the next thing she knew, the world stopped.

Or maybe that was just her heart.

Rule was exploring her lips as if they contained the key to the gates of heaven. Abby was pretty sure they didn't, but Rule seemed determined to find out for himself.

But she would be willing to swear on her grandmother's silver rosary that she would never in a million lifetimes forget the feel or the taste or the heat of the demon's mouth on hers. It had etched itself permanently not just on her memory but on her soul as well.

That's when Abby remembered just who she was kissing.

Stiffening, she flattened her palms against Rule's chest and pressed. He made a low, rumbling sound in his throat and tightened his grip on her arms. She felt the way his muscles tensed, but his mouth unexpectedly softened.

Ooooh, he was devious. Or was that delicious?

An attack she would have fought against. It would have made her mad and cold and perfectly willing to put a knee to a place she assumed was as sensitive on demons as it was on mortal men. But Rule knew his stuff. The minute she got her back up, he regrouped and switched to stealth tactics.

His grip remained firm, but Abby could feel his thumbs rubbing small circles on her upper arms as he held her in place. The rigidly contained sensation raised gooseflesh on more than her arms and had her leaning closer to him instead of pulling away.

A tremor ripped through her, like the aftershock of an earthquake, which was no wonder, since she could swear the earth was moving. She had to struggle to suppress a whimper when he dragged his mouth with drugging slowness over hers. He tasted like heat and pleasure and gingersnaps, crisp and spicy and just barely sweet. She swore to herself that she would not kiss him back, even as her lips parted and he slid inside like a cat burglar, quiet and subtle and devastating.

That time the moan slipped out. She couldn't help it. Her knees collapsed and his arms slid around her to catch her to him. The red haze of rage dissolved in the bright light of lust just as the door to the library swung open behind them.

The voice she heard next belonged to Tess, not God, but that didn't change the fact that Abby swore she heard the angels singing.

"Well," the woman said, laughter rich and bubbling in her voice. "I suppose this pretty much counts as a meeting of . . . er . . . minds."

CHAPTER TEN

"I brought you some towels." Samantha set a stack of fluffy linens on the end of the bed and offered her a tentative smile.

Abby turned away from the window overlooking the street four floors below and reminded herself not to take her frustration out on the Lupine. Of the Others Abby had met today, Samantha had been the most sympathetic, even if she hadn't managed to talk Rule and Rafael into letting Abby go home. Frankly, Abby didn't think that much talking was possible.

I warned you to knee him in the balls while you had the chance.

Abby groaned as the voice that had gone blessedly silent after her bout of unconsciousness reared its ugly tongue. At this point, slamming her head into a brick wall sounded almost fun, if it would get rid of the thing permanently.

Hey, that ain't nice. You keep thinking things like that and you'll hurt my feelings.

"Would you shut up!" Abby yelled, throwing her hands up and glaring at . . . nothing. Unfortunately,

Samantha seemed to think it had been aimed at her. She paled and looked like a puppy who'd just been kicked.

Forcing herself to at least a semblance of calm, Abby sighed and offered the Lupine a weak smile. "Sorry, I didn't mean you," she explained. "But the voice inside my head is driving me crazy. If hearing a voice inside my head doesn't count as evidence that I'm *already* crazy."

Samantha murmured something sympathetic, which just served to make Abby feel like a heel as well as a prisoner. No matter how often one of the Others told her they understood how she felt or that they didn't like the current situation any more than she did, their sympathy didn't extend toward straying from their decided course of action.

They'd vetoed letting her go home alone, letting her go home to her brother, letting her go upstate to her parents, letting her go anyplace with a body- guard, and even letting her go to the police. Not that she'd held out much hope about the last one, but she'd have settled for the FBI or even the bloody KGB if it got her out of the nightmare she'd landed in. She felt so out of control at the moment that making any decision for herself, even a stupid one, had become her only goal. Make that obsession.

Nothing had made the others so much as blink. Rafael had pulled rank as head of the Council of Others—which still didn't mean much to Abby but seemed to settle the matter for everyone else—and decreed that Abby would remain in protective cus- tody until Uzkiel was captured. The custody turned out to be so protective that she wasn't even allowed to leave the building. The night manager of Vircolac had set up a room for her on the private top floor of the club, and she'd been hustled up here unceremoniously by an annoyingly amused Tess and an at least guilty-looking Samantha.

The only concession abby had been able to wring from her jailers had been the agreement that they would at least look for a way to get her body back under her sole ownership by moving Lou into some other kind of non-human, volunteer host. They could exorcise it into a Tibetan meditation bowl, for all she cared, but she wanted to be the only voice talking inside her head again.

"I know I hate getting into a nice clean bed when I'm feeling all grubby. I thought you might want to take a shower."

At least Samantha's voice had the courtesy to be coming from someone else's body.

Abby gestured at her grubby jeans and even grubbier sweatshirt. "Thanks, but I don't have anything to change into."

"Oh, Missy sent over some sweats from next door. She always keeps spares around. They're under the towels."

Abby looked down and saw a corner of navy cotton peeking out from beneath the oatmeal-colored towels. "Who's Missy? And why does she keep extra sweats around? You guys do the kidnapping thing often?"

Samantha ignored the kidnapping comment. "Missy Winters. Luna of the Silverback Clan."

Samantha tugged down the sheets of the bed she'd helped make up a few minutes ago. "She and the Alpha live next door. He owns Vircolac."

The research Abby had done on one of the station's werewolf stories flashed into her head along with a mental picture of one of the Other faces that had been most prominent in the news over the last few weeks. Graham Winters was another one of those Others like Rafael De Santos—too sexy to possibly be human. Honestly, it could give a girl a whole new perspective on her dream man.

"Missy always keeps extra changes of clothes around, because there always seems to be someone showing up around here without them." Samantha folded the duvet neatly down toward the end of the bed. "You might have noticed earlier that when we shift, our clothes don't make the change with us."

Abby sighed. "I had a few other things on my mind at the time, but yeah. I remember thinking I usually know a person for longer than fifteen minutes before I see them completely naked."

That may be one of your big problems, sweet cheeks. You're a prude. You need to relax. Let your hair down. Let your pants down. . . .

She really wanted to punch the dirty-minded little fiend right in its nasty little mouth. Since that wasn't possible, she settled for ignoring it.

The werewolf grinned at her and fluffed a big down pillow. "You did blush a little, but I thought it was cute. When you grow up in the pack, it's easy to forget that humans don't have the same perspective on things like nudity and sex that the Others do."

"There's an official Others' perspective on sex? Was it part of the media kit?"

Samantha laughed. "No, but we do tend to be more relaxed about physical stuff than you guys are. Lupines especially. Maybe it's our 'animal instincts,' but the pack looks at skin and sex as natural. There's no reason to hide either of them."

Which reminded Abby . . .

"Listen here, you little creep," she said to Louamides, "I am *not* going to have an audience while I get out of these clothes and take a shower."

A gusty sigh echoed inside her head.

"I mean that, too," she said firmly. "I swear by everything holy, if you think you're gonna get an eyeful, you disgusting little fiend, you've got another think coming. I don't care if I have to shower with my eyes closed in the pitch dark."

Ignoring Samantha's very wary expression, Abby grabbed the towels off the end of the bed and was about to turn toward the connecting bathroom Samantha had pointed out earlier, when she noticed that the werewolf wasn't leaving. Her hands lingered on the third pillow, the same one she'd been fluffing for the last ten minutes.

"Is something wrong?" Abby sighed. "Surely no one thinks you need to watch me while I sleep so I don't try to climb out the window? I'm the human one, remember? I don't do stunts."

Samantha shook her head. "No, of course not. It's just—" She broke off and her expression turned even guiltier. If that were possible. "I brought you something else."

Abby watched while the other woman reached into the pocket of her own borrowed sweatshirt and pulled out something small and silver and shiny.

She looked over her shoulder, and when she spoke again, her voice was barely more than a whisper. "I can't leave the phone with you, but I can't stop thinking about how worried my family would be if I disappeared and they didn't hear from me. The Felix said you shouldn't be allowed to make any calls, but I thought . . . you know. If you sent just one text message . . . at least you could let someone know you're safe."

Abby stared at Samantha and fought the urge to grab her by the cheeks and kiss her smack on the mouth—

Aw, yeah, baby! Now that's what I'm talking about!

—Abby contented herself with a squeal and a big hug and grabbing the proffered phone like a lifeline. This was exactly what she needed, and she didn't even need to think about whom to text or what to say.

She typed in the phone number she knew by heart and used a trembling thumb to pick out the one-word code she and her brother, Noah, had developed when they were kids.

"Thanksgiving."

Vircolac didn't stock enough brandy for Rule to get as drunk as he wanted to. Hell, he doubted even faerie wine would have offered him the oblivion he longed for tonight, but he was damned sure going to do his best to find some kind of substitute, even if it killed him.

At the moment, an untimely demise had a lot to recommend it.

What in the sun's name had he been thinking? He would have been better off sticking his tongue in an electrical socket than in the mouth of Abby Baker. Not only was she human and apparently *just* pious enough to have bought into all the bad publicity her religious leaders had spent centuries concocting about his people, but she was also the key to defeating or being defeated by the most dangerous fiend it had ever been Rule's misfortune to encounter. And to top it all off with a nice, shiny ribbon, she now resided quite securely under his protection.

Rule slouched in his chair and brooded, a large glass of brandy in one hand and his gaze trained on the flickering flames in the hearth. After Rafe and Tess and the others had left, Rule had remained at Vircolac and settled here in an upstairs sitting room he'd been told was often used for private meetings and gambling. He'd denied any interest in retiring to the bedroom he used while he stayed in the Above—or any room with a bed just then—and the night manager had offered Rule the library. The last thing he needed was to stare at the site of his own folly for a few hours, so instead he'd come up here to sulk in peace.

Too bad his mind wouldn't let him rest. It kept reliving the feel of Abby's lips beneath his, the warm, sweet taste of her, her subtle feminine scent filling his nostrils. If he had wanted to devise a particularly insidious form of torture to inflict on himself, he could not have chosen better.

The Watch had become far more than his job over the centuries he had spent serving in it. Perhaps part of that came from the fact that his father had served before him and his father's father before him, back to the dawn of the order. Maybe it had truly come to be in the blood of Rule's family. He knew for certain that somehow it had fused with his identity. He had become a Watchman in truth as well as in name. Protecting people from the evil of the fiends was his mission, the reason he continued to draw breath after so many long centuries of existence. Taking advantage of someone under his care, setting his own desires above the need to guard and defend, counted as the greatest heresy he could name. It went against everything he believed and everything he stood for.

So why the hell had he done it?

Groaning, he let his head fall back against his chair and scowled up at the ceiling. Was he going soft? At a thousand years of age, he should just be reaching his prime, but the prime he had imagined for himself had never involved taking advantage of a human woman under his care. It had never involved taking anything from a human woman.

Like most of his kind, Rule had grown up with a sort of acquired disdain for humanity. A primitive species with no magic to speak of and a clear but inexplicable desire to exterminate itself. They dabbled in forces they didn't understand and abused the forces they did understand. They held about as much attraction for most of his kind as a common slime mold. Until this woman.

"If you were anyone else, I'd say I recognize that look."

Rule glanced over his shoulder to see Graham Winters propped negligently against the wooden frame. He cast the Lupine a dark look and turned back to his mental self-flagellation.

"I've seen it too many times, my friend, on the faces of my friends and cousins, and in my own mirror to boot." Cheerfully ignoring his lack of welcome, Graham sauntered into the room and settled himself into the armchair to Rule's left. "In my world, that look only comes from one place. Woman troubles. I didn't know your kind shared that particular vulnerability."

In general terms, Rule liked Graham. He possessed a fierce loyalty, a ferocious honesty, and razor-sharp fangs that Rule knew personally came in handy in a fight. But right now, he would just as soon toss the Silverback Alpha out the window as have this conversation.

"Considering how little you know about my kind, that is hardly surprising." Rule raised his glass to his lips. "But I fear you are mistaken. I do not have a woman to cause me trouble."

"Then who exactly is upstairs sleeping in one of my VIP rooms?"

"I'm sure Rafael has filled you in on the current state of affairs."

"Oh, he told me a pretty interesting story. Missy

and I found him and Tess waiting in our living room when we got back from the movies." Graham leaned back in his chair and stretched his legs out to plant his heels on the low wood-and-metal coffee table. "But what he said doesn't explain the look on your face. Or the eyeful Tess described seeing when they barged back in on you and not-your-woman in the library."

Rule cursed, low and fluently, in the language of the Below. "That meant nothing."

"Interesting. That's a pretty different summary than the one Tess gave me. From what she described, I was thinking we'd be celebrating another mating around here any day now."

That earned Graham a glare. "I am not a Lupine. I do not make a commitment to a female merely because my hormones become slightly unruly."

"Then what does make a demon take the plunge? Presumably some of you do, or there wouldn't be any little demons pitter-pattering around the Below."

Rule's shoulders shifted in a reluctant shrug. "Of course some do, but it isn't like one of your matings. We don't believe that one soul has been preordained to join with ours and make us complete. We forge alliances or partnerships based on mutual compatibility."

"And lust."

"That, too."

Graham shook his head. "That sounds almost human, Rule. They pick their mates in the same arbitrary manner you've just described. I've always thought that's why so many of them get divorced."

"And I have always thought being tied to another for all eternity was the reason why so many Lupines die young," the demon snapped. "But this conversation is pointless. I have no interest in the human woman. We certainly do not share the sort of similarities in mind and character that could forge a lasting relationship."

"Just a lasting lip-lock, huh?"

Rule's growl was succinct and illustrative.

Graham smirked. "Right. But it's not woman trouble."

"Not the sort you are imagining." Rule tossed back the remainder of his brandy and rose to pour himself another glass. "I have no doubt the woman will be trouble, but that is because she is alone, afraid, and, I suspect, reckless. She doesn't seem to comprehend the gravity of her situation."

"Which is?"

"If Uzkiel locates her and wrests the *solus* spell from Louamides? The end of your world as it currently exists."

"Bummer."

Rule snorted and turned back to his chair. "I fail to understand how you mortals, with your finite life spans, can seem to regard matters like the destruction of your existence with such nonchalance."

"We're used to it. Christ, Rule, you remember what happened last year with Fiona and Dionnu. Before that it was the Light of Truth, and before that it was something else." He shrugged. "It's not that we take anything lightly; it's just that if we panicked every time we were threatened with destruction, we'd all be dead of heart attacks."

"And you all view where I come from as hell."

Graham grinned. "That's just because you guys don't get ESPN."

Rule shook his head and swallowed more brandy. He still didn't even feel a tingle, let alone a healthy buzz.

"Seriously, Rule, I hear what you're saying, but I still think you've got more trouble than you're admitting to. Unless you tripped and fell on her lips?"

No, he'd tripped and fallen on his own damned idiocy. "Something like that. It was purely accidental, and not something I plan to repeat."

The Lupine just looked at him.

"What?" Rule snapped. "I am perfectly serious. I have no intention of so much as touching the woman again, let alone kissing her. Not only is she under my protection, but she is mortal. Human. She is not at all the sort of female to interest me."

Graham's lips twitched. "Right. Just like I never in my life would have looked twice at a mousy human kindergarten teacher too softhearted to step on an ant at a picnic."

Having met said kindergarten teacher and seen Graham's inability to keep his hands off his mate for more than five consecutive seconds, Rule failed to appreciate the analogy.

"This is an entirely different situation. I am not Lupine, I have no pack succession to ensure, and there is no force in the Above or the Below that could possibly compel me to take a mate, let alone one so patently unsuited to me."

Shaking his head, Graham rose and sauntered toward the door. "You keep telling yourself that, buddy. And while you're at it, flip open the dictionary in the desk drawer. There's one particular word you ought to look up. It's called 'fate.' "

CHAPTER ELEVEN

bby had to admit the service at the Vircolac club beat any kind of hotel she'd ever stayed at. She'd been served coffee, eggs, scones, and jam in a private dining room that morning almost before she'd so much as had a chance to tell the caller on the other end of the house phone line that she was feeling a little hungry. While Abby had eaten, her room had been ruthlessly straightened, the clothes she'd worn yesterday had been laundered with a speed that bordered on creepy, and she'd been asked no fewer than five times if there was anything else she required.

She had to give it to them; the Others ran a heck of a swanky club. But that didn't change the fact that they'd be in for a surprise when Noah showed up and drove a tank through the front door of their little bat cave.

She wasn't sure if Noah had a tank at his immediate disposal, but if he decided he needed one to stage her rescue, she had no doubt that he would find one. Just like she knew he would find a way to use her text message from Samantha's cell phone to trace her location. Whether or not it would be quite in keeping with military regulations or the stated mission of his unit, she didn't know, and at this point she really didn't care.

I'm glad you have so much confidence in this brother of yours, Lou whined, *but I'd like to point out that if you're wrong about GI Joe, I'm gonna be the one paying the price.*

"Trust me, as much as I hate to acknowledge this," Abby muttered, "I wouldn't do anything I thought would lead to you getting hurt. At least not while it's my face coming between you and a well-placed fist."

She felt Lou settle down for a sulk and shook her head. Not only because the fiend had turned out to have such easily hurt feelings for such a crude, uncouth little monster, but also because she realized she was beginning to be able to sense it inside of her. That feeling of being watched, she now knew, was a signal that Lou was aware and paying attention to her and her surroundings, even if he wasn't talking. A few carefully placed questions over the last few hours had assured her that when that feeling faded, so had Lou. It couldn't leave her, but it could settle into a different area of her brain and stop paying attention for a while, kind of like taking a nap.

Too bad that feeling didn't come nearly as often as the first one.

The only luck she'd had in all of this nightmare consisted of the fact that her brother's battalion wasn't currently overseas. If it held even a smidge more, he wasn't at his base in North Carolina but on leave somewhere closer.

A glance at her watch made her grimace. She'd sent the text message and marked it "urgent" at just about midnight last night. It was now after three in the afternoon. If Noah had been in the state, visiting friends or their parents in their hometown northwest of Ithaca, he'd have been here by now, which meant she would be home free. Since she was currently pacing a hole in the carpet of a very comfortable sitting room, he must have been at Fort Bragg. She just hoped he had leave coming to him. The last thing she needed added to her conscience was the knowledge that she'd made her brother go AWOL. It was already stinging to the point of needing a spiritual shot of Novocain, stat.

I still vote for bourbon. Neat.

"Only if you want to experience firsthand what it feels like for your host body to projectile vomit. I told you, I don't drink. Even beer makes me queasy."

If you were drinking American beer, I can understand why.

Abby gave up pacing and dropped onto the sofa, burying her face in her hands. She still couldn't get over it. She'd kissed a demon. Shoot, if they hadn't been interrupted just then, heaven only knew what else she'd have done with him. Just the memory was enough to make her blush. She hated to think what a repeat performance would do to her.

Abigail Miriam Baker! Get that thought right out of your head. You can't go around fantasizing about having sex with a demon! Do you have any *idea how many Hail Marys that would be?*

Okay, she was reasonably sure that had been her conscience and not the fiend lurking inside her, especially since she doubted said fiend would be able to calculate the penance she'd be doing from her nursing home if she kept this up.

As if I'd care? I can calculate one thing for you, though. Your uptight quotient is like off the scales. You need to relax more than anyone else I've ever met, sweet cheeks. You ever considered yoga?

In the nude?

Abby very quickly and very deliberately conjured up a vivid image of grabbing the fiend inside her by the neck and stuffing a sock into its mouth. She thought she heard something like a muffled grunt.

Her trouble so far—the demonic rather than the fiendish kind—hadn't been with stopping herself from fantasizing. When she remained fully conscious, she could force those oh-so-sinful thoughts out of her head. After five or ten minutes. The problem was with her degenerate subconscious. The minute she'd drifted off to sleep last night, it had begun bombarding her with dreams of the hot, heady flavor of Rule's kiss and all the other delicious things he could do to her *if* he were just human.

It didn't make sense to her, not that many things made much sense these days, but this really threw her. She'd always assumed, had built her life around the premise, that there was good and evil in the world and that some beings were inherently one or the other, like angels and demons. She considered herself a modern, liberal-minded Catholic. She didn't think the entire global population of Buddhists was going straight to hell just because they didn't see things quite the same way the church did, and she believed the same about the Others. If one lived a moral life and tried one's best to help rather than hurt their fellow humans, she'd be the first to welcome them to the neighborhood. But there was a big difference between turning furry and chasing rabbits once a month and being a demon. She wasn't sure her liberalism was quite so elastic as all that.

Her mind kept traveling back to the story Rule had told, which Tess and Rafael and Samantha and Carly had been happy to corroborate, that what most humans believed about demons and fiends amounted to a front-page story in the *Weekly World News*. Abby just wasn't sure if she believed it. Could centuries— even millennia—of theologians have been wrong? Even worse, could they have been lying? Adjusting her worldview to encompass well-meaning werewolves and virtuous vampires was proving to be enough of a strain. Could she honestly make room for do-gooder demons as well?

And if she did, would it make it right for her to fall madly in lust with one, especially one who had kidnapped, manhandled, and generally been abominably rude to her?

Was there a name to the version of Stockholm syndrome that accounted for the captor being a six-foot, four-inch, outrageously sexy demon?

Sheesh, she had the worst luck with men. The last

one had been an egotistical control freak of a financial analyst, and she'd sworn she'd never get mixed up with another one of those. Talk about out of the frying pan and into the fire. Pretty literally.

The click of the door latch tugged her out of her funk and had her looking up from her morose contemplation of the carpet pattern. Samantha poked her head into the room and offered a tentative smile.

"Hi. The Alpha let me go early this afternoon so I could see how you were doing. Was there anything you needed?"

Sex, drugs, and rock 'n' roll. And maybe a club sandwich. Extra bacon and mayo.

Abby shrugged. "Thanks. After spending all day with nothing to do other than watch Jerry Springer reruns, I'm going a little stir-crazy. But otherwise, I'm fine."

The Lupine nodded and pushed the door fully open. "I thought you might be, so Missy and I decided to see if you wanted to go out to the park for a little while and get some fresh air. There's one just down the street that's private to the neighborhood."

A second figure stepped into the doorway and smiled. The woman had pale, fine skin and ash-blond hair pulled back into a braid. She also had one of the sweetest smiles Abby had ever seen and a tummy slightly rounded with pregnancy.

Hey, not bad for a breeder. Wonder what she'd look like without the tummy. Or the shirt. Abby shushed Lou violently.

"Hi," the woman said, stepping into the room followed by Samantha and extending her hand. "I'm

Missy Winters. I'm sorry my husband and I weren't here last night to welcome you to Vircolac, but it was date night and I was dying to see the new Ryan Reynolds movie. Ever since that man grew a beard it's been like an addiction, and it's so hard to talk Graham into letting me drool at someone else for a couple of hours that I hate to cancel. How are you doing?"

Abby blinked at the friendly chatter and automatically shook Missy's hand, noticing how delicate and human the other woman felt.

"Um, fine. I guess."

Missy grinned. "Right. I recognize that 'fine.' And that expression. But don't worry, eventually the whole thing starts to sink in, and eventually it'll even seem normal. Come on. It's chilly out this afternoon, so we brought you a jacket. The fresh air and exercise will do you good."

Feeling slightly dazed, Abby shrugged obediently into the denim coat Missy held out for her and followed the other two women downstairs and out the back door of the Vircolac club.

"Graham won't let me go in or out through the front anymore, not with all the protesters." Missy wrinkled her nose. "He's generally pretty protective, but when I'm pregnant he turns into some sort of monstrous maiden aunt. Which I will kill anyone for repeating," she added, raising her eyebrows at Samantha.

The Lupine just grinned and made a zipping motion over her mouth.

"It's lucky for everyone concerned that not only

do I love kids, but I get a kick out of the other benefits of pregnancy, too."

Aw, man. I can see it now. This is going to turn into one of those girl chats about the horrors of labor and delivery and the best brand of baby ass wipe. I'm outta here.

Abby felt the fiend's presence in her mind click off and nearly cheered with relief, but she was feeling a bit too surreal right then. Instead, she just trailed along beside the talkative wife of the Alpha werewolf of the Silverback Clan and tried not to look as nonplussed as she felt.

"My favorite, of course, is the calorie burning," Missy continued, leading the way across the street and toward the wrought-iron gate at the park entrance. "The only time in my life when not only do I not have to watch what I eat, but I'm practically required to pig out at regular intervals, just to keep the little wolf cub happy. It's bliss."

She patted her stomach with obvious affection and led the way in onto the cobbled path of the little neighborhood green space. Guiding them to a bench placed in the shade of a huge old oak tree, Missy sat and patted the wood beside her.

"Sit down," she urged. "I figured you'd be more comfortable talking about all this and asking questions and generally bitching about the heavy-handed, managerial, and authoritarian tendencies of nonhuman males in a more neutral location. So, have at it. I'm volunteering as your sounding board."

Abby just stared at her for a second, wondering

which part of the rabbit hole she'd fallen into this time.

"Um, I don't mean to be rude or anything," she finally managed, "but I'm not sure I'd feel comfortable complaining about them to one of them if we were at the UN headquarters under armed NATO peacekeeping forces."

Missy laughed. "Oops. I thought you knew." She glanced up at Samantha, who was, oddly enough, standing a couple of steps away from the bench and watching the park like a Secret Service agent. "You didn't tell her about me?"

The other woman looked down at them and frowned. "Tell her what, Luna?" She paused. "Oh! You mean that you're human? I didn't think about it. You've been with us so long now that I tend to forget about that kind of thing."

"Typical Lupine. If you can't eat it, mate with it, or play catch with it, try ignoring it." Missy shook her head.

Abby stared at her. "You're *human*?"

"Born and bred. Well, I suppose at the moment, since I'm currently breeding and sharing a blood-stream with a Lupine-human hybrid, you could consider me something kind of in between human and Other. But for the other seven months out of the year, I swear I'm as human as you are."

"Other *seven* months?"

Okay, the question was totally inane given the subject matter at hand, but twelve minus seven only equaled five in the kind of math Abby remembered.

"Yup. That's the third-best thing about having Lupine babies. Full-term is only five months. Not that labor and delivery are any easier, but a girl has to count her blessings where she finds them."

Abby collapsed back against the bench and blew out a deep breath. "Toto, I don't think we're in Kansas anymore."

Missy laughed out loud. "Trust me, honey, I know that feeling. I've *lived* that feeling. When I first found out the man I had a giant, secret crush on wasn't human, it took a little getting used to, too. And back then, we all thought werewolves and vampires and demons—oh my!—were figments of Hollywood's imagination."

"How did you—" Abby broke off and felt her cheeks heat. How was she supposed to feel comfortable about being rude to these people if they were going to keep being nice to her?

"Go ahead and ask," Missy said, smiling. "I promise not to be offended. I mean it when I said I understand how you're probably feeling."

Abby snorted. "Sorry, but unless you met your husband when he kidnapped you, I'm not sure you can really say that."

She wasn't sure why Missy found that so funny, but the other woman laughed long and hard before she managed to respond.

"No, actually. I knew Graham for a couple of months before he kidnapped me," she said, still chuckling. "But kidnap me he did. Dragged me off to his lair and refused to let me go for an entire weekend. And by the time that weekend was over, he'd apparently decided he was never going to let me go. So, if you don't mind, just go ahead and decide to trust me."

Abby fought the urge to stare at the top of Missy's head for the halo that must be there. If this woman had really been through half as much as Abby had and had still been able to forgive and forget and even fall in love with the Other who'd done that to her, Abby had to remember to write to the Vatican and nominate Missy for canonization.

"So what were you going to ask?"

It took Abby a second to rewind her mental tape recorder and remind herself.

"I was going to ask how—" She spent a second searching for a polite way of phrasing it but gave up. "How did you end up getting mixed up with vampires and werewolves and demons? I mean, if you're human and you met them before the news broke . . ."

"Well before. Like several years. It's a bit of a long story, but suffice it to say my best friend met a man in a club and fell madly in love with him, and it turned out that he was a vampire. Of course, when we, her friends, found out, we staged a valiant rescue," Missy smiled, clearly remembering something amusing, "but it turned out she didn't need to be rescued. She was perfectly happy where she was. Her husband was head of the Council of Others when they met, and Graham, my husband, was a close friend of his. We met through the two of them."

"And it didn't bother you that they . . . weren't human?" Abby frowned.

"Sure it did. When I first found out that the guy

Reggie had hooked up with liked a high-protein liquid diet, I freaked. All her friends did. But that was because we didn't know anything about the Others. All we had to go on was the same stories you've probably heard. *Nosferatu* and *An American Werewolf in London.* But you might have noticed that it's pretty hard to maintain an irrational hatred and fear of someone once you've spent time with them and discovered they're not so different from anyone else. And in my case, once you've been maid of honor to their best man."

Abby stared across the grass at a gray-haired woman in a fur-trimmed coat walking an apricot Pomeranian on a retractable leash. The setting sun gilded the dog's fur until it matched the bright gold shining from the woman's earlobes. "I don't know. You throw in being held somewhere against your will for reasons you don't fully understand, and you'd be surprised what you can maintain."

"Do you really mean that?" Missy shifted and curled one leg up onto the bench so she could face Abby more directly. "Are you sure you hate Rule and all the Others? Or are you just angry and frustrated and confused? Like I was."

"I don't know what I am right now."

"Well, personally, I know what I am." Patting her knee, Missy smiled and pushed to her feet. "I'm starving. The deli on the corner has killer roast beef sandwiches the size of a Mack truck. I think I can fit one or two in before dinner. Sam, stay here with Abby and give her a few minutes to think. I'm going to run and grab a snack and I'll be right back."

Samantha shook her head, looking very unhappy with that idea. "Luna, I'm sorry, but you know I can't do that. Alpha has said that you're not to go anywhere alone until the protests die down. Especially now."

"The Alpha is a paranoid mother hen. I'll be fine." Missy rolled her eyes. "You know perfectly well that Abby's in a lot more danger at the moment than I am. She's the one who needs a bodyguard. Stay and keep an eye on her."

"Luna—"

"I'm just going across the street. Look. You can see the deli entrance from here." She pointed through a break in the greenery at the brick-fronted store. "If it makes you feel better, stand over there and you'll be able to see me and Abby at the same time. Now I gotta go. I said the *b* word, and if Junior doesn't get some red meat in the next five minutes, he's going to make me a very unhappy mommy."

Without giving Samantha time to protest, the woman offered a jaunty wave and jogged out the park entrance and across the street. Samantha swore roundly and shot Abby a glance so stern, she wouldn't have thought the Lupine was capable of it a couple of minutes ago.

"Don't move," she ordered. "I'm going to stand right over here so I can watch the deli, but *don't* move. And scream if anyone tries to talk to you."

Since she was still feeling more than a little confused by her conversation with Missy Winters and remembered that Samantha was way too fast for her to outrun even if she tried to make a break for it,

Abby had no trouble obeying the order. She sat on the bench and watched the fading sunlight dapple the grass as she wondered yet again what on earth had happened to her life.

She would like to have thought that it was her distraction that kept her from hearing anything behind her in the moments before a large hand clamped over her mouth and a dark figure whispered in her ear.

"Where's the gas leak?"

CHAPTER TWELVE

*I*t would be nice to think that it was distraction that allowed someone to sneak up close enough to touch her without her ever noticing, but in reality her brother was in the Special Forces, and he was just that good at his job.

She waited a couple of seconds for the rush of panic to pass and for her adrenaline to register that the voice she'd heard had belonged to Noah. Samantha was still watching the deli, and Abby had no intention of screaming. Not that she could have until the hand shifted off her mouth to let her speak.

"Two o' clock. About ten feet away. Next to the water fountain."

Noah remained completely silent, and Abby knew better than to look backward to try to see him. He might be right behind her, but between her body, the bench, and the shrubbery surrounding them, she knew he'd be very well concealed.

He never made a sound, but she knew he'd made a comprehensive survey of the situation. The careful, modulated tone of his nearly soundless voice confirmed it.

"Abigail, you're going to have to tell me that you didn't send me an SOS in the middle of the night using our secret 'the end of the world is upon us' code because you've had a fight with one of your girlfriends."

She had known Noah would recognize her text message and take it for the 911 call it had been. It was a silly code they'd developed as kids, when the greatest torture they could imagine was being dragged to their great-aunt Ruth's house for Thanksgiving dinner and being trapped in her living room listening to her tell them for the nine billionth time about the year her sister had forgotten to turn the oven on for the turkey. It was like being in an airtight room and discovering a gas leak. One's sanity and very survival depended on getting out using any means necessary as soon as possible.

Since then, "Thanksgiving" had been their way of politely and secretly saying to each other, "My life is on the line here, and I need your help *now*."

It reassured her to know the old signal still worked. Especially given the current circumstances.

"That's not one of my friends," she whispered, keeping her eye on the Lupine. "That's a werewolf, one of a couple who kidnapped me last night and have been holding me in the Vircolac club ever since. You've got to help me escape."

There was a moment of silence behind her.

"Have you tried hailing a cab?"

Now was not the time for sarcasm. "I'm serious, Noah. This is not a joke. They brought me out for fresh air, but in a few minutes they're going to take me back to the club and keep me there, and isn't it lucky you found me here where there's one guard instead of in the building down the block, which I've been informed has one of the best security systems this side of the Pentagon!"

She could picture her brother's shrug. "The Pentagon isn't that secure." She sensed rather than heard a stir of movement behind her, but when Noah spoke again, the words were music to her ears. "Okay. I'm gonna get us out of here. You know the drill. Do what I say when I say it, no questions. And believe me when I tell you that I intend to hear all about whatever it is you haven't told me as soon as we're secure." His voice moved back and to her right, and Abby knew he was getting himself into position. "Oh, and you're buying me some really good beer for this."

Abby would buy him a brewery for this. She didn't care if she had to hock her every last possession and spend the next forty years digging ditches to do it. Maybe if she put enough distance and enough of her brother's weaponry between herself and the demon called Rule, she could get her hormones to settle down and go on a mission to a leper colony in India to atone for the sins she'd already committed and all the ones she'd wanted to commit but thankfully hadn't had the opportunity for.

She sat forward on the bench and tensed her muscles in preparation for movement. Thank goodness only her clothes were borrowed and not her sneakers. Running would be bad enough. Running in someone else's shoes would have been painful.

"On my signal, you're going to get up to stretch

your legs. You're going to smile and wave at the brunette, who's pretty damned hot for a dog, and you're going to hear something on the south side of the park that's going to make you turn."

Abby had to remind herself not to nod and to keep her expression impassive while Noah gave his orders.

"When you do, a guy carrying two big bags of groceries with all sorts of crap sticking out of the top is going to walk between you and her. I can see him coming as soon as he's completely blocking you from her sight, you're going to turn and run hell for leather due west into the trees. I'll be covering your ass. Got it?"

"She's a werewolf, Noah. I can't outrun her. Neither can you."

"We don't need to outrun her. We just need to put enough distance between us and her that no one will see when I take her down."

A twist of conscience made Abby hesitate. "I don't want you to hurt her, No. She's actually been pretty nice to me. She's the one who let me text you."

"You wanna stay where you are?" he hissed. "I promise I'm not going to kill her, but I have to at least knock her out if you want me to get you away. Otherwise, you're right; she would catch us."

"Okay, fine." Abby took a deep breath and squared her shoulders. "Ready on your signal."

"Good girl." She felt the slightest brush of air as her brother rose into a crouch behind her. "On three. One. Two."

The three was silent, but Abby didn't need to hear it. Her brain screamed it loudly enough all on its own.

She stood and followed Noah's directions precisely. Her hands went into her pockets and she rolled her shoulders as if stiff from sitting. Samantha immediately caught Abby's movement out of the corner of her eye and looked sharply in her direction. Abby raised one hand in a wave and offered a grimacing smile along with another shoulder roll to indicate the reason for her change of position. Samantha nodded with a half smile of her own and turned back to watch the door of the deli just as the grocery-toting bystander crossed between them.

Abby didn't waste a second. Heart pounding in her chest, she spun on her heels, tucked her head down, and ran directly west as if the hounds of hell were on her heels. If her luck and Noah's skill panned out, hopefully nothing like that would happen.

Nobody screamed, no shots were fired, no alarms sounded, but apparently the change in air pressure Abby's abrupt takeoff caused or the sound of her footfalls on the turf was enough to tell Samantha something was wrong. Abby glanced over her shoulder just in time to see the Lupine turn her head, catch sight of her fleeing charge, and bellow an order that she stop.

Abby ignored her and ran faster.

"Didn't I teach you not to look back, Ab?" Running with apparent effortlessness by her side, Noah growled the question even as he kept one eye firmly on the Lupine who looked set to launch a hot pursuit.

"Looking back wastes time you can't afford to lose. You'll get yourself caught."

"You're doing it."

"I'm the rear guard. It's my job."

"Abby! Stop! Come back here!"

Samantha's shout sounded much too close for Abby's comfort. She reached down inside herself for another burst of speed. She was afraid it wouldn't be enough. She was really afraid when she heard Noah curse.

"Left!"

Abby veered left without question, even though that path seemed designed to send her running straight into the trunk of a rather immovable maple tree.

"Down!"

Abby took a nosedive into the dirt and hoped nothing vulnerable was sticking out and asking for a bad case of road rash.

"Move!"

Without even taking the time to catch her breath, Abby rolled several times as if she were on fire and was glad she hadn't stopped for questions when two very heavy bodies hit the ground exactly where she'd been lying a second ago. One was her brother, and the other had a lot more hair than the kind of woman he normally tried to pin beneath him.

Abby scrambled out of their way and knelt in the debris at the base of one of the pine trees next to the maple she'd narrowly avoided. A quick glance around told her that everything must have happened fast enough not to catch the attention of any of New York's famously mind-your-own-business citizens. Plus, the small copse of trees provided just enough cover that once the sun slipped past the tree-tops and threw the park into shadowy twilight, it got difficult to see much of anything.

It probably helped that Noah and Samantha conducted one of the most silent struggles Abby had ever witnessed. Neither of them made a sound as they grappled together on the carpet of pine needles. In any other fight, Abby would have counted her brother's victory as inevitable and moved on, confident he'd catch up with her in a few seconds so they could be on their way, but this was no ordinary opponent.

In her wereform, Samantha stood at least half a head taller than Noah's six feet. Her fur-covered limbs rippled with muscle, and her movements were so fast, Abby could barely make her eyes focus on them. Her brother clearly had his hands full.

Abby looked around for a weapon. She didn't *want* to hurt Samantha, any more than she'd wanted Noah to hurt her, but Abby needed to make good on this escape. Now that she'd begun, she felt pretty much compelled to follow through. If she could find a tree branch or a big rock or something, maybe she could knock the Lupine out, and she and Noah could make their getaway.

Unfortunately, the landscaping company charged with maintaining this particular park appeared to be meticulous in the execution of their duties. She couldn't find so much as a twig or a pebble to suit her purposes.

"What the heck happened to the wild and untamed

beauty of nature?" She growled her frustration. "Does everything in this part of town have to be manicured within an inch of its life?"

"Well, I don't know about manicures," a rough, grating, thoroughly unpleasant voice growled from somewhere over her head. "I'm more of a manacles sort myself. And I've got a pair with your name on them, little human."

Later Abby clearly remembered the sound of that voice and the sickening, unnatural gleam of glowing red eyes, but just at that moment Lou reared back inside her and yelled, *Holy fucking sonofabitch shit!* at the top of its uncouth and hysterical little lungs.

Then everything went black.

CHAPTER THIRTEEN

ule didn't know what made him more nervous: the tingle in the back of his neck that told him that the current situation was about to go very wrong or the fact that the Vircolac employee who seemed to think Missy and Samantha had everything well in hand.

"The Luna and Samantha took the girl for a walk," the member of Graham's security staff said. "Just to the park down the street. Apparently, she was feeling a little restless. They should be back in twenty minutes or so."

It would be dark in twenty minutes. At the moment, the sun had already gone down far enough to make Rule seriously anxious.

It took every shred of self-control he had ever possessed not to reach out and snap the burly Lupine's neck like fireplace kindling.

"Which way?" Rule demanded instead through clenched teeth.

"South," the Lupine said, taking a wary step back. "Next block down, opposite side of the street."

Rule didn't thank him. He just ran.

Almost straight into Missy.

The Silverback Luna had a plastic deli bag in one hand and her cell phone in the other, but she wasn't heading back toward the club. She was dashing across the street and into the park, and her normally pale skin looked as white as tissue.

Rule felt his gut clench. "What happened?"

"She bolted. Just now. That way."

Not bothering to cast blame—there would be plenty of time for that later, he would make sure of it—Rule followed the direction of Missy's pointing finger and took off again. Part of his mind noticed that the human Luna seemed to have little trouble keeping up with his breakneck pace, but the greater part of his mind was already firmly fixed on finding his runaway charge and planning how in the name of everything holy and un- he was going to keep from blistering her ass as soon as he caught her.

"To the left," Missy shouted. "In the trees. I can smell her."

Rule immediately veered left and broke into a strand of trees. He spotted Abby just in time to see her eyes roll back in her head and her body throw itself ten feet to the side. Then he saw why.

Standing in the space where her body had just been was a tall, human-looking figure with medium brown hair, a remarkably average build, and eyes that glowed with fiendish evil.

"Seth!"

Rule roared the name, immediately recognizing one of Uzkiel's minions. The fiend heard him and turned, the lips of his human host curling back in a feral snarl.

"Stay back, Watchman," Seth warned, stepping toward where Abby had landed and was already trying to scramble out of reach on all fours. "You'll never reach them before I do. And it would be such a shame to break the pretty little human before I got Louamides out of her."

At the sound of the voices, the two forms wrestling near the base of a nearby tree stilled. Two heads turned toward them, one an unknown human male, the other, Samantha. The man swore and shoved the werewolf away, leaping to his feet in one smooth movement. He took a step forward and locked everyone other than Abby in a menacing stare.

"Everyone better get the hell away from my sister before I get cranky."

Rule saw the man's curse and raised him one. *Of course she has a commando for a brother. I was expecting something easy?*

"You are outnumbered, Seth," Rule said aloud. He kept his eyes on the fiend, but his peripheral senses focused closely on the brother. "Let the girl go. We would be on you before your hand could even fall."

"The only hand likely to be falling soon is mine." Noah let his glare hone in on Rule. "I've been on the road for the past eight hours on no sleep, and I swear I think it took me that long to park once I got here. I don't know a single one of you, and since as far as I know every single one of you could have been involved in my sister's kidnapping, I'm inclined to take my bad mood out on all of you. Indiscriminately."

Rule wanted to tell the human that his show of bravado probably wasn't proving that big a comfort to his sister, since his sister didn't appear to be listening. Abby had gone for a quick vacation, and in her place stood—or, rather, trembled—a clearly terrified Louamides.

The fiend had reason to be afraid. Seth was no lackey foot soldier to Uzkiel; it was the archfiend's right hand, second only to Uzkiel in cruelty and evil. The fact that Seth was here gave testimony to how badly the fiends wanted the *solus* spell.

"Abby, come here," the man ordered.

Louamides didn't move, which at the moment meant that neither did Abby.

"Abigail," her brother repeated with a scowl, "it's time for us to be leaving. Now."

Before Rule could decide how to break the news to him that the body standing a few feet away from him wasn't exactly his sister anymore, the man did what humans always did and leaped in where wiser creatures knew enough to hold back.

The entire area erupted into chaos. The human threw himself forward, intending, it looked, to grab his sister and rush her out of harm's way like a linebacker. Had the current danger been human, Rule had no doubt it would have worked. The human looked to be built of solid muscle, but he moved with the speed and grace of a much smaller man. Unfortunately, even a much smaller man may as well have operated in slow motion compared to a demon.

Louamides saw the attack and screamed like a little girl. Samantha saw and howled something in Lupine that Rule figured he was better off not understanding, and Seth saw and grabbed Abby by the hair, throwing her down onto a bed of pine needles.

"Rule!" Lou screamed. "Help me! You gotta do something!"

Abby's brother froze, his frown shifting into something less certain. He searched the face of the sister he'd recognized only moments before and hesitated.

It was all Seth needed. With a guttural snarl, the fiend fell on the possessed woman, teeth bared, fingers curling into claws. Rule roared and charged forward, but Samantha made it there first.

The Lupine went straight for the fiend's throat, but Seth saw her coming and raised a hand to block the savage bite. She locked her powerful jaws around the fiend's forearm, teeth ripping through the flesh of the creature's host body and crunching down on bone. The resulting bellow should have raised Revolutionary War heroes from their graves, or at least brought the public running. Unfortunately, Rule didn't have time to worry about that.

He halted his momentum a split second before he would have impacted in the spot Samantha now occupied, and spun the energy into a restrained tackle that brought Abby's brother thudding to the ground safely out of the fiend's reach. Judging by the curses the human uttered and the series of powerful, well-placed blows he landed on Rule's solar plexus, nose, and throat, the man failed to appreciate the efforts made on his behalf.

Grimly Rule struggled to subdue the human without harming him, a nicety he only observed for Abby's benefit. He finally got the man pinned, twisting his arms up behind him and planting a knee in the small of his back to hold him in place. Then Rule took a look around to assess the situation.

Samantha seemed determined to sever the fiend's arm and any other body part it was foolish enough to place in her path. She worried it like prey, attacking and then dancing out of reach, keeping its attention focused on her rather than on the possessed human woman lying on the ground nearby.

Moving too fast for Rule's comfort, the last traces of sunlight retreated out of the park to the far side of the street and crawled up the sides of the buildings. No hope of using the fiend's natural intolerance to the light against it, and Rule hadn't had time to grab his sword before he dashed out the door of Vircolac.

He berated himself for the total lack of preparedness. He'd been hunting fiends far too long to make this kind of amateurish mistake. Abby must have short-circuited his brainpower more seriously than he had imagined. As things stood, he would have to improvise.

Too bad the same thought occurred to Seth at approximately the same time.

Shrieking in rage, the fiend caught Samantha with a blow to the head and sent her flying. She landed with a yelp nearly twenty feet away and had to struggle to regain her feet. It was already too late. Seth grabbed Abby's body, cuffing her hard to silence Lou's caterwauling, and slug her over its shoulder. When it turned to go, Rule heard a sound like a thunderclap and felt the earth move beneath him.

Abby's brother bucked with a force greater than Rule could have predicted and managed to free his left hand from the demon's grip. Faced with a challenge on two fronts, Noah spat out a curse and sent up a fervent wish for whatever shreds of luck fate could see fit to send his way.

Levering himself off of the struggling human, Rule lowered his head, tensed his muscles, and charged the fiend. Behind Rule, he heard a Lupine howl and two voices shouting. A loud crack echoed around them and he felt a searing pain slice through his left side. He ignored it and poured on even greater speed. He had to catch Seth before the fiend managed to escape with Abby and Louamides in his grasp.

More voices joined the din, but Rule didn't have time to wonder who they belonged to. As long as they weren't more fiends or the police, he wasn't sure he cared at the moment. His long strides ate up the distance between himself and Seth, but the fiend had a considerable head start and a destination in mind. He also had night vision even better than Rule's. Seth could see in even the blackest of the deepening shadows and knew where to step to make it difficult for Rule to track it.

But Rule wasn't about to give up. He might not have managed to grab his sword before he rushed off after Abby, but he never dressed without at least some other weapon secreted somewhere on his body. A short burst of speed managed to narrow the distance between him and the fiend. Muttering a chant for luck, Rule skidded to a stop and yanked a small, devilishly sharp knife from his left boot. A sharp glance and a flick of his wrist sent the blade spinning through the air straight toward the demon's heart.

It burst into a ball of bright golden light just before it made impact squarely between Seth's shoulder blades.

The fiend screamed. More important, it stumbled, landing on one knee just inches from the fence separating the small park from the neighborhood beyond. The jarring force of its landing loosened its grip on Abby's body, and she thumped to the ground, her head smacking the corner of a paved path and knocking both her and Louamides unconscious.

Rule took quick stock of the scene and moved forward, only to almost trip over the human again. The man didn't know when to quit.

Abby's brother at least had the sense to come in fast and low, but he clearly hadn't spent a lot of time fighting fiends in the past. He had a weapon in one hand—a gun—and an object gripped in the other that Rule could only hope wasn't a hand grenade. Noah reached the fiend before Rule could stop him and placed himself between Seth and Abby's motionless body.

Rule could see the man's trigger hand flex along with the muscles in his jaw and prayed he would have more sense than to shoot. A bullet would have no effect on Seth, but it would certainly prove fatal to the fiend's human host.

"What did you do to my sister?" the man demanded, his voice cold and fierce as winter.

The fiend laughed and pushed itself slowly to its feet. "How charming that one worthless human should be so concerned about the fate of another." Its voice dripped with poison, and its eyes blazed with hate. "I'd like to tell you she fought well, mortal, but they never do. Their souls tear like tissue paper the instant I touch them. Barely worth the effort, but I was feeling a mite peckish."

The shot rang out before the last word faded, but Seth had anticipated it. It dodged, not to the side but forward and down, using the most formidable weapon the body of its human host possessed. Hard, white teeth closed down on Seth's enemy's calf muscle, sinking through heavy cloth to rend into the skin and muscle beneath. Seth's fiendish strength turned a nasty bite into a vicious one, and the human shouted as he felt his flesh tear.

Rule had tensed to leap forward when another burst of golden light flared, not on a weapon this time but on the back of the fiend's head. It reared back and shrieked, pain and fury clear in its shrill and inhuman voice. The foul odor of burning flesh filled the air, and Rule thought he saw flames when the fiend turned and leaped over the six-foot wrought-iron fence and into the street beyond. Only the feel of a small hand on Rule's arm—digging into his wrist like iron cuffs, actually—stopped him from launching himself after Seth.

"It's gone," Tess said, her voice clipped and her mouth tightly pinched, "and with that injury, it will be in a new body before you can locate it. Don't waste our time. Help me get Abby back to the club, and we'll figure out what to do next later."

"You'll be taking my sister just as soon as I'm laid in my cold, cold grave." The human's voice had everyone looking as he struggled to his feet, the uniform shirt he'd been wearing tied around his lower leg in a bloodstained makeshift bandage. He leveled his pistol squarely at Rule's head. "Now how about everyone takes five steps back and keeps their hands in plain view."

Noah took two limping steps backward toward where Abby still lay, unconscious, half on the pavement.

Samantha crouched at Tess's feet and growled, but none of them moved. They stood perfectly still, their eyes fixed on Abby's brother as he positioned himself between them and his sister.

"I said five steps back." He raised his free hand to the butt of his pistol and sighted down the short barrel. "Now."

"We don't have time for that."

A small hand clutching a very large brick came crashing down on the back of the human's skull, and the man crumpled to the earth like a marionette.

Missy dropped the brick and dusted her hands on

the legs of her jeans. "It's getting late. Let's get them back to the club before someone blabs to Graham that I went out without his permission. I won't hear the end of it for another pregnancy or two."

CHAPTER FOURTEEN

*t*he first thing Abby realized when she woke up was that it was a good thing she didn't drink much, because she would rather be dangled over the Grand Canyon by her thumbnails than experience blackouts on a regular basis.

At least, she assumed she'd had a blackout. The last thing she remembered was standing in the little grove of trees in the park watching her brother and Samantha wrestle around in the pine needles. Since the surface Abby lay on felt a lot more like a mattress than a rocky park surface, something must have happened to her between her last memory and her newly conscious thoughts. Judging by the turn her life had taken in the last twenty-four hours or so, it would be asking too much to hope she'd just been knocked unconscious for a few hours. The thing inside her must have taken over again.

Frowning, Abby searched her awareness for any sign of it. She didn't feel anything, but then, she hadn't before. Apparently being possessed could turn out to be a relatively painless experience.

Um, hello? she thought.

No one answered.

Abby realized she had no idea what that meant. She knew the thing could talk to her while she was conscious, since it had offered all kinds of suggestions, most of them obscene, since it had first taken up residence within her, but being able to and actually doing it seemed to be two different things.

Hey, are you in there?

Silence.

Was the fiend ignoring her? Now, that would be rude. If she was going to give the thing a home for the next few days, the least it could do was answer when she rang the doorbell.

Come on. Wake up, she thought. *I want to know what happened. I need you to tell me what's going on. Are you there? Can you hear me?*

"Great." Abby opened her eyes and gazed up into a darkened room. "Even the damned are giving me the silent treatment. This should be fun."

The room around her was pitch black, not even enough light to read her watch when she brought her wrist right up next to her face. She glanced around for an illuminated clock face but saw nothing. She didn't hear any ticking, either, so she couldn't hope for an old-fashioned alarm clock on the bed stand. Not that she could see if there was a bed stand. She couldn't even see the faint outline of light around the edges of a window's heavy drapes. She may as well have been in a tomb.

"Oh, great thought, Ab. Real cheerful."

Bracing herself, she prepared to throw back the blankets that covered her and go feeling her way to a wall and, she hoped, a light switch. Before she could even sit up, a door opened and a warm, golden glow spilled in from the hallway.

The figure silhouetted in the doorway didn't bother to reach for a light switch, but she did leave the door open enough for Abby to identify her.

Samantha.

If Abby's conscience hadn't already been pro-grammed to hypersensitivity by twenty-eight years of Catholicism—twelve of them spent in a school run by Benedictine nuns—the look on Samantha's face when she regained consciousness would have sent her running to the nearest confessional at top speed. The Lupine wouldn't even look her in the eye, let alone speak to her.

Abby felt about as tall as your average cockroach.

She had woken in a different bed from the one she'd occupied last night, and this time the soft cot-ton sheets felt more like sackcloth. The faint light spilling in from the hall was all Abby needed to see that Samantha bustled around the room with her head occasionally tilted at such an awkward angle that she had to be giving herself muscle spasms just to avoid looking in Abby's direction.

An apology burned in the back of Abby's throat, but she couldn't seem to force the words out. She felt terrible for lying to the Lupine, but she couldn't tell Samantha she was sorry for trying to escape; she wasn't. She hoped that if their positions had been reversed she would have expected the Lupine to do the same thing, but Abby felt like the worst sort of slime for using Samantha to do it. She'd probably gotten the woman in all kinds of trouble for giving her the cell phone and not watching her more closely in the park, and that had never been one of Abby's goals. She just wanted to get out of this mess, not cause a bigger one for anyone else.

Who knew what the others would do to punish the Lupine? Maybe there was some sort of ancient ritual of shunning or stoning or head-shaving.

Abby almost worked up the courage to ask. But another figure stepped in through the open doorway, behind Samantha. This one flicked on the lights.

"It's just as well you're awake," Tess said, her voice brusque. "I've been checking your pupils every so often, but this way you can answer all the standard questions about your name and who's president at the moment. If I don't tell your brother you're hale and whole and concussion-free in a few minutes, I'm going to have to turn him into a three-toed sloth just to shut him up."

Abby sat up and pushed her hair out of her face. "I feel fine. No dizziness, no nausea."

"Good." Setting the glass she carried down on the table beside the bed, Tess leaned forward and peered into Abby's eyes. "Any pain?"

Abby thought about it. "I feel like someone whacked me upside the head, but it's not bad. My sinus headaches during allergy season are a lot worse than this."

The woman nodded. "Fine. Drink this." She pushed the glass into Abby's hand. "Samantha, you don't have to stay any longer. Rafe and Graham will have security outside the door all night. She's not going anywhere."

The Lupine nodded, said something in a low, tired voice before she slipped out of the room, pulling the door shut behind her.

Abby swallowed the last of Tess's brew—a sweet, herbal concoction that tasted of green and cinnamon with a faint note of bitterness in the background—and frowned over the rim of the glass. "Did she get hurt in the park?"

Tess raised an eyebrow and looked at Abby for a long moment. "No, it wasn't in the park."

A flush of guilt crept up Abby's face, and she frowned down into her empty cup. "I didn't mean to upset her. I just wanted to get in touch with my brother."

"Right. And of course, you should always get what you want. Even when what you want is immature and selfish and a serious threat to your safety and the safety of the people trying to take care of you. The world always works that way."

Tess snatched the glass out of Abby's hands and headed toward the door.

"Hey, I don't think you have the right to get mad at me." Abby's voice stopped Tess just as the other woman reached for the doorknob. "In case you've forgotten, I'm being held here against my will. I never promised to be an obedient little hostage. I'm not going to let you feel all bent out of shape just because I slipped my leash. I didn't hurt anybody. I just left."

The look Tess shot Abby nearly singed off her eyebrows. "You didn't *hurt* anybody?" Tess repeated quietly. "I realize you might not remember everything that happened in the park, since Rule and Samantha said Louamides took over the instant Seth showed up, but if you think your little escapade didn't hurt anyone, let me explain to you how very wrong you are. Not only is Samantha having to deal with the disgrace of having failed to carry out orders given to her by the Alpha of her pack, but the wife of said Alpha is having one of the loudest fights in the history of interspecies relationships because she put herself and her baby at risk to save your ungrateful behind. A man who has done nothing but grab you out of harm's way since the moment he set eyes on you has a bullet wound in his side, and I just finished putting twenty-four stitches in your own brother's calf." She finished her summary on a hiss, her chin jutting out and her blue eyes crackling with anger. "So don't tell me no one got hurt because of you. I've seen the casualty list. And let's just take a peek at how many other people will be hurt because of you if you don't stop being a conceited, selfish, blind little girl."

Tess raised a hand, muttered something under her breath, and slapped her palm against Abby's forehead before the other woman could so much as blink, let alone duck.

If Abby had even for a moment forgotten that Tess De Santos was a witch, what she saw in those moments while the other woman touched her mind ensured she would never forget again. Not for the rest of her life.

It came in flashes, shorter than commercials, more real than movies. More horrifying than her worst nightmares. She saw her own body lying bloody and broken at the base of a huge stone altar in the middle of an open space. The air seemed to burn with foul, gaseous heat. All around, the world seemed cloaked in blackness while the sky above glowed with a bloodred fire that shed no light but cast shadows everywhere, thick, dense pools of black that seemed to pulse and throb with sentient evil.

On top of the altar stood a figure so grossly misshapen and twisted in its being that it took several slow heartbeats for Abby to even recognize it as a living being. If you could call something animated with the pure spirit of malice alive. It had bent, broken legs like no beast Abby had ever seen stride upon the earth and a long, disproportionate torso that swayed back and forth like a great snake. Its arms seemed too long for its body, huge, swollen knuckles dragging on the ground like a gorilla's.

A huge, vaguely bovine skull sat atop wide, muscular shoulders, but the skull looked nearly bare. What little flesh still clung to it looked stringy and rotten and vile. Huge horns grew from the center of its forehead, spearing up toward the dark, cursed sky.

It was a figure Abby knew she could never have conjured even in her darkest moments, and while she watched, it threw back its head and gave a mighty bellow that sent her flesh crawling. It sounded like a thousand tortured souls screaming all at once, and its echo set the earth to trembling. As it raised its great fists, she saw that it held a ball of fire the same sullen red as the sky in one hand. In the other it clutched a child.

Helpless, Abby watched as the perspective of the image shifted, pulling back like a camera to show a wider shot. Around the altar, Abby began to see the city, now smoldering and ruined beneath the crimson darkness. Bodies lay strewn in the streets, creatures ghastly and cruel hunted the living, and small groups of fighters waged doomed battles against the hordes of fiendish creatures that seemed to pour like an infinite flood through a portal near the altar.

Saint John the Divine had never envisioned an Apocalypse so complete and so terrible.

"Tess, that's enough!"

The shout was accompanied by firm hands grasping Abby by the shoulders and yanking her out of the reach of the burning hand on her forehead. Blinking through a veil of tears, she saw Samantha standing between her and the witch and snarling. Not at Abby but at Tess.

"Leave her be! She doesn't understand what you're talking about! You can't just rip her illusions away and leave her with nothing familiar in her entire reality! It's not right!"

Tess wiped a hand across her own eyes and shot the Lupine a red-rimmed glare. "Someone had to show her the truth. If she keeps thinking what happens to her doesn't matter, she's going to doom us all. I'm not going to let that happen."

"And you think showing her the worst-case scenario is going to help? Come on, Tess. She's not

Ebenezer Scrooge and you're not the Ghost of Christmas Future."

"Someone has to be."

"Is that really what will happen?" Abby croaked, feeling as if her throat had been singed by the flames she'd seen in her vision. "Did you show me the future?"

"No."

"Yes."

"Tess . . ." Samantha spoke a warning.

Tess sighed. "One of them."

"One of what?" Abby wondered if she felt as confused as she looked.

"One of the futures." Tess's anger seemed to be dissipating, leaving behind a fatigue Abby found it easy to sympathize with. "The future changes all the time. Every time we make a decision, we're turning off one path and onto another. Every time we take a new path, the ones we didn't take and the futures they led to cease to exist. Life is like a great big Choose Your Own Adventure novel."

"You're psychic?"

Tess tucked a stray curl behind her ear and sat down on the edge of Abby's bed. "Only in the loosest sense of the word. Really it's like I have déjà vu a lot, only the things I see didn't already happen. They're things that might happen in the future. I've spent a lot of time over the last few years trying to develop it into something like precognition, but what I showed you is as close as I've gotten."

"Which isn't very close," Samantha pointed out. She shut the door she must have left open when she reentered the bedroom and sat on the bed corner opposite Tess. "What she comes up with tend to be like fantasies or nightmares. Either the best-case scenario or the worst. I don't think I need to ask which one you got."

"Hey, what I showed her is a very real possibility," Tess said, crossing her arms over her chest. "If Uzkiel and his goons get ahold of Louamides and force him to give up the *solus* spell, the future we're looking at wouldn't necessarily be so different from what she saw."

Abby leaned forward over her knees and braced her temples on her palms, burying her fingers in her hair. Then she fisted them as if she would yank the stuff out by the handful.

"I just can't make this make sense," she said, staring at the embroidered coverlet in her lap. "What I do or didn't do has never been important to anyone but me. And maybe my family."

"Well there's been a major change there."

She looked up into Tess's expression, which had settled back into its normal expression of mild amusement.

"I'm sure this is a job for one of you. For an Other, I mean. Someone with special powers or supernatural strength or speed. I'm sure you could handle this all a lot better without me getting in the way."

"It's not a matter of you being in the way. It's a matter of Louamides being in you." Samantha reached out and patted Abby's knee. "Trust me. It'll get less weird once we get Lou out of you."

Abby sighed and finally managed to look straight

at Samantha. "I'm sorry if I got you in trouble before," she said. "That wasn't my intention."

Samantha gave her a half smile. "It's not the first time I've been in trouble. And I somehow doubt it will be the last. Besides, the Luna stepped in and deflected the worst of it. Alpha was too busy worrying about her to keep yelling at me." She pursed her lips. "But if I were you, I'd probably try to avoid running into him for the next few days. Or, you know, decades."

"Right. Real easy, given he happens to own the place where I'm being—where I'm staying."

Tess must have noticed that catch, but she just grinned. "Oh, did I happen to mention earlier that he and Missy live right next door?"

Abby collapsed back against the pillow. "Yeah, but thanks for reminding me."

"Don't worry about it. If you want my opinion, I think your brother looked almost as pissed off as Graham. Didn't you tell him what was going on when you sent your little bat signal?"

"How? It's not like I sent him a blueprint of the joint and a schedule of shift changes in the guardhouse by carrier pigeon. I had a cell phone for seventeen seconds. Not even a thirteen-year-old can text that fast. I just let him know I was in trouble."

Tess tilted her head. "You may be in even bigger trouble now."

Abby just sighed and continued staring at the ceiling.

"I don't think the brother is anything to worry

about," Samantha said dismissively. "The demon, though . . . now he's another story."

"Ugh. Stop. You'll give me nightmares."

"Fair's fair," Tess snickered.

"Says you." Abby turned a pleading expression on the blonde. "But there's no reason I have to see him again, right?" Her mind rushed back to the kiss she'd almost managed to forget and she contemplated pulling the covers over her head. "I'm safe and sound back at the club. There are plenty of people here to look out for me. If I promise not to try to leave until this is all sorted out, can't you send him out to hunt down that Uz-whoever guy? The sooner he does that, the sooner I can get out of everyone's hair."

Tess and Samantha exchanged a speaking glance over Abby's head. She didn't think she wanted to hear what it had to say.

"He's a multitalented fellow," Tess said. "I'm pretty sure he can manage to fit in hunting the fiend *and* reading you the riot act. In fact, when I left to come upstairs, he was rehearsing in the library."

"Gee. Isn't that swell."

Samantha rubbed a reassuring hand over Abby's forearm. "I'm sure it won't be all that bad. I mean, he knows you're human, so he'll probably be trying really hard not to hurt you."

Abby glared at her. "You're such a comfort."

"I've found there's only one sure strategy for dealing with situations like these. You have to go on the offensive. Even if he's the one in the right, you have to throw him off balance. Make him forget that."

Tess's beautifully manicured hands punctuated her instructions with decisive gestures. "You'll have to seduce him."

"What?!" Abby sprang upright like a jack-in-the-box. "I have to *what*?!"

"Seduce him. If you want him to forget about being mad at you."

Abby looked over and saw Samantha nodding, her expression serious, as if the idea weren't completely insane.

"Absolutely," the Lupine agreed. "I mean, I don't have a mate myself, but the Luna swears by the tactic, and if it works on the Alpha . . ." She shrugged. "It's got to be worth a try."

Abby's stomach felt as if someone had just installed a hamster wheel with a very energetic rodent inside. And then fed it diet pills. "That's—I . . . I mean . . . I-I can't."

"Sure you can. It's all in the lips." Tess wriggled her eyebrows up and down.

"No. I can't. Really. I can't."

"Why not?"

Abby just shook her head and wondered if someone had slipped her something. Her heart felt like it might beat a hole straight out of her chest. In double time.

"I just . . . can't."

"Well, I know you're not gay," Tess said, sounding exasperated. "I saw that kiss, remember? If I had been wearing glasses, the things would have been fogged up. *Before* I opened the door."

Samantha looked impressed. "That good?"

Tess fanned herself with one hand and rolled her eyes to the ceiling. "Oy. You should only know like I know."

"That's not the point."

Both women turned their heads to stare at her, their expressions mirror images of polite curiosity. Neither said a word. The silence stretched on for minutes.

"What?" Abby finally demanded.

"Then what is the point?" Samantha asked.

"We assumed you had one," Tess nodded.

Members of the media had been right. There was a massive Other conspiracy, only it had nothing to do with taking over the world and enslaving humanity. It had to do with driving Abigail Miriam Baker totally and completely out of her mind.

"I—I can't . . . I can't just *seduce* someone to distract him from being mad at me," she sputtered. "That's . . . just not right."

Samantha blinked. "It's not?"

"Is it a personal problem? STD?"

Abby grabbed a pillow and covered her face with it. How long would it take, she wondered, to smother herself this way? "I do *not* have a sexually transmitted disease."

"What did she say?"

"I think she said 'no.' It's hard to hear through all that goose down."

Lowering the pillow just enough to glare at the women over its edge, Abby decided the time investment might be worth it.

"Because it wouldn't be anything to be ashamed of if you did," Tess continued. "One in five humans in the country has one. Besides, it's not like you could give it to Rule. Others are immune to human diseases."

Twenty-three seconds and counting.

Samantha tilted her head and eyed Abby consideringly. "I don't think that's it. Female sexual dysfunction? Up to forty percent of human women suffer at some point in their lives."

Abby slammed the pillow down onto the bed. "Do you people work for the National Center for Health Statistics or something?"

"We're well informed." Tess studied Abby for a moment, her eyes traveling over what was probably the rat's nest of her hair and the face that probably looked as if it had been dragged backward through a gravel pit and coming to rest on a spot just beneath her collarbone. "Is it a religious thing? You're not a nun, are you? I mean, don't they still wear habits and everything?"

"Just because I don't sleep around doesn't make me a nun."

"Are you a virgin?"

"What is the sudden fascination with my sex life?" Abby crossed her arms over her chest and scowled.

"I'm not asking for details; I just want to know if you have one," Tess said. "It's a purely academic question. If you're a virgin, the seduction thing gets a little . . . trickier."

"I'm not a virgin," Abby snapped. "There are days I wish I was, because trust me, that wasn't my finest moment, but I'm not. Not that it matters. There isn't going to be a seduction."

Samantha and Tess gave each other another one of those looks.

The Lupine cleared her throat. "Um, what exactly do you mean, 'finest moment'?"

"I thought you guys didn't want details."

"You can answer in general terms."

"It was just a bad idea." One Abby preferred not to dwell on. It only made her feel inept. "I was young, stupid, and drunk, and I thought I was in love; he was young, horny, and male, and he thought I was easy."

Tess raised her eyebrows. "Had he ever spoken to you?"

"Har-har."

"Okay, this might require some strategizing." Samantha drummed her fingertips on the bedspread. "The Luna must have a negligee you can borrow. . . ."

Abby squeaked. The idea of appearing before Rule in anything short of full body armor sent chills up her spine.

She told herself they were bad chills.

But not even she bought that one.

"I'm not borrowing anything, and I'm not seducing a demon."

"You're not going to go to hell, you know." Tess smiled.

"How would you know? Are you the Pope? Are you even Catholic?"

"I don't need to be. Think about it for a second. God is supposed to be loving and forgiving, right? So why would he send a good person to perpetual torment for doing something as natural as having sex? I mean, if it wasn't for God, it wouldn't feel so good, right?"

Abby grumbled. "What makes you think it feels so good?"

Tess laughed. Loudly. "My husband. But I'm afraid he's not going to be able to prove it to you. You'll have to go to Rule for that."

"I am not going to sleep with Rule!"

"Look, I'm not here to talk you into it," Tess said, standing. "Frankly, it's no skin off my nose either way. But judging by what I saw in the library yesterday, it's going to happen sooner or later. Anything that produces that much steam produces an equal amount of pressure. I just thought that if it were me, I'd want to be the one deciding when and where to let it off."

CHAPTER FIFTEEN

*t*he tension in the library made Rule doubly thankful Graham's security had disarmed Abby's brother before allowing him into the club. Hostility exuded from his every pore.

In fact, he bore a striking resemblance to his sister.

It wasn't just attitude that the siblings shared. Her brother might be nearly twice Abby's size, but there was no mistaking their relationship. His features were decidedly more masculine, but Rule recognized the stubborn set of the jaw, the same wide, thickly lashed eyes. Unlike his sister's, the man's eyes were both the same color, a dark, mossy hazel, but their stubborn, suspicious expression was nearly identical to Abby's. His hair was a little darker, a little curlier, and his skin had the look of being habitually tanned, but the two humans obviously shared more than a couple of genes.

The man had remained silent and relatively co-operative while Tess stitched up his leg, even if he did watch her every move as if he expected her to trade the suture needle for a bayonet at any moment. Of course, he wasn't the only one with suspicions. Rule made sure two of the club's Lupine security staff stayed in the room with them and on alert while he allowed Tess to fuss over the graze the man's bullet had left in his side. Fortunately, his own accelerated healing had meant he didn't need any stitches. By morning, all that would be left of his wound would be a red mark. In a week, even that would be gone.

The human didn't look so lucky. He didn't complain, though, just grunted when Tess warned him to keep the bandage dry and try not to scratch, as if he'd heard it all before. Rule wouldn't have been surprised if he had.

The only time he'd given them trouble had been when Tess tried to leave to go check on Abby.

"I want to see my sister."

"You saw us settle her into bed upstairs," the witch had said. "Trust me when I tell you she hasn't moved, Mr. Worrywart. If I had to guess, I'd say she's probably still unconscious."

"My name is Noah. I want to see her now." His hard expression discouraged argument. Rule bet it probably worked on the soldiers under Noah's command, but Tess wasn't a soldier. She was a witch, and she was mated to a Felix. Intimidating her practically required an act of God. "And then I want to know what you've done to her."

Tess narrowed her eyes and planted her hands on her hips. "The only thing any of us has done to your sister is make sure she stayed alive despite every attempt she's made in the last twenty-four hours to change that situation."

Noah's eyes glittered. "My sister is not suicidal."

"No, but I have at times wondered how smart she can be. She's certainly not one for looking before she leaps; otherwise she never would have landed in this mess."

"And what mess is that?" he asked, his voice managing to be smooth and menacing at the same time.

Tess looked suitably unimpressed. "Sorry, Rule will have to explain. I have a severe testosterone allergy. The atmosphere in this room is getting toxic. I'll have someone come down and let you know when Abby's awake."

Tess shut the door behind her with a speaking click, and silence descended over the remaining occupants of the room. Abby's brother eyed Rule up and down with the assessing gaze of a warrior. It was a look the demon recognized and respected.

"Is this the part where you kill me and dispose of my body where no one will ever find it?" The man sounded more curious than worried. "I should warn you that Abby's not just resourceful; she's vengeful."

Rule snorted. "Somehow, the news fails to surprise me. But I have no intention of harming you, any more than I have of harming your sister."

Noah's expression remained flat and distant, but his hands flexed open and closed with a restless anger. "You have a funny way of not harming her, because what I saw in the park definitely didn't look pleasant to me."

"That was Seth's doing, not mine. In case it skipped your attention, I was among those trying to rescue Abby."

"So you could keep her prisoner? I'll remind her to thank you."

Rule sighed. "Apparently she had time to give you her side of the story."

"Is there a side that doesn't involve a felony?"

"This was never meant to be a kidnapping. Your sister was never meant to be a prisoner. We are merely trying to protect her."

"Interesting. And Delilah was merely trying to give Samson a makeover."

"I see you two must be very close. You have a lot in common," Rule muttered.

"It's the dimples."

"What did your sister tell you?"

"So you can prepare a tidy counter-story?"

"I was hoping to get an idea of how much she understands, but I suppose the point is moot. Whatever Abby understands, whatever she believes, is beside the point. She is in danger."

"I figured that when she asked me to come rescue her."

Rule struggled to keep his patience. The ability to make him lose it was a talent shared by these humans. "I am not the danger, and neither is anyone in this building. Your sister is possessed."

Noah blinked. "She's what?"

"Possessed," Rule repeated. "That is why she did not respond to you in the park when you called her to your side. She could not hear you. The spirit inside her was in control, not Abby."

"You're serious?"

"Did she act like herself?"

Noah frowned. "Not after that guy showed up. Or maybe before that. I got distracted when the were-wolf tried to rip my throat out."

"If Samantha had tried to rip your throat out, you would not be talking to me right now. But the reason why the spirit inside your sister took over at that point is because it recognized Seth and knew that fiend meant your sister harm. Its panic caused it to seize control of your sister's body and mind."

"But where did this 'spirit' come from? Was that a particularly haunted city park?"

"Louamides came to your sister yesterday. She did not tell you?" Noah just raised an eyebrow and Rule sighed. As concisely as possible he outlined the events of yesterday. Then while he was at it, he explained the reason he was in Manhattan to begin with.

Unlike Abby, her brother did not give in to hysteria. In fact, his expression barely flickered.

Noah was silent for a long moment before blowing out a deep breath. "Well, shit," he said, his tone mild. "I wish she'd told me ahead of time. If I'd known I was dealing with a fiend, I'd have brought iron and silver ammo, instead of silver and copper."

It was Rule's turn to blink, nonplussed. "If you had known it was a fiend? You know about fiends?"

"Sure."

"You know the difference between fiends and demons?"

Noah shrugged. "One's evil; one's not."

Rule shook his head. "I think you are the first human I have ever met who I didn't have to explain it all to. You may be the first being in all of the Above

I did not have to explain it all to." He frowned. "How is it that your sister knew nothing about my kind?"

"She never joined the army." Noah's mouth quirked. "Abby and I are tight, but there are certain things I don't tell her. I *can't* tell her about my job. She and our parents know I'm in the army, but I haven't been able to tell them anything about my assignments since I made Special Forces. I'm in the Spook Squad."

Rule shook his head. "I am not familiar with—"

"Not many people are. We're a division of the Special Forces set up about five years ago, when command first began to get suspicious that not everything that showed up in an episode of *The X-Files* could be fiction. The alien thing's been pretty thoroughly debunked, but they hit pay dirt with the supernatural stuff. Since not all you folks are law-abiding citizens, my team has been around to keep you in line." He made a face. "At least, that's how it was. Since the Unveiling, we've been scrambling to retrain and redeploy. Now we're taking on Other team members and focusing on expanding our mission to handle all national security matters with supernatural or paranormal aspects."

"I had no idea the humans could be so . . . sensible."

"Yeah, well, we'll surprise you from time to time." Noah shifted his weight against the edge of the desk he'd been leaning on and frowned again. "But you still haven't explained why my sister is possessed by a fiend. Other than the obvious reason why fiends usually possess people. They like to use us as disguises. But why hasn't anyone done an exorcism?"

Rule told him about Uzkiel and the *solus* spell.

Noah swore. "Well, that sucks some serious monkey nuts. What the hell are you going to do now? Because I sincerely hope it doesn't involve leaving my sister as the target of a fiendish hit squad."

"I have no intention of allowing Abby to come to any harm. This is why she is staying here where the Silverback Clan can see to her protection twenty-four hours a day."

"No wonder she's so pissed."

"I have little choice."

Noah said, "I think we need to be a little proactive here. Have you seriously considered exorcising Abby and hiding Louamides in another host? Someone a little more able to defend themselves than my baby sister?"

"The fiend appears to be stuck," Rule explained about Tess's failed exorcism. "Besides, no human would stand a chance against Uzkiel and his minions. As I explained to your sister, it's not just a matter of keeping her in custody to keep her safe. As high a priority as they may be for us, it's equally important that we keep Louamides safe as well. An Other would unlikely be to volunteer, for they have little more liking for those from Below than the humans. I cannot imagine they would line up for the privilege of being possessed."

"Then what about me?"

"You?" Rule did a double take. He had not

doubted the strength of Noah Baker's affection for his sister but had not expected the suggestion.

"Why not? This Louamides obviously didn't bring a body of his own, so he'll need one, and there's a heck of a lot more of me to hide in," Noah said with a crooked grin. "Also like Abby, if I get myself into a sticky situation, I have the training and the equipment to handle it. No matter how many tricks I've taught my sister, she's still about a hundred and twenty pounds of soft."

Rule didn't need anyone pointing that out. Especially not Abby's older brother. Her extremely protective older brother. Rule shook his head slowly. "It is not that I do not trust your ability to handle yourself, or to handle Louamides," he began.

"You just don't trust me in general?"

"It is Uzkiel I do not trust. I do not trust him not to go after Abby anyway. He knows Louamides was in her today. Even if we performed an exorcism, it would not surprise me if Uzkiel tried to capture Abby and make her reveal Louamides' new location. Or use her as bait to force me to do so."

That sent Noah's eyebrows winging toward his hairline. "Why should Uzkiel think Abby would serve as a lever over you? You've only known her for a day. It's not like she's special to you."

"Of course not." Rule ignored the niggling voice inside of him that suggested he shouldn't speak so hastily. "But Uzkiel knows I am on the Watch. It knows my duty is to protect others from its kind. Your sister would be no exception."

"Wouldn't it be better to put the fiend into me? That way, even if they found Abby—and trust me, I'm not about to let that happen—they wouldn't have anything to gain from her."

"That would not stop Uzkiel from torturing her just for the pleasure of hearing her scream."

The look that passed over Noah's face had Rule's complete sympathy. "So she's damned either way."

"In a manner of speaking." Rule sighed. "I did not want to alarm your sister or to give her a false sense of confidence, but right now the fact that Louamides is within her is at least a small advantage over not having it. The strength it provides might become critical if the unforeseen were to occur."

Noah studied Rule's face for a long moment, though the demon wasn't certain what he was looking for.

After a moment, the human shrugged. "In that case, as far as I can tell, we only have one choice," he said.

"Which is?"

"If Uzkiel needs to be returned Below, then we're going to have to find him and bring him there."

Rule's eyes narrowed. "What exactly do you mean by 'we'?"

"Just what it sounds like, *kemosabe*." Noah smiled, but the firming of his jaw belied the sunny expression. "There's no way in hell or on earth I'm leaving my sister in the middle of this mess. From here on out, I'm on the team."

Just what he needed, Rule thought, another human

to worry about. "This is not a military exercise," he warned. "Uzkiel is no rogue vampire to be staked and be done with."

"I never said it was."

"It is a more dangerous monster than any you have ever encountered. I cannot allow you to put yourself in harm's way and I do not have time to protect you as well as your sister."

Noah's eyes narrowed. "I don't recall asking for protection. I may be human, but I'm no lightweight. I have eighteen years of military training and experience, five of which have been on the Spook Squad dealing with all sorts of bad eggs who could have physically pounded me into the dust if they'd wanted. We're not trained to go hand-to-hand with an Other; we're trained to outthink him, and from everything I've heard about fiends, they may be clever, but they're not real smart, if you know what I mean."

"Uzkiel is not stupid. It will not be taken in by primitive tricks." Rule crossed his arms over his chest and had the sinking feeling that if Noah possessed half his sister's stubbornness, this fight could end badly. "This is one of the most powerful and most corrupt fiends I have ever encountered. It is immortal by human standards. It cannot be killed with bullets or holy water, and it will not shrink before symbols of human faith."

Noah snorted. "I wasn't planning on attacking it with a palm frond and a string of rosary beads. And trust me, anything can be killed with bullets if you put enough of them in the right places. Fiends die when you behead them, don't they?"

"Their corporeal manifestations can be destroyed that way, yes. But the immaterial entity must be trapped in a proper vessel and destroyed magically."

"Fine. I'll do the shooting; you do the chanting."

Rule scowled. "You are going to need something bigger than a handgun if you intend to injure Uzkiel seriously enough to destroy its physical body."

A slow grin spread across the man's face. "Trust me. I have bigger."

That expression made Rule stop for a moment. A thought occurred to him. "I do not think you ever told me your specialty on your team."

The grin widened. "Nope, I didn't."

"Well?"

"Demolitions," Noah answered with great good cheer. "I blow things up for a living."

Rule grunted just as the latch on the library door clicked open. "Funny. Your sister seems to do it as a hobby."

CHAPTER SIXTEEN

bby paused outside the door of Rafael De Santos's office on the second floor of the club and took a deep breath. The taste of crow was becoming a familiar one to her, but she couldn't say she was learning to like it any better for all that. Since the incident in the park yesterday, she had apologized to Samantha, made her peace with Tess, and even managed to smuggle a note to Missy expressing her regret at getting the Luna in trouble with her mate. All of that had been easy compared to the lion Abby was about to beard.

She rapped briefly on the door and decided the muffled grunt she heard in response would do as well as a command to enter. Her hand closed around the cool metal of the knob and she paused to say a quick prayer for courage—and patience—before she turned it and entered the dimly lit room.

Rafael De Santos had apparently given over to Rule the space in which he normally conducted his business as head of the Council of Others. Instead of the Felix, the demon sat behind the massive walnut desk poring over sheets and sheets of yellowed

and brittle paper with a kind of intensity that failed
to surprise her in the least. She imagined he focused
that kind of intensity on everything he did.

In fact, she couldn't seem to stop herself from
imagining him focusing it on making love. . . .

"Oh, for Pete's sake. That fiend's dirty mind must
be rubbing off on me."

"I beg your pardon?"

Abby jerked her gaze up off the floor to meet
Rule's across the width of the room. The cold, con-
trolled expression he wore made him look nothing
like she remembered from yesterday afternoon, right
before she had passed out, or whatever she was supposed to call it when Lou took over her body. Then
Rule had looked positively feral.

"Um, hi," she began. He simply stared impassively. "I was just, um, wondering if . . . you had a
minute. To talk to me."

"About?"

"Yesterday."

He dropped his attention back to the papers spread
before him. "I do not believe that is something we
need to, or should, discuss."

Abby sighed. Not a single one of them was going
to make this easy for her, were they? "I don't agree.
I think we absolutely need to discuss it. The whole
thing demonstrated pretty clearly to me that this situation is even more complicated than I thought it
was and that it's not going to end nearly as quickly
or as easily as I was hoping."

"Indeed."

He didn't say, "I told you so," but Abby could

practically see the phrase floating between them, as if a pixie in a crop duster had broken into the club and written it in the air in plumy exhaust.

"That being the case, I thought . . ." She rubbed her damp palms against the legs of her jeans. "I wanted to tell you . . . I'm sorry. For some of the things I said to you yesterday. Not the stuff about wanting to leave, or about finding this whole thing insane, 'cause those are both true. But I attacked you personally, and that wasn't fair. So . . . I'm sorry."

"Apology accepted."

Abby stood there a moment in silence while Rule continued to pore over his research materials, or whatever it was he seemed so engrossed in. She could almost hear the crickets chirping.

"That's it?"

"What is it?" He shuffled some papers aside, pulled out new ones. Never looked up.

"That's all I get? That cool little 'apology accepted' and we both go on our merry ways?"

Finally he looked up, but his expression said he wasn't at all happy about it. "You do not want me to accept your apology?"

"Of course I want you to accept my apology! You *should* accept my apology! You should—" Abby cut herself off and pressed a hand to her forehead.

"I beg your pardon?"

"Don't beg my anything. I think it's time we all decided no more begging." She closed the office door behind her and crossed over to the desk, sinking into one of the chairs opposite Rule's position of elegant authority. "My olive branch may be kind of wilted, but I swear, I came to make peace."

And since her stomach still insisted on fluttering and her heart on racing and her libido on shifting into overdrive every time she got near him, she figured it was a darned impressive gesture she was making, too.

"We were never at war," Rule dismissed, seemingly oblivious to the tension and attraction she could have sworn sparked between them. Maybe it was all on her side, a kind of latent teenage attraction to the ultimate bad boy. Because Rule didn't look like he lusted after her. He actually just looked annoyed, especially with that muscle in his jaw twitching as if he were grinding his teeth together in irritation.

"So why do I feel like we need to declare a truce?"

"I am not qualified to speculate on your beliefs."

Abby felt her own jaw beginning to clench. "You know, I'm beginning to think that you want me to hate your guts, for some insane reason. That can't be possible, can it?"

"It is none of my concern how you feel about me. My only concern is to see you safe and to keep the spell you carry out of Uzkiel's hands."

"Wow. I bet you have to beat the girls off with a stick, don't you?"

"I do not believe it benefits either of us to discuss personal matters." His tone was cold and dismissive, but Abby saw something almost like anger sparking behind those pitch-black eyes of his.

"You should have thought of that before you kissed me," she goaded, her eyes narrowing. "'Cause that felt pretty personal to me."

Even before the words left her mouth she recognized them as a supremely bad idea, but by then it was too late to stop them. They fell between the two of them like an undetonated nuclear warhead. Abby could almost swear she heard ticking.

"You humans have a tendency to read too much into simple tactics," he said after a moment in which Abby could have sworn the atmosphere in the room visibly thickened. "You had launched into a tirade. I simply chose an expedient method of quieting you."

Something prodded Abby to her feet, moved her like a puppet, and braced her hands on the paper-strewn desk, urging her to lean forward until her nose was just inches from his. She tried very, very hard to blame it on the fiend inside her, but that would have been a big, fat lie. And what was worse, Abby knew it.

She knew very well that the only one to blame for the challenging quirk of her eyebrow and the teasing parting of her lips was her. But she did it anyway.

"If all you wanted was to shut me up," she murmured, her gaze falling to his mouth and lingering there, remembering the heat of it over hers. The rich, spicy taste of it. "Your hand would have done the trick, and you know it. That kiss was either overkill . . . or undertow. Which one do you want to lay your money on?"

As if in slow motion, he reached a hand out to her, curled it in the knit fabric of her top, and began to pull her inexorably closer. "By the light of the sun, I swear I tried to keep myself from this."

"This" turned out to be another of those searing, mind-bending, toe-curling, heart-pounding, brain-scrambling kisses, and all Abby could do was sigh her pleasure.

The fact that he tasted so incredibly good to her, that his lips could make her knees melt and her stomach flutter, only served to reinforce what a bad idea this probably was. Anything that felt this good had to be a sin, she reasoned through a blurry fog of arousal, and at that moment she didn't care.

His fist tightened around her shirtfront, tugging her across the polished wood of the desk, sending papers shushing to the floor, and ending with her tumbling off the edge and into his lap. She tensed for a moment, feeling suddenly trapped by his enormous body, his heavy, muscled arms closing around her. Nervous, she tried to ease back a fraction, but his lips just softened against her, teasing, beguiling, until she relaxed against him once more.

Hard, gentle hands eased up the length of her spine, drawing shivers in their wake, before trailing back down in a long, fluid caress that left her sighing into his mouth. She leaned closer, let her tongue tangle with his, set her hands on his shoulders, her fingers kneading him like a cat. He made her feel as sinuous as one, as lazy and eager for petting.

One large hand firmed on her back, slid down over the waistband of her jeans to cup around the curve of her bottom and pull her closer against him. She moaned softly, a deep throaty sound that took on a sharp edge of surprise when another hand slid up her rib cage to close with gentle purpose around her breast.

This time, Abby didn't even bother to stiffen. Rule's touch felt nothing like the clumsy groping of the boy she'd slept with in college, the one and only other man to have touched her. Then, giving in had felt like an obligation. But this . . . this felt like heaven.

It was Rule who finally lifted his head, staring down at her with those fathomless black eyes. "This is not wise, Abigail."

Shivering, his hands still holding her to him, warm and arousing at her breast and bottom, Abby leaned forward to nip at his chin. "I know. But wisdom can be highly overrated."

"As can my self-control," he muttered.

His hands slid away to grip her hips and lift her away from him. Abby blinked, as if she'd been in a dark room and someone had just turned on the lights.

She shivered. "What's the matter?"

Rule set her on the edge of the desk and slumped back in his chair, running a hand through his disheveled golden hair. "Circumstances have thrust us together, but that does not mean we should allow ourselves to be ruled by these illogical impulses. We do not suit."

Abby's breast, still tingling where he'd touched it, begged to differ. "Why do you say that?"

He leveled her a long stare. "First, because you are under my protection."

"Euphemistically speaking."

"Also, We come from two different worlds, quite literally. We can have nothing in common other than this . . . strange attraction."

Abby crossed her arms over her chest. "You make it sound like some sort of disease. And I'm sure we have to have something in common; otherwise I doubt we'd feel anything for each other but dislike."

"What could you possibly believe we could share?"

"Well, I think it's pretty clear that both of us have a well-developed sense of duty," she said, wondering why she was trying to convince this man, this demon, that he was wrong about their incompatibility when she'd been reminding herself of it for nearly twenty-four hours. "And we both seem to find Louamides deeply annoying."

"Every living creature on every plane of existence finds Louamides annoying. It is hardly a foundation on which to build a relationship."

Abby blew out a breath and pushed herself off the desk to stand on her own two feet. There was something reassuring about the movement. "I don't believe I asked for a relationship," she dismissed, ignoring the niggling in her chest. "I'm not trying to convince you we're perfect for each other. I may be possessed, but I'm not insane . . . yet."

He looked up at her, his expression brooding. "Then what did you come here for?"

"I told you. To apologize." She wrapped her arms around herself and took several steps away from the desk and the danger that lurked behind it. "Which I've already done. And to thank you."

"For?"

"For helping my brother. I know he'd just been holding a gun on you, so I'm sure helping him get back here to the club when you already had me to

worry about wasn't the top on your list of priorities.
But I wanted you to know I appreciate it."

Rule shrugged. "He is human. It is my duty to
protect him."

"See what I mean?" Abby's mouth quirked.
"Duty. Why do you think I haven't found a way to
scale the outside wall up to the roof and flag down a
helicopter?"

"Because you know I would stop you."

"No. Because every once in a great while, what you
say almost starts to make sense. I figure if that starts
to happen more frequently, I'll go see my doctor."

"Once we have dealt with Uzkiel and can be assured of the safety of you leaving this club alone."

Abby laughed and headed for the door. "Right.
And stubbornness. Did I mention that was another
thing we have in common?"

ule watched the door click shut behind Abby
and blew out a deep breath. Then he leaned
forward and let his forehead thump down
onto the heavy desk.

Hard.

What in the sun's name had he been thinking? Kissing Abby once had been bad enough, but to repeat the
exercise clearly indicated he had the common sense
and the self-control of a chaos imp. He must be going
out of his mind.

"Wow. When De Santos told me I might find you
like this, I thought he was kidding."

Rule looked up to see the brother of his current
obsession standing in front of the desk. The fact that

Rule hadn't heard him open the door or approach the desk provided testament to either his skill as a soldier or Rule's doom as a single male.

"I'll let you in on a little secret," Noah continued, his expression deadpan and his eyes twinkling. "You may not have noticed this, but Abby is a little . . . determined. The two best ways to deal with her are to either go along with her or to ignore her completely. I'm an advocate of door number two."

Right. And that had been working so well for Rule thus far. He pushed back into his seat. "Somehow I do not believe you have come in here to talk to me about your sister."

"Nope. I came to ask if you were up for shaking a few trees to see if our raccoon might just fall out."

The demon raised an eyebrow. "What did you have in mind?"

"A guy in my unit grew up on Avenue A. There's a bar down there he says gets a pretty interesting clientele. The exact opposite of the cream of the crop, if you know what I mean."

"Well, if we were going to find info about Uzkiel in a bar, that sounds as if it would be the perfect one. Perhaps we should pay a visit."

"Sundown's in two hours."

"Good. I think I'm suddenly feeling parched."

*t*he bar turned out to be every bit as unsavory as Noah's teammate had promised, a fact that he and Rule took an odd sort of delight in. Not because either of them was the type to hang out in seedy bars, though Rule at least had certainly been in worse, but because at this point, anything that smelled like a lead would be enough to get the Watchman as excited as a high school quarterback on prom night.

The patrons of the low-ceilinged, badly lit room had obviously never heard of the city's smoking ban, but then, the owners had obviously never heard of soap and water, so Rule figured it might be a fair trade.

He pushed through a haze of cigarette smoke and led the way to the bar with Abby's brother trailing behind him. The soldier had traded his fatigues for a battered pair of jeans borrowed from Graham Winters and a well-worn chambray shirt softened by many washings. He didn't look so entirely different from the other occupants of the bar, but then, neither did Rule, with his scruffy stubble, deliberately rumpled clothes and ball cap pulled low to disguise his features.

It just went to show that appearances could be deceiving.

They laid claim to a couple of rickety bar stools, and Noah managed to catch the eye of the hulking but less-than-enthusiastic-looking bartender.

"Whaddaya want?"

Noah met the man's sullen gaze with a steady one of his own. "I got a friend says your beer's good. Gimme two of those."

The bartender's eyes narrowed. "What's this friend's name?"

"Billy. But mostly we just call him Badass."

Rule watched the man closely and saw when the tension about him eased just slightly. He also saw that the man had the kind of craggy, rough skin and thick, dense build that marked him as the descendant of a stone giant.

"How is the bastard?" the bartender asked, his small, dark eyes watching Noah steadily. "He still got that stupid heart tattoo on his chest?"

"Badass has a lot of tattoos," Noah said, "but the only one I've ever seen on his chest isn't a heart. It's a one-fingered salute."

The man's chin jerked in a nearly imperceptible nod. "Two beers. Get those for yas."

Rule waited till the bartender trundled off to the tap before turning to his companion. "A secret password of some sort?"

"I guess. Billy didn't say anything to me about it, but he did say these guys don't warm much to strangers."

"I would wager."

The mirror behind the bar was spattered and dingy, but Rule could still make out most of the patrons scattered around at tables behind them. It was early yet, so the bar was mostly empty. Only about half-a-dozen regulars had shown up, and none of them looked familiar to Rule. More significantly, none of them smelled familiar.

The bartender thumped two mugs down on the bar in front of Rule and Noah. "Anything else?"

"Maybe." Noah wrapped a hand around the handle of his mug and met the bartender's gaze steadily. "Badass said there was a guy here named Crank who knows everything that needs knowing in the neighborhood."

"That's me. Whaddaya looking for?"

"A who." Reaching into his shirt pocket, Noah drew out an enlargement of the grainy photo Missy's camera phone had snapped of Seth's human host in the park. "This guy look familiar?"

Crank hesitated for a moment before leaning down to squint at the photo. "He ain't no regular, that's for damn sure."

"Have you ever seen him before?" Rule asked.

"Maybe once." Crank looked from Rule to Noah and back again. Maybe the Badass blessing only extended to one friend at a time. "I mostly mind my own business, but this guy stood out. I mean, look at him. Not many yuppies bother to come to a place like this, you know what I mean?"

Rule did, but he refrained from answering.

"When?" Noah prompted.

" 'Bout three, four days ago. Got into it with a weird guy, Lenny, likes to sit in the corner of the bar and nurse shots of Jäger. Usually this Lenny fellow's real quiet, keeps to himself. But that night, it was like he was lookin' for a fight. Laid into the rich guy the second he walked in here. Eventually, I had to persuade them to continue their discussion outside."

Rule followed Crank's nod to the heavy wooden baseball bat prominently displayed above the cash register.

"I'm sure you did," Noah agreed. "You see anything that happened after that?"

"Nah. Two of 'em go outside, and next thing I know, the yuppie's gone and Lenny's propped up against my stoop sporting a couple of broken ribs, two broken wrists, and a cut nearly chopped his ear off. Paramedics loaded him into an ambulance and took him off right then. Ain't seen either of 'em since. And Lenny still owes me for the Jäger."

Noah thanked the man and waited until he moved to the other side of the bar before turning to Rule. "Sounds like Lou isn't the only one hopping around the city. I suspect the change in Lenny resulted from a possession by Seth that then transferred to the man we met in the park."

"I am not surprised. To remain undetected for as long as possible, Uzkiel and his minions would want to appear as normal humans, which requires them to take possession of human bodies."

"That'll make them damned hard to track down."

"I never expected much else."

Swearing, Noah pushed aside his beer and stood. "Well, shit. Sorry this turned out to be a dead end."

"It was not." Rule followed suit. They tossed money for the drinks on the bar and exited into the deepening night. "We have confirmed our suspicions of where the fiends are hiding, and we may have another lead to trace. If this Lenny person was taken to the hospital, there will be records. If he filed a police report after the possession ended, there may even be an investigation or a name of the other man, the one who was hosting Seth. It is more than we had to go on a few minutes ago."

"My, aren't you the optimist?"

"It is never productive to give in to the belief that nothing can ever change."

"I used to think that way," Noah mused. "Then Abby learned to talk."

Rule shot him a sidelong glance. "What do you mean?"

"Just that my baby sister is what physicists mean when they start talking about an immovable force."

"She seems very young to be so set in her ways."

"She was born set. And I'm not convinced the way our parents brought us up was much help in the flexibility department. They meant well, and they loved us both, but they're kind of old-fashioned. A little unbending themselves."

"I would not have called your sister unbending," Rule mused, thinking of the supple flex of her spine beneath his hands.

Noah's eyes narrowed. "I'm going to pretend I didn't notice anything odd in the way you said that, Rule, because I like you. I'd hate to have to kill you."

"And I would hate for you to have to try. Rest assured, I have no plans to corrupt Abigail. She will always be safe with me."

For a moment, the only sound came from the light fall of their feet on the pavement. Then Noah glanced over at Rule, his mouth beginning to curve with amusement.

"Hm. I wonder how long you're going to be safe with her?"

CHAPTER SEVENTEEN

For the first couple of days, Abby just kept repeating to herself that it would all be over soon. Rule and Noah had teamed up in the quest to locate Uzkiel's hiding place, so at least someone was *doing* something, even if she wasn't. Even Louamides managed to leave her mostly alone, probably still traumatized by its run-in with Seth.

During the next couple of days, the reminders stopped being enough. She took to wandering the halls of the club during the day, when it was mostly quiet, and pacing the confines of her room at night. If she kept moving, it seemed easier to control the frustrated scream welling inside her. Samantha and Tess took turns trying to keep her occupied with movies and games and girl talk, and even Missy stopped by after a couple of days to take a shift.

The first time the Luna showed up, Abby had apologized.

Missy dismissed it with a wave and a smile. "Honey, I'd have tried the same thing if I were you," she said. "In fact, come to think of it, I did try. Only let me tell you, it's a lot harder to stage an escape naked from an Alpha's bedroom than it is fully clothed in a public park with a military escort. You, at least, get points for planning."

Missy's easy forgiveness almost made Abby feel worse.

Noah spent time with her every day, but when he had chastised her, she didn't enjoy it so much.

"You didn't tell me the whole story, Ab," he'd said over a hand of rummy. "If I'd known about the fiends rebelling and the spell they're trying to get their hands on, I'd have told you to stay put. You're safer here than just about anywhere else I can think of, except maybe Faerie."

And that was another thing. Here she was with her universe rocking back on its heels, and she finds out her brother is practically an authority on all things Other. He seemed perfectly comfortable with magic and the supernatural power, and judging by the glances she occasionally caught him shooting at Samantha, he didn't appear to have any problem with inter-species relations either.

She knew the rest of the world was like her, still struggling to adjust. She watched the news occasionally on the big-screen TV in the club's second-floor media room, so she knew the protests hadn't died down. In fact, there had been rioting in St. Louis and Houston over the past few days. Other people were having an even harder time with this than she was, so why did she feel like such a jerk about it?

By day five, Abby was ready to surrender her mind and body to Louamides just so she wouldn't have to deal with the waiting and the confinement anymore. The times when he'd taken over had left her blissfully unaware and with no memory of anything that had happened. Just then that sounded like heaven.

She knew she was reaching a boiling point, but she never expected to blow her top quite as soon or quite as spectacularly as she managed. In the end, she blamed it on her brother.

*t*he door to Rafe's office slammed open hard enough to send the knob bouncing off the wall behind it, and Abby stood in the center of the opening, hands braced on her hips like one of the nuns who had so terrified her all during her school years. Fortunately, none of the rest of the Council was present.

"What *exactly* did you mean by telling my brother that it could be weeks before you manage to find Uzkiel?"

Rule and Rafe looked up from Rafe's desk, and two sets of eyebrows headed toward the ceiling. Rafe's remained in that position, but it only took a second for Rule's to descend into a glower.

"I do not have time to listen to your temper tantrum, Abigail," the demon dismissed. "You will have to wait for another time."

Through the red haze of her anger, Abby just barely heard Rafe's hiss of indrawn breath. "I would advise you to choose your words more carefully, friend," the Felix said quietly. "You speak as if you've never been faced with a warrior's woman in all her glory."

Rule glared at him. "She is not my woman."

"At the moment, my goal is to be your worst night-mare," Abby bit out. Her jaw felt so tight, she was amazed she managed to get it out at all. "There is no way on earth or in heaven I am going to stay cooped up in here for that long! Why aren't you out there right now looking for him? Are you expecting him to knock on the front door and climb right into your lap?"

She didn't even bother to glance at Rafe, but out of the corner of her eye she saw him purse his lips and ease himself out from behind his desk.

"I think perhaps I had better leave the two of you to sort this out yourselves," he murmured, and began to inch toward the exit.

Abby cleared his path by blazing ahead on her own straight toward the object of her fury. "What have you got to say for yourself?"

Rule leveled a stare at her. His expression remained cold and distant, something she was beginning to recognize was his "on duty" mask, but his eyes blazed with dark fire. "I was not aware you required a response. You seem to have drawn your own conclusions about the matter at hand without any assistance from me. Or from logic or good sense."

"You arrogant bastard!"

In the back of her head, Abby had a vague moment of wondering if her shout had managed to register on the Richter scale. It wouldn't have surprised her.

She sucked in a deep breath, but before she could let it out, a headful of blond curls poked in from the hallway.

"Did someone commit a murder in here, or have I gotten here in time?"

Rafe strode to the door and put his hands on his wife's shoulders. "I doubt anything could halt the violence at this point, sweetheart, and for the sake of our son, I would rather you did not make the attempt."

"Oh, I don't want to stop it," Tess laughed. "I just wondered if I'd have time to make popcorn before the good parts."

Abby never took her eyes off Rule. "There aren't going to be any good parts, but if Mr. High-and-Mighty over here doesn't come up with some really good answers to my questions really fast, there just might be some NC-17-rated gratuitous violence."

Rule shoved back his chair and stretched to his feet, his gaze just as steady on Abby. "I have no intention of coming up with anything until you can behave with reason, maturity, and self-control."

Behind them, Abby heard Tess make a tsking sound.

"Yikes. Isn't he supposed to be like a bunch of centuries old?" she asked her husband. "You'd think he'd never done this before."

"Perhaps if he survives this round, I can give him a few pointers," Rafe answered.

Rule looked up, focusing over Abby's head at the couple in the doorway. "I think perhaps it would be better if the two of you left us for a moment."

"They're fine," Abby growled. "I have no problem with ripping you a new one in front of witnesses."

Tess whistled. "Wow. For a nice Catholic school-girl she's got a mean streak, doesn't she?"

"Come, love. I think Rule is right. Let's give them a bit of privacy."

Abby was too busy struggling with the unfamiliar urge to commit an actual act of violence to watch them leave, but she heard the door shut behind them with an ominous click.

"If you have a problem with me," Rule said, his voice low and dangerously smooth as he prowled toward her in the suddenly quiet room, "I would appreciate your bringing it up with me, rather than airing it in front of an audience. No matter how appreciative they might be."

"And I would appreciate it if you would stop making decisions about my life and my captivity with my brother and letting me find out second-hand," she hissed. By the time Rule stopped, he was looming over her like a golden-haired, black-eyed mountain, but Abby was too angry to be intimidated. "This is my life! Or it used to be. I'm sick and tired of being treated like some kind of inanimate object that can just be put up on a shelf or locked up in a closet without so much as a by-your-leave. I want my life back!"

"You can't have it."

"That is exactly what I'm talking about!" Abby threw her hands up, surprised one didn't land knuckles-first smack dab in the middle of his infuriating mouth. "You make these decrees on high and expect me to meekly go along with them! Well, it's not going to happen."

"The last thing I expect from you is meekness,

Abigail," he said. "But I do expect obedience. And I'll have it."

She almost choked on a laugh. Not that she was amused, it was just either laugh or scream, and she knew she'd need her vocal cords to be in tip-top shape if she was going to get through that mile-thick demonic skull. "Do you even hear yourself? You sound like some sort of feudal lord. This is not the Middle Ages, my unholy friend, and I am not some serf to be ordered about on a whim."

Rule's dark eyes narrowed, and she saw a flicker of anger beneath the impassive mask. "You have no right to call me that."

"What? My friend? I realize we're not all that close, but since you're one of only about ten people I'm allowed to talk to these days, I'm not ready to shortchange myself on possible companions."

"Unholy." He took a step closer until she had to crane her neck to look up at him. A flicker of unease shivered through her. "You are no more entitled to sit in judgment on me than you believe I am to hold you prisoner."

A devilish voice inside her prodded Abby to take another step, never mind the chasm she sensed stretching before her. "Oh, am I hitting a little too close for comfort? It's not my fault you're a demon, Rule. It's not my fault you've been forsaken by God and condemned to a life outcast from heaven."

She could almost hear his self-control snap. One minute he loomed before her, a wall of icy control, and the next he had her by the shoulders, hauling her up against a body she could now vouch for as being a long, long way from cold.

"If you would condemn me as a monster, then at least I will give you a reason."

And his mouth came crashing down on hers like a landslide.

CHAPTER EIGHTEEN

*I*nside Abby's head, voices sang suspiciously like choirs of angels, and the explosion behind her eyes banished any thoughts of darkness more quickly than sunrise. If this was a sin, Abby would hang up her rosary and surrender herself to eternal damnation without a twinge of regret. It would be worth it, to feel this man's hands on her forever.

He swept inside her mouth like a conquering army, bulldozing past any tentative explorations and plundering her heated response. Abby whimpered and sucked on his tongue, pressing herself closer against him. He went to her head like a shot of whiskey but tasted a whole lot better. He sent the same fire curling into the pit of her belly with none of the bitter acid on her tongue. Instead, he was smooth and rich and sweet like fine chocolate, and for once in her life, Abby didn't worry about the treat going straight to her thighs. She rather hoped he would.

Rule, though, seemed determined to take the long road. His hands glided over her shoulders and down her arms, raising goose bumps in their wake. Everywhere they touched, she tingled, her nerves on high alert. Her breasts pressed against his chest, molding to his hardness, and when she shifted restlessly, her denim-clad thighs rubbed against his, pushing a moan through her swollen lips.

A growl rumbled in his chest, a low, thrumming response. She felt his hands slide beneath her arms to close around her ribs, tightening as if to warn her against trying to escape. As if the thought had even crossed her mind. She wanted to put less distance between them, not more. She wanted to be skin to skin. Closer if she could manage it.

The intensity of her need surprised her, but she didn't stop to think about it. She didn't want to waste that kind of time. For the first time in her life, she burned with desire. She'd always assumed, especially after her disastrous first and only sexual experience, that when people wrote about lust in terms of aches and fevers and trembling needs, that was why they called it fiction. People didn't really feel that way. She didn't. She'd lived without sex for almost a decade, and she was none the worse for the wear. Or the lack thereof.

Oh, how naïve she'd been.

Rule had kick-started her sex drive, and the power of it now drove her on with a vengeance. She felt it like the sting of a whip driving her on, driving her closer, driving her to tempt him into a frenzy she had no idea if she could handle.

She had a feeling she was about to find out.

In the back of her mind, her conscience whispered at her. She had known this would happen. When she'd come storming down here driven by her frustration and the anger that had welled when Noah told her it might be weeks before she could go back to her old life, she'd known the spark of her fury would light this inferno. Yet she'd done it anyway.

It was the coward's way, her conscience chided her. It wouldn't let her get away with putting the responsibility for this on Rule's broad shoulders. She had known she didn't have the guts to follow through with Tess and Samantha's suggestion that she seduce the demon, so her subconscious had decided to shift the burden onto him. If she prodded him in just the right way, at just the right time, she'd get her seduction, and probably her vindication of her anger, and she'd never have to make a move for it to happen.

Cowardly.

But Abby's hormones didn't care. They were too busy glorying in the feel of his thick golden hair beneath her fingers, the heavy weight of his muscular body pressed against hers. They were too busy urging her to spread her legs, to wrap them around his waist and push him past the next barrier, to care about why she had made this move. They just celebrated that she had.

Abby moaned into his mouth, moaned again when those lips shifted off hers to blaze a trail along her jaw and down the side of her throat. He nibbled his way along, all but consuming her, tongue and teeth tasting every square inch of pale, heated skin. Her body quaked in his arms, and as she hooked her ankles together in the small of his back she realized her hormones had won that particular battle. She held his hips cradled against hers, the heat of his erection pressed snugly against her center.

Her eyes flew open and their gazes locked. She saw the fire of passion in his and something else, something simultaneously fierce and protective, greedy and giving. And beneath it, a question. One more step and neither would be able to turn back. He may have led her this far, but as she drowned in the black depths of his gaze she knew she would have to cross that last distance on her own.

Breath frozen, heart pounding, she slid her hands to his shoulders and braced herself against him. She felt his hands gripping her hips, felt his fingers flex as if to force her into the place he wanted her, then they eased, and he began to lift her away from him.

No way was she going to let that happen.

Fingertips digging into his flesh, Abby caught his gaze again and held it while she tightened the grip of her thighs and rocked her hips suggestively against his.

The dam broke and swept away the last of her doubts in a torrent of rushing need.

Large hands slid from her hips to her butt, gripping and shifting her, pressing her heat more firmly against him. Abby felt a moment's astonishment that the two layers of denim between them didn't spontaneously combust and dissolve in a cloud of ash. No such luck. The heavy cloth separated them, but even through the barrier her center ached, empty and wanting.

Her entire being felt empty and wanting. With any luck, he wasn't planning to let that continue.

Abby felt the earth move. It took a minute to realize it was actually Rule, walking backward across the room to a large leather chair in front of the fireplace. She tightened her thighs around his hips to steady herself and heard him growl in response. Curious, she repeated the motion and got the same response along with a light smack on the ass.

"Don't tease," he rumbled, his gaze burning into her. "I don't want to hurt you."

"Would you?" she asked, leaning forward to drag her tongue over the pulse beating visibly at the base of his throat. She felt as if some other Abby had taken control of her body, but it was too pleasurable for her to care.

"You tell me."

He shifted her weight into one hand and used the other to grasp one of hers. Dragging it between them, he slid it down and down and down until he wrapped her shaking fingers around the insistent ridge of his erection, pressing eagerly against the fabric of her jeans.

Abby trembled, not with fear but with the force of her desire. He felt enormous, hot and hard and heavy through the dulling veil of the material. Dragging her gaze back to his, she caught her bottom lip between her teeth and managed a little shrug. "Won't know till we try."

Her husky taunt seemed to have roughly the effect on him as a waving red cape had on a bull. Rule cursed in a language she didn't recognize, something low and harsh and guttural, and took two more giant steps back until the backs of his legs bumped up against the edge of the chair. Carefully he eased himself down, keeping Abby's hips pressed tight against him, guiding her knees to the cushion beside his legs.

She felt her breath speed up, saw her field of vision narrow until all she could see was his face, harsh and set in the light of the fire. His features might have been carved roughly out of granite, all sharp planes and angles, weathered by time and experience. Now, lust had made them even more jagged, even more heavily shadowed, and Abby lifted one hand to his cheek to reassure herself of his living warmth.

Only to feel his teeth close around the plump flesh at the base of her thumb.

A shiver of need wracked her, and he pulled her more snugly against him. His hands slid down her thighs, pulling her knees forward until they pressed up against the back of the chair and his cock pressed up against the very heart of her. Her eyes closed for a moment as the need threatened to overwhelm her, and she had to fight to force them open again.

"What now?" she asked, her voice so rough and throaty, she almost didn't recognize it.

"Impatient?" His hands slid back up her thighs and around to cup her ass, kneading with heated intent.

A moan tumbled unbidden from her lips. "Empty."

"Not for long."

If she had been capable of thought, or voluntary muscle control, she might have tried to move, to lift herself off his lap and fight free of the clothes that had suddenly become her greatest enemy. She needn't have worried. He leaned forward, a dark, overwhelming presence that blocked off the light, and his lips settled once more on hers. This time, his mouth devoured, hungrier, more demanding. If such a thing were possible. She went under as if grasped by a riptide, barely registering the movement of his hands on the waistband of her jeans. But she couldn't mistake the sudden wrenching pressure or the loud hiss of protesting fabric as he ripped the thick denim into shreds and tossed the remnants of her jeans onto the floor behind her.

Gasping, Abby pulled back and stared into his eyes, seeing nothing there but a need that mirrored her own.

She swallowed hard and shifted, gasping at the feel of him pressing the thin cotton of her panties against her achingly wet core. "I, uh, I guess that superstrength comes in handy, from time to time."

"From time to time," he agreed.

He slid one finger over the bare skin of her hip, curling it around the narrow strip of cloth that covered her. One tug and the panties went the way of her jeans, leaving her hot and bare and spread open across his lap like a banquet.

He looked very, very hungry.

She didn't even have time to catch her breath. Rule wouldn't let her. His hand on her bottom held her firmly in place while the other slid relentlessly over the soft mound of her belly and down through the tidy nest of curls between her legs. His fingers parted them, slid lower, discovered the slick moisture that waited for him, and sank deep.

Abby cried out, high and aching, and arched reflexively into his touch.

She felt, more than heard, his purr of satisfaction. Her head fell back, her neck no longer able to support its spinning, dizzy weight. She felt him shift, felt his fingers slide deeper, parting her soft folds, seeking her center. His lips touched her throat, slid down, his tongue dragging across the hollow above her collarbone just as one long finger pierced her snug opening and thrust inside her with torturous slowness.

She clamped around him like a vise, every muscle tensing at the unfamiliar intrusion. She heard his murmur of pleasure and squirmed, looking for an ease she couldn't find. Her whole body felt tight and restless, empty and needing. Not a single memory of her last sexual experience intruded. Rule's hands felt too right, too perfect on her overheated flesh.

"Tight," he whispered against her throat. "Sweet."

Abby moaned and squirmed again. His finger stroked deep inside her, but she wanted him deeper, wanted it with a fierceness that shocked her.

"Please," she gasped.

He nuzzled aside the collar of her blouse; teeth nibbled the sensitive skin, the light teasing contact a stark contrast to the invasive intimacy of his thrusting finger.

"More?"

She could barely nod, but her muscles clenched around him in avid encouragement. A low chuckle drifted through her fog, and she felt his finger slip out of her. Her hands clenched on his shoulder in panic. He couldn't leave her now.

"Hush," he soothed, stroking his tongue in a hot path to her shoulder. "Have more."

His touch returned, two fingers this time, the thickness of them stretching her opening with a heavenly, aching burn. He probed deeply, fingers curling to drag along the inner walls of her passage, and Abby found herself thrusting back against him, struggling to take him deeper, to urge him into the possessive rhythm her body longed for.

Her body had been empty so long that even his two fingers filled her, feeling as thick as a cock inside her. She rocked against them, high, desperate whimpers begging for more.

The rough denim of his jeans rasped against her inner thighs, and her tightly beaded nipples stabbed at the fabric of her bra and blouse, reminding her he was still completely dressed while she writhed, half-naked and aching, like a wanton on his lap.

Rule didn't seem to mind. He murmured encouraging noises against her throat, his hand on her ass dragging her firmly into the thrust of his fingers. She gripped his shoulders, her nails biting into him, trying to steady herself against the raging tide of lust that threatened to overtake her.

God, it had already overtaken her.

"Please," she gasped, her voice raw, reduced to begging for pleasure. "More. Please."

She didn't know exactly what she was asking, whether it was for him to stop teasing and come inside her, whether to keep teasing until she fractured into a million tiny shards on his lap. It hardly mattered. She wanted more. She was begging for more.

"More."

His hand shifted between her legs, two fingers sliding through the hot slickness of her desire, teasing her opening with tickling touches before returning to press against her again. This time, it was three fingers, and the pressure at her entrance stretched Abby wide, threatening pain that didn't quite materialize.

"Rule? . . ." Her voice shivered from her, a question, a warning.

He soothed her with the light brush of his lips against hers and pressed more firmly at her entrance. "Come, little one," he urged, his voice dark and magic. "Take me inside. You can do it."

She swallowed a cry and dragged in a shaking breath. Blowing it out in a long, steady stream, she concentrated on forcing her muscles to relax and let her body ease down around his thick, probing fingers.

"That's it," he praised, his voice all rasping heat and growling urgency. "Beautiful."

Abby wasn't sure she felt beautiful. She felt tense and stretched and shivering on the edge of pleasure. Her nerves were on high alert, registering every shift, every slide, every nudge of his fingers inside her slick sheath. If his fingers filled her this full, she shuddered to think what it would feel like when his cock tunneled through the oversensitized flesh.

A quick hiss of breath told her Rule had felt every ripple of that shudder. She forced her heavy eyelids up again and found him watching her with almost frightening intensity. She shivered again and watched as he softened, felt as his fingers stroked slowly and steadily inside her clinging body.

"All right?"

She managed a nod, barely.

"Good girl. Hold on."

Before she could wonder what he meant, she felt his fingers thrust deep, high, and hard inside her. He kept them there, his gaze searching her face. He must have seen what he wanted, because his gaze flared with hungry satisfaction as his free hand slid from her bottom up over her hip, under her button-down blouse to curl around the vee of the opening, his fingers peeking out from between her breasts. Abby had one second to blink down at his fingers before they tightened and yanked down, sending buttons flying to the four corners of the room and pulling her body down hard onto his invading touch.

Abby's scream startled her. Rule just looked pleased.

He brushed the sides of her blouse out of the way and tugged it off each arm before settling her hands back into their places on his shoulders. Certain she would drown if she loosened her grip for an instant, she clung to him as if he were a life raft. He tossed her blouse aside and looked down at the little plastic tab between her breasts that held her bra closed. The last tangible barrier between her and his devouring gaze.

"Perfect."

With exaggerated care, so incongruous after the ruins he'd made of the rest of her clothing, Rule used his thumb and forefinger to flip open the tab and watched with apparent fascination as the two sides parted, peeling away from the insides of her breasts to expose soft, white skin.

"Perfect," he repeated.

His fingers resumed a slow, steady thrusting between her legs, making her body feel as if it were melting into a little Abby-flavored puddle in his lap. She whimpered uncontrollably as he leaned down and nuzzled her bra away from each breast, baring her nipples one at a time like tiny treasure hoards. He greeted each with a slow, lazy glide of his tongue that made her clench around his fingers, before he finished removing her last garment with excruciating delicacy.

Abby figured she was about three and a half seconds away from losing her mind.

She leaned forward, sobbing as the movement drove his fingers higher inside her, and rested her sweat-dampened forehead against his chest. "Rule, please."

For one horrible moment, she thought he was going to ignore her. She thought he was going to continue to torture her until her heart gave out and she died of unfulfilled need in the office of the head of the Council of Others. Sure, she wouldn't have had to witness the snickers of the crowd when they came to remove her body, but it was a fact she'd still rather avoid.

Turning her head, she pressed one feverish cheek to his chest and closed her teeth over a smooth expanse of heavy muscle.

That seemed to do the trick.

With a smothered roar, Rule pulled his fingers from her body and yanked at the fastening of his jeans. In the space between heartbeats, he had the fabric open and out of the way and shifted his hands to close one around Abby's hip, holding her steady against him. The other curled around his erection, his knuckles brushing against Abby's clit and making her jump.

"Don't move," he ordered, tense and breathless, as he set the head of his cock against her opening and began to push.

Abby's eyes widened and her spine tensed as she felt the width of his erection demanding entrance to her body. He felt even thicker than his fingers, hotter, smoother, and she wondered in a brief moment of panic if she had bitten off more than she could chew.

Then Rule shifted his grip, both hands clamped down hard on her hips and drawing her slowly, steadily, inexorably, down upon him.

All Abby could do was take a deep breath and relax.

Their eyes locked, black on brown and blue, both intent as he forged his way deeper.

Abby shuddered and froze, every muscle locked against the intrusion. She wanted him inside her so badly, but she couldn't seem to relax enough to admit him. Frustrated, she whimpered and pressed hard against him.

Rule's fingers tightened on her hips. "Slowly."

She didn't want slow. She wanted now. Biting into her lip to distract herself from the sharp sting between her legs, Abby firmed her thighs against his hips and pressed herself steadily down over him.

He cursed, his fingers biting into her hips for a

breathless heartbeat. She could almost see his struggle against the sensations of wet heat and tight welcome closing around him. If it was anything like
what Abby was feeling, he probably couldn't even
remember his name just then.

But she could. It was engraved in flaming script on
her mind and someplace else that felt suspiciously
near her heart.

"Rule."

She whispered it, sobbed it, as he slid deeper,
deeper, mind-bendingly deep until he came to rest
pressing up against the very heart of her. Then she
tightened her body around him and screamed it.

"Rule!"

If he made an answer, she didn't hear. She leaned
against him, trembling and aching, feeling the heat
of him through the soft cotton of his shirt as he
shifted his grip to pull her tighter against him. One
hand pressed against the small of her back, guiding
her hips in a sliding, rocking motion that sent him
nudging over and over against a spot high inside her
that made brilliant points of orange light burst and
shimmer behind her eyelids.

His other hand slid up the bare, supple length of
her spine, tunneling through the weight of her silky-
fine hair to settle possessively over the back of her
neck. He cradled her with a touch that felt distinctly
like a brand, but Abby didn't care. She wanted him
to be possessive, wanted to be possessed by him. If
she could have sunk beneath his skin, she would
have. She needed to be closer to him, to be part of

him, the way she had begun to fear he was becoming a part of her.

She opened her mouth to cry out, but the sound caught in her throat. She lacked the breath to force it out. He drove it from her with each deep, gliding stroke.

Her muscles began to shake, pulled tight to the point of breaking. She could feel something looming over her like a tidal wave about to break. She knew when it struck, the undertow would drag her to the rocks and the sand, leaving her battered and bruised in the aftermath. She didn't care.

The last vestige of her strength went to forcing her eyes open one last time. Her gaze locked with Rule's, saw the same dazed acceptance in his that she knew shone in hers. Aching, writhing, keening soft and high with the need, Abby leaned forward and spoke the only word she could remember. The only one that mattered.

"Rule."

It was the crack in the dike. With a roar, he crushed her against him, his fingers digging into her flesh with bruising force. His thrusts battered at her, sending him almost painfully deep inside her, forcing out the memory of what her body had felt like when it had been separate from his. She felt his possessiveness, felt it and gloried in it. Her own fingers tightened on his shoulders and she knew she would fight just as hard to hold on to him. They had become interdependent, one burning, twisting, desperate entity, unable to sustain themselves apart.

Tilting her head back, Abby looked up into the mouth of the wave and felt her lips curve into a smile. Let it come. She was ready.

Body arching, heart pounding, she gathered herself and threw her heart into the tidal wave, knowing that when she washed ashore, she would never be the same.

It didn't matter, because neither would Rule.

CHAPTER NINETEEN

*I*f demons were allowed into heaven, Abby was the gate through which they would enter.

Rule acknowledged the truth of that an instant before he frowned. That shouldn't have been plural. Only one demon would ever touch her, and he'd make damned sure only one ever entered her.

The office had fallen silent. Even the fire seemed to burn on without a sound. All Rule could hear was the slowly steadying sound of Abby's breathing and the too-rapid beating of his own heart.

She had destroyed him.

He had no other words to describe it. She had torn down every barrier he'd ever erected around himself in all the thousand years of his life and had used every last one of them as so much kindling for the flames that had consumed them. For a small, relatively quiet human she packed the destructive wallop of a class-five hurricane.

No one would ever guess by looking at her. He tilted his head and gazed down at her where she lay limp and boneless against his chest. She still had the average features and the baby-soft skin he'd noticed the first time he saw her. She still had the fine ash-brown hair and the soft, plump curves, the utter, forgettable humanness he'd made note of. She still looked as ordinary and unimpressive as he'd judged her from the first moment, and if anything, she had even more power to stop his heart and start his libido than any female of any species he'd ever met.

It defied all reason, that she should leave him so helpless. Someone so small and so plain should not be able to fell him with a single touch of those slender fingers, but Abby could. The evidence was overwhelming.

She stirred in his lap, shifting against him like a sleepy kitten, and his arms tightened reflexively around her. He watched, utterly fascinated, as her forehead wrinkled in a frown, then cleared when she gave in to a jaw-cracking yawn.

He was doomed.

"I can't feel my legs," she muttered against his shirt. Her voice was thick and husky with sleepiness and remembered pleasure. "They're still there, right?"

Unable to resist, Rule slid his hands over the limbs in question and felt her shiver.

"Um. That's a yes. I guess they fell asleep." She yawned again.

Rule shifted forward in the chair and helped her straighten her legs. He thought she would slide them to the floor and let both him and her up out of the chair, but instead, she unbent her legs from their cramped position only to wrap them around his waist, ankles locking behind his back.

She pillowed her head against his chest. "Mm. Better."

Rule felt himself hardening. "Abby . . ."

He didn't intend to upset her. Powers knew he liked the feel of her against him, the warmth of her body still cradling him inside her, but something unexpected had happened, at least unexpected from his point of view, and he needed to process it.

She stiffened and pulled away to look up at him. "That was a 'we need to talk' voice."

Damn it, they *did* need to talk. He needed to talk. He just wasn't sure yet what he needed to say.

Abby sighed, and he felt the liquid softness seep out of her, felt her stiffen and distance herself even while she remained locked in his arms. "I guess I got better at some of the sex thing, but not all of it, huh?"

Rule scowled, an expression that deepened when she braced her hands against his chest and separated their bodies, wincing a little when he slipped free of her tender opening. "What are you talking about?"

She shrugged and tried to push away from him. "I wasn't very good at this when I was eighteen, either. I guess some people just don't have the knack, huh?"

"You're positively dripping with knack," he assured her, feeling completely at sea. "Did you somehow mistake the signs that I enjoyed myself thoroughly? Did my explosive orgasm not clue you in?"

A blush stained her cheeks but didn't provide him with any clues as to where on earth her brain had gone to. Whatever train of thought she had boarded, she had clearly left him at the station.

"Fine. You enjoyed it at the time, but you don't seem to be having a lot of fun now." She tried once more to push away from him and once more he refused to let her go. "Guys only use that 'let's talk about this' voice when they're about to tell you that it's been fun, but this isn't going anywhere because they don't think about you that way."

That at least made her look at him, even if she was frowning. "I am. You know I am."

"Then would you mind telling me what makes you think you can read my mind?"

"I never claimed I could—"

"Exactly!" he roared, unable to resist the urge to shake her, very gently. "Stop jumping to conclusions before you fall and hurt yourself."

He watched a blush rise from where her breasts pressed against his chest and climb into her cheeks, staining them a fiery crimson. He made a mental note to find out exactly where that color started next time and follow it from top to bottom.

"I'm sorry," she muttered, looking at his shirt instead of at him. "I meant it when I said I wasn't good at this."

"You were wrong. You happen to be very good at 'the sex thing,' " he said, stroking his hands down her back. "You simply need to work on the bits where you start talking."

She gave a half smile and played with one of his shirt buttons.

"You were correct when you thought I wanted to talk to you," he said, stroking a hand over her hair, marveling at the fact that it felt almost as silky as her skin. "I do, but not to criticize you or to drive you away from me. I want to make sure you are well, that I did nothing to hurt you."

Her blush deepened. "Not in a bad way."

He resisted a primitive urge to beat his chest. "Good. And I want to try to understand why you decided to goad me into taking you."

That brought her eyes to his, wide and startled. "What . . . I mean . . . what makes you think I goaded you—"

"Abby . . ."

She bit her lip and looked back down at his shirt. "It wasn't like I planned it. I was really mad. I'm going stir-crazy, and having Noah tell me there was no end in sight drove me a little crazier, but I didn't come storming down here with this in mind." She shook her head. "Trust me, I couldn't have dreamed this up if I'd tried. I'm not that creative."

Rule had a sudden vision of helping her discover her creative side that had his arms tightening around her. Before he could make any suggestions, though, he heard a brisk knock at the door and someone counting down from ten on the other side.

"What the—?"

"Ready or not, here I come." The door swung open and Tess hurried inside. She took one look at the room's occupants and shut the door behind her. "Looks like you aren't ready."

"Tess, what are you—?"

"You can yell at me for interrupting later," she said, striding forward and tugging her sweatshirt off over her head. Beneath it, she wore a black tank top with a round neck and wide straps. She held the shirt out to Abby. "Here. Put this on."

"Why?"

Tess raised an eyebrow. "Because while you might have forgotten about the fact that you're sitting there stark naked, I can assure you that that fact will not escape your brother's notice when he gets here in approximately," she glanced at her watch, "thirty more seconds."

Rule watched the color drain from Abby's face, then return in a rush as she disappeared and then reemerged from the neck of the sweatshirt. It was oversize, so it covered her all the way past her hips, but her legs were still bare and pale in the lamplight.

Tess ushered her to the sofa. "Sit. Put this over your legs." She grabbed a soft knit throw off the back of the sofa and tucked it around Abby's legs. Nodding decisively, Tess grabbed a book from the coffee table, opened it to a random page, and thrust it into the other woman's hands. "Here. You've suddenly developed an intense fascination for . . ." Again she paused, this time to glance at the cover of the book. "Pennsylvania's covered stone bridges."

Leaving Abby dazed but compliant on the sofa, Tess turned her assessing eye on Rule. Then she rolled both of them. "For God's sake, zip up, pal."

Rule nearly blushed himself as he adjusted and refastened his jeans.

"And next time, try not to leave torn clothes all over my husband's office, will you? He works hard in here and doesn't need you providing fodder for his overactive imagination." Tess grabbed a handful of fabric scraps and shoved them into a wastebasket before she took a last glance around the room and nodded in apparent satisfaction. "Good."

She had barely gotten the word out when the office door swung open again and Noah walked in. He made one sweeping survey of the room before he turned directly to Rule.

"There's someone here to see you," Noah said, his tone calm and casual. "Big guy, red hair. Won't talk to me. Graham put him in his office by the main entrance." He turned to Tess and raised his eyebrows. "I looked for Rule in the billiard room, like you said, but your husband told me he'd last spotted him in here. When the two of you were leaving."

Tess didn't even stutter. "Was *that* when? I knew I'd seen him recently, but I have the worst memory for details."

"Right."

Rule looked from the witch to the warrior and was glad neither of them was working against him. At the moment. He cleared his throat. "I'd better go down and see what's going on. Keep an eye on your sister."

When he strode out into the hallway, it felt like the closest escape he'd managed in a long, long time. He just hoped Noah wouldn't notice the unmistakable bruise he'd left at the base of Abby's throat. Like he'd already decided, he didn't want Noah working against him.

*T*ess made her excuses and left the office right behind Rule, leaving Abby alone with her big brother. The big brother who had scared away every male who had ever looked at her for just a few seconds too long while she'd been growing up. He circled around the end of the sofa and settled onto the cushion at her feet.

"New hobby of yours?" He nodded to the book in her hands, his expression utterly bland.

Abby looked down at the forgotten prop and tried to make her shrug casual. "Just something to do. You know how bored I've been the last few days." She closed the book and laid it down in her lap. "How's the search going?"

"About like it was when you asked me a couple of hours ago," he said. "You going to snap again when I tell you that?"

"No. I know you're doing your best."

Noah nodded. "Glad to hear that."

A moment of silence stretched between them and Abby tried not to squirm under her brother's gaze, but that was easier said than done when she could feel how wet and sticky she was from her and Rule's recent activities. She really wished she'd had time for a shower before she'd had to face Noah again.

"So," he said, his voice just as bland as his expression, "have you been managing to entertain yourself?"

She drew in a quick breath, then blew it out and slumped against the arm of the sofa. "How did you know?"

He shook his head. "It wasn't hard to figure out, Ab. You and Rule both looked like kids who'd gotten caught sneaking cookies before dinnertime. His hair looked like someone had been running their fingers through it for the last couple of hours, and you have a hickey on your throat the size of a Bradley Fighting Vehicle." His mouth twisted. "Plus, I'm pretty sure that's your bra on the floor next to the fireplace."

Abby buried her flaming face in her hands. "God, this is so embarrassing."

Noah snorted. "Why? I'm not Mom and Dad. It's not like I expected you to stay a virgin until your wedding night. Not," he held up a hand, "that I want to hear any details, but I'm not your keeper."

"That's not how you felt when I was growing up."

"Christ, Abby, you were eight years younger than me, and the guys in my platoon were horny dogs. You're damned right I told them I'd kill 'em if they touched you."

"Just as long as you've changed your mind."

"Well, I'll kill anyone who hurts you," Noah qualified, "so I have to say that on a practical level, I kind of wish you'd gone for someone a little easier to take down, like a professional wrestler or something. But like I said, I'm not your keeper. And I'm not your conscience."

Abby grimaced. He'd had to bring up the *c* word. She plucked at the throw blanket's braided trim. "Yeah, well, I don't think anyone's being my conscience at the moment. Not even me."

"What are you talking about?"

She pulled a face at him. "I just had sex with someone I've known for less than a week, No. My conscience is clearly on the fritz, along with my common sense and any sense of self-preservation I may once have had."

Noah shook his head. "Abby, from what I can tell, you just slept with an honorable, responsible, capable guy who happens to go all twisted with lust every time you step into the room." He looked at her expression and snorted. "Yeah, I noticed that. I think the staff in the kitchens downstairs noticed that. You're both healthy, consenting adults. What's wrong with that?"

"What's wrong with that?" she repeated and waved a hand in front of his face. "Hello! Anybody home? Aside from the whole known-him-less-than-a-week thing that I already mentioned, there's the fact that the meeting happened when he kidnapped me."

"He didn't stuff you into a van and call Mom and Dad for a ransom, Ab."

"So what? He's responsible for me being confined someplace against my will. There's a term for stupid idiot girls who fall in love with their kidnappers. It's called Stockholm syndrome. I'm thinking of changing my name to Inga."

"You do not have Stockholm."

Abby crossed her arms over her chest and glared at her brother. "Oh? Then what would you call it?"

He thought about it for a second. "The hots?"

"Noah—"

He heaved a put-upon sigh. "Abby, what is this really about? What has you so bent out of shape about this? Rule seems to be a great guy. Why are you so freaked out by the idea of having some kind of a relationship with him?"

Darn it, why did her brother have to understand

her so well? She squirmed in her seat. "You mean aside from the kidnapping thing and the fact that he's not human?"

"Demon or not, he's an improvement over a couple of the guys you've dated. Like that jerk you were all over in college."

"Improvement in whose eyes?"

"Anyone with half a brain." He ticked off points on his fingers. "Rule is responsible, intelligent, and capable of kicking the butts that need it. He's also a hell of an interesting guy and according to the whispers of the waitresses in this place, 'sexier than he has a right to be.' So what really has you knotted up like a macramé project gone wrong?"

With a drawn-out groan, Abby let her head fall back against the arm of the sofa and stared up at the plaster-worked ceiling. "You just said it all yourself."

Noah was silent for a moment, then another one. "Okay, you've lost me. I said what?"

"Oh, for Pete's sake, No, you've seen the guy yourself, haven't you?" She lifted her head so she could glare at him. "He's like a walking female fantasy. He's big and built and gorgeous. I know the female staff around here must be talking about him, because I've seen them drooling over him."

"And you have a problem with that?"

Abby tried to laugh, but she wasn't really amused, and the sound reflected that. She spread her arms. "Look at me, Noah. He's like a cover model, and I'm like the girl next door's less remarkable younger sister."

He wrinkled his brow and stared at her in confusion. "What the hell are you talking about? You sound like a blithering idiot. You're—"

"He's out of my league, Noah!"

Her bombshell shut his mouth with a clack. He sat looking at her for so long, she wondered if they'd been caught in some sort of time warp. If she listened hard, she figured she'd hear the crickets chirping.

"I'm sorry," he finally said slowly, "but *what* did you just say?"

"You heard me."

"I heard something, but it didn't make a whole lot of sense to me. Care to explain?"

She glowered at him. "You're not stupid, Noah, and you're not blind. Well, neither am I. I have a mirror and eyes and I can see that women who look like me don't attract men who look like Rule."

"You're sure you're speaking English?"

"Don't be an—"

"No, hold on," Noah interrupted. "You need to stop talking like an idiot. There is nothing wrong with the way you look. You're making yourself sound like some sort of deformed hag."

"That's not what I'm saying. I know I'm not ugly. I don't have a wart on the end of my nose, or a hump on my back, or snakes for hair."

"Glad to hear you realize that."

"But I'm average," she continued, talking over him. "I have average features, average hair, an average body. I blend into the woodwork. Men who look like Rule don't find me attractive."

Noah pointed off toward her bra lying on the

floor near the desk. "I'd like to draw your attention to some evidence to the contrary."

"Maybe he has Stockholm syndrome, too," Abby muttered. "He was cooped up here with me, and he needed to get laid. I was convenient."

He shook his head. "Seriously. You need therapy here, Abby. You're a beautiful girl. Not every woman needs to be blond and stacked. And not every guy even likes the ones who are. Some of us like girls who look capable of rubbing a couple of brain cells together."

"Right, because all my life men have been falling in love with me for my keen intellect."

"Abby, no offense, 'cause you know I love you, but all your life, your taste in men has pretty well sucked. When you've even bothered to date."

"Why do you think I do that so rarely? Men aren't exactly lined up at my front door."

"How would you know? You barely ever open it. This stuff about you being unattractive . . . these are not rational thoughts."

She bit off a laugh. "What about this situation is rational?"

"More than is irrational. Look, I know I've had longer to deal with the supernatural thing than you have, and I'm sorry about that, but I think it's time to forget about being freaked out by reality and find a way to deal with it."

"Trust me, I'm open to suggestions."

Noah rested his hand on her foot and squeezed through the blanket. "First off, I'd suggest you stop fighting things so hard. It's obvious to everyone but you that Rule is pretty much crazy about you, so I think you can stop thinking it's Stockholm or boredom or a lack of attraction that makes his tongue hang out every time you walk into a room."

Abby couldn't help the surge of pleased warmth that filled her at hearing that. "Yeah?"

Her brother rolled his eyes. "Honestly, Ab, have you considered therapy for these hang-ups of yours?"

Helplessly, she laughed. "I'll keep that in mind." She poked him with her foot. "You think sex therapy would help?"

"Don't be gross. That's my little sister you're talking about." He pushed her foot away playfully. "I also suggest you stop tying yourself up in knots like this. I like Rule. I think he's a good guy, and I think you're the only person in the known universe who hasn't noticed that in his eyes, you're like Helen of Troy and Venus Aphrodite and Miss Universe all rolled into one."

Abby remembered the look on Rule's face when he'd first fit himself against her body, remembered the heat and the unexpected tenderness in his gaze, and felt a flicker of hope and possibility spark in her belly. She smiled. "Thanks, No."

He grinned. "That doesn't mean I ever again want to walk into a room with you two and find you half naked with him, but if you're going to have to get mixed up with anyone, at least you're showing some good judgment. I know Rule will take care of you."

"I'm not half naked," Abby protested, managing a half-smile of her own. "I'm covered from head to foot."

"You're not wearing pants, Abigail. That counts as half naked. I don't care if you're covered in pixie dust and moonbeams."

"Pixie dust and moonbeams? Sounds kinky."

"Shut up, Ab."

CHAPTER TWENTY

ule strode directly from Rafe's office to Graham's, and with every step he took, a strange sense of foreboding began to fill him. By the time he stepped into Graham's office and saw who was waiting for him, he felt not even a twinge of surprise.

"Good evening, sir." Rule shut the door behind him and waited to be acknowledged.

The figure on the side of the room was just as large as Noah had judged, a tall, burly-looking man with thick arms, dark copper skin, and improbably bright red hair.

"Rule." The prime minister of the Parliament of Below turned away from the window he'd been gazing out of and fixed his Watchman with a dark stare. "I had expected to hear word of your progress well before this. Where is Louamides?"

Rule's jaw flexed and his spine straightened, but he didn't blink. "He has been located, but I have not been able to find Uzkiel. I am certain he must be somewhere in this city, but so far he has eluded me."

"Not surprising. Uzkiel and his minions have

been eluding the Watch since before you were born, Arulnagal."

Rule flinched at the use of his real name, but he masked it well. The full names of demons had power; that much of the human folklore was correct. A name could be used as a summoning, or a name could be the component in a curse. Either way, few demons cared to share their names casually. Only three beings knew Rule's full name: Prime Minister Bal; Rule's mentor in the Watch, Kurien; and Rule himself. All others who had known it were dead. It was Bal's way of reminding Rule of his authority.

"I believe I am getting closer, Prime Minister Bal," he said calmly. "I am certain I will have him in just a few more days."

"If you tell me this, I will not doubt you," the ancient demon said, "but we cannot take any chances in these matters. If you have located Louamides, you will bring him to me so that I can return him to the Below. He will stand trial before the Parliament and be sentenced to a suitable punishment. If you wish, you may remain here and continue to search for Uzkiel."

Rule felt his jaw clench. "I'm afraid that isn't possible, Prime Minister."

Bal stared hard at him. "Why should it be impossible, Arulnagal? You have the fiend, and I have the authority. You will turn it over to me."

"With all due respect, I cannot do it, sir." Rule stood his ground and sent up a fervent wish that the gamble he was about to take would pay off. "The fiend is currently trapped inside a human and cannot be exorcised. It cannot be returned Below in its present state."

Bal waved a hand. "Humans are expendable. One will not be missed."

"I'm afraid I cannot agree with you."

The door opened and Rafe strode in from the hallway, looking characteristically elegant and nonchalant. Before the door swung shut behind him, Rule caught a glimpse of Tess standing in the hallway. It looked as if she was shooing her husband into the room.

"I requested a private meeting." Bal scowled. "I have not given leave to any interruptions."

"Ah, but I have not given leave for your visit," Rafe said, his tone mild, his expression easy, and his meaning clear as glass. "It is considered polite, and in observance of all current treaties, that a visitor from another realm present himself to local authorities before completing his business."

"I do not intend to stay long. There is little time for formalities."

"There is always time for formalities. They make life so much more . . . lasting, don't you think?"

In that moment, neither Rule nor Bal had any doubt that the Felix head of the Council of Others had lethally sharp claws of his own.

Bal gave an abrupt nod. "I will be leaving momentarily. Please convey my regards to the proper authorities."

"There is no need. I am the authorities." Rafe's smile was charming and sharper than steel. "Rafael De Santos, head of the Council of Others and Felix of the City of New York. At your service, of course."

Bal nodded again. "I am Bal of Infernium, prime minister of the Parliament of the Below. I merely came to discuss with my Watchman the progress he has made in his current assignment."

"I informed the prime minister that while Louamides has been located, we have not had such luck in finding Uzkiel," Rule explained.

"Ah, yes. Most unfortunate. But I have every confidence in your abilities, Rule. As, I'm sure, does your prime minister."

The redheaded demon puffed out his chest and scowled. "No one doubts . . . Rule's abilities, but the situation is most grave. While Louamides is in possession of the *solus* spell, it presents a danger we cannot ignore. The spell must be destroyed."

"I understand your concern, but I admit to a certain innate curiosity." Rafe flashed a very white, very toothy smile. "It is in my nature. And I have had my wife do some research on this spell. What she has found has proved to be most interesting."

This was the first Rule had heard of Tess's investigation. He'd known Rafe had been trying to gather more information on the spell and on Uzkiel in hopes of leading them to the fiend's hiding place, but the Felix hadn't mentioned any discoveries.

"From what my wife tells me," Rafe continued, "there are only two ways to destroy this spell. One is to cast it."

Bal didn't react, just watched Rafe through unblinking black eyes.

"The unfortunate thing is that casting the spell also

destroys the caster. Rather inconvenient, wouldn't you agree?"

"And what is the other way?"

Rule suspected Bal wouldn't like the answer to his question, but he had to ask it.

"To kill the one who knows it." Rafe turned his gaze on Rule, and beneath the urbane façade the demon could see a powerful swell of anger. "Destructive little bit of magic."

Rule's gut clenched, and he nodded abruptly. "So it would seem."

"And I haven't even told you the best part," Rafe continued, his mouth curving in a feral smile. "The spell has one other nasty little surprise that the fiend Louamides failed to tell us. Anyone who teaches the spell to another will also die. A sort of magical sowing the fields with salt, as it were."

That time it wasn't Rule's gut clenching. It was his heart. In his mind he heard the echo of Lou's words telling him the spell would kill it if it gave it to Uzkiel. Rule hadn't understood what that meant at the time. Now he did. The *solus* spell was like a time bomb lurking inside Abby, just waiting to be set off. When he'd called it a Doomsday device, he'd been right. No wonder the spell had been hidden and forgotten after the wars.

"Yes, you see how destructive it is," Bal said. "That is why it is so important that it be returned Below where our people can develop a way to disarm it."

"Not while the spell is hidden inside the human. I will not risk her life over this."

"Her? Louamides and the spell are concealed inside a human woman?" Bal snorted. "What more proof do you need that the hiding place is expendable? One human woman will not be missed. Let me take her to the Parliament and have done with it."

Rule felt a growl beginning to vibrate low in his chest. Rafe sent him a warning glare.

"No. In my city, no humans are expendable," the Felix said. "We are on the verge of war with the humans as it is. I will not add this girl's disappearance to the tally of our sins."

The prime minister's mouth curled in a sneer. "So the tales are accurate. You have gone and revealed yourselves to the humans. It's disgraceful. And no good will come of it, mark my words."

"You are not the first to speak them, and you are not the last I will ignore. This is not your world, and your opinion holds no weight here. But this is not at issue. The woman is, and she remains under my protection."

"This is none of your concern, mortal." Bal's voice held a clear warning. "Do not meddle in the affairs of the Below."

Rafe arched a dark brow. "At the moment, you are here in the Above, and in this world, *my* word is law. She stays. You, however, are invited to take your leave at the earliest possible opportunity."

"I am not accustomed to being denied."

"Think of it as a learning experience." Rafe reached behind him to open the office door. Looking out, he beckoned to a Lupine security guard stationed in the hall. "Evan, the prime minister was just leaving. Please escort him to the gate outside the Council chambers and see that he gets off safely."

"Yes, Mr. De Santos." The guard stepped into the office and attached himself to Bal's side without so much as a blink.

The demon snarled. "I suggest, De Santos, that when Uzkiel seizes the girl and the spell, you not come begging to the Parliament for aid. You will find we have long memories."

"And you will find that I never beg."

With a parting glare, Bal stormed out of the office and down the hallway with the guard a silent, steady presence at his heels.

When the pair disappeared through the doorway leading down into the cellars, Rule turned to the Felix and frowned. "Abby is in even worse danger than I thought. We have to find Uzkiel now. And I want her under twenty-four-hour guard until we find that fiend."

Rule knew he sounded dictatorial and paranoid, but he couldn't seem to ignore the clenching that had begun in his gut when he'd listened to Bal suggest offering Abby up as a sort of sacrifice to the greater good. No good was great enough be worth the loss of her. He would do anything he needed to do to keep her safe.

The knowledge of what that meant struck him with the power of a catapult blast. He fought to keep from listing to the side as the full weight of his concern for the mousy, ordinary, thoroughly beguiling human woman dropped on his heart.

Graham had been right all along. Abby Baker had captured not just his reluctant attention, but his heart as well. She was the woman he would take to mate, the only one he could envision spending any stretch of eternity with.

And spending eternity with her required that he keep her safe. At any cost. In fact, if he could help it, he planned to keep her within arm's reach beginning now and ending never.

Rafe smiled. "It's a good thing I am such a mellow sort, or I might take offense at being given orders by a second demon in the space of a few short minutes."

"You know what they say about demons. We have no manners to speak of."

"I had heard that," Rafe said conversationally as the two men stepped into the hall and headed toward the stairs. "But I didn't really believe it until I saw the evidence with my own eyes."

"So what happened?" Tess demanded, falling into step beside them.

"It was as we thought. The prime minister wanted to take Abby back Below with him." Rafe tucked his wife's hand into the crook of his arm and led the way upstairs.

Rule noticed that on them the oddly old-fashioned gesture looked entirely natural.

"I hope you told him where he could shove that idea."

Rafe laughed. "Not in so many words, my crude little darling, but I believe he understood the implication."

"Good. Imagine thinking we'd just let him take Abby away like that. I mean, how stupid can you get?"

"He was right about one thing. Abby is not safe while Louamides and the spell remain inside her."

"I'm working on that," Tess frowned, "but it's tricky. Traditional exorcisms banish a fiend back to the Below or bind it to an inanimate object. If we cast Lou back Below, we'll be in almost the same position as if we let that creep take Abby with him. And the *solus* spell can't be cast into an object, so neither can a fiend who knows it."

"Keep working on it." Rule reached the top of the stairs first and turned immediately toward Rafe's office, the last place he'd seen Abby. "In the meantime, Noah and I will resume the hunt for Uzkiel. If he's in this city, we'll find him."

Tess nodded. "Don't worry. I'm not a quitter. I've also asked a friend of mine, another witch, to whip up some mojo. She and her coven had a talent for finding lost things. It can't hurt to have some extra eyes on the lookout."

"Fine. Let me know as soon as you hear anything."

He slipped into the office and shut the door firmly behind him. Outside, Tess and Rafe looked at the door, then looked at each other. They both heard the snip of the lock sliding home.

"The demon has locked me out of my own office," Rafe mused, half-smiling.

Chuckling, Tess pressed herself against her husband's side and nodded. "It's getting late, and Gabriel will be ready for bed in a couple of hours. Once he's asleep, I can show you that our bedroom is much more comfortable than your office." She leaned close and pressed her lips to the side of his neck. "And it has an even better lock."

Rafe grinned. "Let's go home and say good night to our son. After he takes his bath and hears his bedtime story, I know another story I would like to tell you."

"Ooh, I hope it has a happy ending," Tess purred.

"Of course." Her mate grinned wickedly. "But this tale is definitely not suitable for children."

CHAPTER TWENTY-ONE

Abby stirred in the middle of the night and bumped up against something solid. It took a moment for her sleep-clouded mind to register that not only did the something belong there, but also she'd asked it to be there. Not that Rule had seemed at all inclined to say no. Still, it was the kind of thing a girl should remember, the first time she asks a man to spend the night with her. Especially since she'd fallen asleep with him still buried inside her, his heavy weight pressing her deep into the mattress. It had been a little tough to breathe, but what did that matter? He felt like home.

He had eventually moved off of her and now lay sprawled on his stomach across the wide mattress, one arm draped across her body as if anchoring her to his side. Not that she had any desire to move. In fact, if she could have lived forever in this moment, lying in the dark beside Rule, listening to the rhythm of his breathing in the late-night silence, she would be perfectly content.

She stared up into the darkness, her fingers instinctively stroking the velvet skin of her lover's bare arm where it pressed her into the mattress. She knew the visit from the prime minister had upset Rule. Even his carefully edited version of their meeting told her that. By the time the men had emerged, she'd been too tired to ask the questions swirling around inside her head and had obediently let Rule lead her up to her temporary bedroom, but she hadn't let him drop her at the door.

He hadn't struggled too hard.

Abby smiled and shivered at the memories of his hands on her, as eager and urgent as if he hadn't had her only a few hours before. She had always dreamed of the man who wouldn't be able to keep his hands off of her, but she hadn't expected to find him. She was hardly a femme fatale, after all, and shy, plain women with hang-ups about religion and her own attractiveness didn't usually find the men beating down their doors. Heck, men didn't even usually bother to stop by. They were too busy rushing over to the beautiful girls' apartments.

This time, though, the man hadn't just stopped; he'd also lingered. Deliciously.

Abby shivered again and felt Rule's arm tighten around her.

"Cold?" he murmured.

"No. Just thinking."

"That usually leads to trouble."

She pinched him. "Not plotting, just thinking. I promise I wasn't hatching any elaborate escape attempts."

His arm dragged her closer against his side. "Good. Because I would come after you."

Abby had been teasing, but Rule didn't sound like he was. She rolled onto her side to face him and found his dark eyes watching her. They picked up the few stray shards of light that managed to sneak into the room and reflected them back to her. "Would you?"

He nodded. "Anywhere."

Maybe it was the darkness; maybe it was the intimacy of lying beside him, skin to skin, feeling the beat of his heart against the hand she laid on his back. Either way, Abby felt her heart clench and grew suddenly serious.

"I didn't . . ." She paused, took a deep breath. "I hadn't planned to meet anyone, to find anyone special in the middle of a riot on a night when I should have been curled up on my sofa reading a good book."

"And I hadn't planned to kidnap a woman and carry her off like a prize of war, let alone keep her prisoner for my own nefarious purposes." His voice rumbled out of the darkness, as warm and rough as a cat's tongue.

Abby stroked her hand over his shoulder. "I want you to know I'm sorry for those things I called you earlier. I don't really think you're unholy."

"I am not sorry," he said. "They led us here."

"But where do we go next?"

There was a moment of silence before Abby felt the soft heat of his lips pressing against her forehead. "I am not certain, but we do not need to make a decision just yet. We have a little while, still, to enjoy the moment."

Abby swallowed against the lump in her throat,

but she knew he was right. They had too many other decisions to make, too many other battles to fight, to tackle this one prematurely. She turned and kissed his bare shoulder. "I am enjoying it. I promise."

His hand slid across her rib cage, closed warm and possessive over her breast. "Let me help you enjoy it even more."

She didn't think that was in any doubt.

His lips found hers unerringly, brushing over them in light, teasing caresses. When she tried to catch him in a real kiss, he closed his teeth lightly over her bottom lip and tugged a playful warning. For a man who looked and sounded so serious most of the time, his capacity for play and teasing astounded her, and he seemed happy to exercise the talent on her. She whimpered and stabbed her fingers into his hair, holding his head in place and chasing his mouth with her own.

His chuckle teased her senses, just as his fingers teased her nipple. They brushed over the crinkled skin, flicking the taut peak, circling and pinching and making her arch up to press herself against his hands.

"Don't tease," she hissed, hooking a leg over his hip and pressing herself against the length of his erection. She rocked her pelvis against him, letting him feel the slick welcome awaiting him. "I want you."

All his playful intent vanished in a ragged groan. In an instant, he shifted over her, his weight pressing her into the soft mattress. He surrounded her, overwhelmed her, and she welcomed him with eager touches of her hands, with the rocking motion of her hips, with the soft, greedy clinging of her lips.

He tucked his hands beneath her arms and curled his hands over the tops of her shoulders, holding her in place. His eyes caught hers and held as he shifted and found her snug entrance. In one smooth, effortless motion, he pressed inside her, filling her in a steady, heady wave of pleasure that sent her senses spinning and her heart soaring.

Tears gathered in the corners of her eyes and slid silently down her cheeks when he came to rest inside her, buried to the hilt, two bodies now one, flesh and breath and hearts joined in perfect union.

"Rule."

She breathed his name into the pregnant hush, watched him take it in and return her own.

"Abigail."

She gripped his forearms, feeling them flex and ripple as he held her steady and began a slow, rocking rhythm inside her.

The feeling that filled her this time was different, less urgent but somehow more intent. She felt no need to rush headlong into the pleasure, but instead wanted to savor the connection, the warm, solid, tangible weight of him above her, inside her, around her. She saw her need mirrored in his fathomless eyes and spoke his name again.

"Rule."

She felt him shift above her, nudge a fraction deeper, and the world started to dissolve around her. Just before she tumbled over the edge, she sensed him lean closer, felt his breath stir the hair at her ear, heard his low, gravelly voice whisper. The words filled her head, the way his body filled hers, and her heart recognized them even if her mind was too clouded to comprehend.

"My Abigail," he breathed. "My heart. My mate."

He slid another breath deeper, and she began to unravel around him. He tumbled after her, his cock pulsing within her sheath, filling her with a warm rush of seed.

"My name is Arulnagal."

CHAPTER TWENTY-TWO

S he woke slowly, stretching beneath the warm sheets, feeling them glide over her skin in a casual caress. The bed beside her was empty, and she had a vague recollection of Rule slipping from it earlier and urging her to go back to sleep. She hadn't had any trouble complying.

It's about time you woke up, though considering the two of you went at it like Energizer Bunnies for half the night, I can't say I'm surprised to see you sleeping in.

Abby frowned, her eyes still closed, her brow wrinkling. Something wasn't right.

By the way, did you know you snore?

Squeaking with outrage, Abby clasped the sheet to her breasts and shot up in bed, glancing frantically around the room. It was empty.

"Louamides?" she asked, feeling like an idiot.

A naked idiot.

Call me Lou, the voice inside her head replied. *After all, the two of us are pretty close, wouldn't you say?*

The laughter inside her head definitely wasn't coming from Abby. She didn't find this at all amusing.

And she hoped she didn't snort like that when she did laugh.

"No, I wouldn't," she muttered aloud. "That's like saying the Lindbergh baby was close to his kidnappers. You're inside my head. That doesn't mean I have to like you."

Yeah, well, you ain't nothing to write home about, sweet cheeks. Rule might find you distracting, but I don't think I've ever been so bored in my life. If it hadn't been for the free porn last night—

"Shut up!" Abby screeched, feeling her skin staining a telltale red. Only for once in her life, she wasn't sure if it was from embarrassment or rage. "Just shut up right there. Not another word. If you don't want me to do a naked jig down Fifth Avenue while shouting Uzkiel's name at the top of my lungs, you will shut your mouth and never, *ever* mention anything about my sex life to anyone, *ever* again. Do I make myself clear?"

She asked that last question in a tone of voice that would have done Sister Mary Joseph proud. Apparently, it worked on more than misbehaving schoolkids, too.

Yeah, whatever, the fiend muttered, sounding chastised, if not precisely repentant. *Listen, now that you're awake and not, uh, otherwise occupied, what do you say to getting us some food? I'm starving in here. Well, actually, you're starving, but it's driving me crazy.*

Come to think of it, Abby *was* pretty hungry. Her stomach growled in testimony, and she managed a reluctant nod. "Fine. I'll go down for breakfast. I assume that when I eat, so do you?"

If you can call what you do eating. You had a cup of yogurt and half a sandwich for lunch yesterday. What the shit is that? Birds eat more than that.

"Yes, well," she muttered, "some of us are trying to avoid acquiring a layer-of-heat-conserving-blubber. And watch your mouth. While you're in my head, you can keep a civil tongue in yours."

Of all the gin joints in all the world, I had to walk into this one.

"Trust me, Rick, neither one of us is all that happy with the situation."

She started to throw back the covers and paused, feeling awkward. Maybe the only eyes Lou had to see out of at the moment were hers, but she couldn't shake the feeling that there was someone else in the room watching her. Especially when she could feel its anticipation. She glanced around and saw the full-length mirror on the back of the bathroom door, the one she'd have to walk past to get to her clothes.

"Nice try," she grumbled, and yanked the sheet from the bed, wrapping it around her and taking it with her into the bathroom.

Spoilsport.

When she closed the bathroom door behind her, she realized the uncomfortable feeling of not being alone was still with her. Crossing her arms over her chest, she blew a stray hair out of her eyes and looked into the mirror. She looked the same as she always had, but that didn't mean she *was* the same.

"Look, this was a lot easier when you were inside

playing dead," she said, pressing her thighs together against the suddenly urgent need to pee. "I'll make a deal with you. You give me half an hour to shower and get dressed and whatever else, and I'll let you pick breakfast. Okay?"

There was a moment of silence inside her head, and Abby had the uncomfortable feeling that Lou was weighing the possibility of eating his favorite foods against the certainty of getting to see her wet and naked.

Deal, it finally consented, grudgingly. *But don't say I never did nothin' for you.*

"Perish the thought."

She waited a good five minutes, against her bladder's fervent protests, just to make sure that un-alone feeling was gone before she hurried to pee and shower. She didn't trust Lou not to come back early and claim it didn't own a watch.

By the time the fiend did reemerge, she was thankfully showered and dressed, and she took great delight in drowning out its grousing, however briefly, in the din of her hair dryer. It turned out her dad had been right all those years. Hair dryers were so loud they made it impossible to hear oneself think.

Bless them.

ule found her an hour later, stretched out on the sofa in the media room, with one arm draped across her eyes and the other cradling her stomach.

"Is something wrong?"

"Many, many things," she groaned, not moving

an inch. "Beginning with runny fried eggs and ending with a deep-fried peanut butter and banana sandwich. If I don't hurl soon, I may have to make a trip to Graceland to desecrate Elvis's grave."

Rule frowned down at her, noticing that the snap of her jeans had been unfastened, exposing the little curve of her tummy to the open air. "Did you eat all of that?" he asked carefully.

"Believe me, it wasn't my idea. And if I have my way, I might never eat again." She paused and sucked in a slow, shallow breath. "In fact, if you don't mind, can we please change the subject? The idea of food is making that hurling thing a distinct possibility."

Frozen halfway into a sitting position on the edge of the sofa beside her, Rule thought better of it and turned to settle onto the coffee table facing her. "Can I get you anything?"

"I need a young priest and an old priest."

Rule groaned. "Is there no one on this plane who has not seen that bloody movie?"

"It's a classic," she defended, but he could tell her heart wasn't in it.

He shook his head. "I take it that means Louamides had something to do with your present discomfort?"

"Try everything," Abby snorted. "He blackmailed me into letting him choose breakfast. *Not* a mistake I'll be making again soon."

There was a moment of silence before Rule heard her mutter something that sounded suspiciously like, "No way, you perv. I'll think of something else to keep you occupied."

Rule raised an eyebrow. "Excuse me?"

She shook her head, then groaned, as the motion clearly upset her stomach. "Nothing," she said, raising her arm to her forehead so she could open her eyes and look at him. "I wasn't expecting to see you this morning. I thought you and Noah would be out pounding the pavement, so to speak."

"Your brother is. I have been talking with Tess."

That brought a little color to Abby's cheeks. "Has she found an exorcism she thinks will work?"

"Unfortunately, no." The animation fled from Abby's face, and Rule felt a squeezing around his heart. It still astonished him that making this woman happy could mean even more to him than keeping her safe. He leaned forward, bracing his forearms on his thighs, letting his hands hang down between his knees. "She is still working on a solution, but in the meantime, we have been debating other possibilities."

Abby frowned. "Other possibilities for what?"

"For flushing the fiend out of hiding."

"I assume you're talking about Uzkiel."

"Yes. I had not expected him to be so hard to locate. This city is large, but there are few fiends here at any given time, since they must wait to be invited before entering."

"I've been wondering about that." Abby lowered her arm, being careful not to jar her stomach, and reached out to take Rule's hand. Almost absently she joined their fingers together, and he again felt his heart contract. "How did Uzkiel get here in the first place? I have a hard time believing even a summoner would be stupid enough to call on him to exact revenge on the girl he couldn't date."

Rule snorted. "I see you share my high opinion of summoners." The question had bothered him, as well, and the answer he'd given Rafe sat no better with him now than it had several days ago. "I am afraid the fiends may have discovered and exploited a loophole in the invitation clause."

Abby looked her question.

"When a summoner casts his spell and issues an invitation to a fiend, what he is doing, in essence, is opening a temporary gate between here and the Below." Rule looked down at their joined hands and twined his fingers with her much smaller, much more delicate ones. "The summoner then names the fiend he wishes to bind, and in doing so, because he uses the demon's true name, he commands the demon to pass through the gate into this world."

She nodded. "That's the impression I got, but I admit I'm far from an expert. Most of what I knew before last month came from watching the late, late movie."

"The assumption has always been that fiends do not enjoy being enslaved, even temporarily, which I believe still holds. But what if the fiends had discovered that by one piggybacking on the summoning of another, the second fiend could pass through that gate as well and enter this world unbound to the human who had opened the gate?"

Rule watched Abby frown as she worked through the scenario, then saw her pale. "Oh, my gosh. That would be . . . horrible. If that's possible, it would allow any fiend who wanted to to come through into this world and just roam around unchecked, killing anything or anyone it pleased." She paused, gripping his hand tighter. "*Is* it possible?"

"Unfortunately, Tess agrees that it may be."

"But that would mean the fiends could just all relocate here if they wanted to and not be under the control of the Watch anymore. They could build an army if they wanted."

That nightmare scenario had also occurred to Rule. He shook his head. "I cannot deny it is possible, but I don't believe the threat is imminent, and Tess agrees. While yes, theoretically any fiend who wanted to could piggyback on another's summoning, the gates opened during those spells are very small and very brief. We believe that at most one additional fiend could travel through at a time. Unless the summoners begin opening gate after gate after gate in a short period of time, the number of fiends here at any one time would be finite."

Abby breathed a sigh of relief. "I suppose that's some comfort."

"Some small comfort," Rule agreed. "In any event, while it does limit the number of fiends in the city, it makes it more difficult to locate one. Uzkiel and any others present at the moment appear to be wise enough to lay low for the time being."

"So how are you going to flush it out?"

This was the part of the conversation Rule had been dreading. "That is why I came looking for you. I thought we should join the others and all discuss it at once. If the idea Noah and I dreamed up is to work, we will need everyone's help."

She smiled at him, her sweet expression glowing

with trust. "Then let's go find them. Just do me one favor." She eased herself carefully into a sitting position and grimaced. "Don't take us anywhere near the kitchens."

CHAPTER TWENTY-THREE

*t*hey convened in the library, which was beginning to gain the nickname around Vircolac of "the War Room." Tess, Rafe, and Samantha sat on the sofa, looking expectant, while Noah lounged in an armchair across from the one his sister had curled into. But his lazy appearance didn't fool anyone. Graham, Rule had learned, had taken Missy on a short trip to the country, because "fresh air would be good for the pup." He wasn't fooling anyone, least of all Missy, who had said, "He's just trying to keep me out of trouble."

Rule couldn't blame the Lupine. If Rule had the choice, he probably would have done the same.

This was not a moment he had been looking forward to.

"Well?" Tess prodded. "Let's hear it, O fearless leader. What's the plan?"

Rule glared at Noah. Tess might have asked the question, but Noah had been just as involved in the planning as he had. The only reason Noah didn't stir himself to answer the witch's question was that he wanted to watch Rule squirm. Apparently Noah wasn't *quite* as nonchalant about Rule and Abby's relationship as he had assured them he was.

"You all know parts of it," Rule began. He stood beside Abby's chair and rested his hand on her shoulder. "I have discussed aspects with each of you over the last few days. Our goal, of course, is to locate Uzkiel and bring the fiend to justice, whether that involves binding it and returning it to the Parliament to face formal charges for its crimes or whether that involves destroying it outright."

"We're not going to be picky," Tess volunteered.

"The trouble has been in locating Uzkiel. He remains well hidden, unexpectedly so."

"Hardly surprising in a city as large and populous as this one," Rafe said. "Especially considering our population of Others and magic users is disproportionately high."

Rule nodded. "Noah and I, however, believe we might have thought of a way to flush him out. To make him come to us."

Samantha looked dubious. "You really think you're going to get a fiend you've been hunting for years to just knock on the door and turn himself in? That doesn't sound like a plan; it sounds like an episode of *Scooby-Doo*."

Noah shot her a sideways glance. "Well, we do have a talking dog on our team."

The Lupine visibly bristled and Rule stepped in to distract her before she could make Abby's brother eat his words. "Of course, we don't expect Uzkiel to voluntarily surrender. We will set a trap and lure him into it."

THE DEMON YOU KNOW 259

"A trap implies the use of bait," Rafe pointed out. His voice sounded mild, but his eyes were sharp.

Rule nodded brusquely. No one was going to like this idea. Even *he* didn't like it, and he and Noah were the ones who had come up with it.

"You are correct, Rafe. The trap will need to be baited. We will need to use Louamides. We will exorcise it from Abby and place it in another vessel. Then we will dangle it in front of Uzkiel and wait for the trap to spring."

Samantha snorted. "I stand corrected. I've seen *better* plans on episodes of *Scooby-Doo*. We'd be better off with a bedsheet, a skateboard, and a washing machine."

While he didn't phrase it so bluntly, Rafe seemed to agree with the Lupine's assessment. "The trouble with mousetraps is that often the prey steals the bait and still escapes the snare. Can we afford to take that risk?"

"We don't have much choice."

Abby shook her head. "Sure we do. We must. What about the coven Tess mentioned? They're trying to track down Uzkiel. Why not wait to see what they come up with?"

Rule's hand squeezed her shoulder. "Time is running short. The Parliament Below is losing patience. They want Uzkiel delivered so they can bring him to justice."

"Well, they can just hold their horses. We're doing the best we can."

"Our best is not counted quite good enough."

"They do have a point, though," Noah observed.

"From what Rule and De Santos tell me of them, I've concluded they're a bunch of whiny little snot-nosed pencil pushers who wouldn't know how to run a location and extraction mission if we drew them a diagram. But they've got a point about needing to move on this. If Tess and Rule are right about how the fiends are getting to town, it's not a far stretch to imagine they're doing it at Uzkiel's suggestion. If that fiend is trying to build himself an army, we need to put a stop to it yesterday."

"Why does that buildup make me think I'm not going to like whatever it is the two of you have dreamed up?"

Noah just grinned at his sister. "Doesn't matter, Ab. If your boyfriend couldn't talk me out of it, there's no point in you even trying."

Abby shook her head in immediate denial. "No way."

"Sorry, Sis. You don't get a vote."

"There is *no way,*" Abby repeated, jumping out of her chair and glaring daggers at her brother. "There is no way in whatever it is you consider hell that I'm letting you take on Louamides and offer yourself up to Uzkiel on a platter. It's not going to happen, so just get the idea out of your head right now."

"Like I said, Abigail, you're not going to be able to talk me out of it. And I'd like to see you stop me any other way."

"You may be older than me, and you may be bigger than me, but I'm sneakier than you are, Noah James. And I happen to know where you sleep."

"I can fix that soon enough. If I want to take

chances, that's my decision. It's not just my decision; it's my job. Or did you think I just spent my days polishing boots and posing for recruitment posters?"

"That's a completely different thing. You're a soldier. You're trained to fight. I get that. But you're not trained to fight fiends, and you're not trained to handle being possessed by one."

"If you can bear up under the strain, I'm pretty sure it won't kill me."

"No, but Mom might. Why don't I just give her a call and tell her what you have planned?"

"Low blow, Ab."

"Children." Rafe rose from his seat on the sofa and stepped between the two of them. "Enough with the bickering. It is not helping matters."

"The only thing that's going to help matters is a swift blow to my idiot brother's stubborn head," Abby muttered. She turned on Rule, her eyes narrowed in anger. "And you're going to let him do this? You were just planning to stand by while he throws himself to the wolves and give your blessing to this ludicrous plan?"

Beneath her furious bluster, Rule could see the real fear in Abby's eyes. He had known the idea of her brother putting himself in danger would be intolerable for her and couldn't blame her. Rule didn't like the plan, either, but it turned out that Noah Baker was almost more stubborn than his baby sister.

"Of course not," Rule said quietly, reaching out to grasp her arms and pull her toward him. She tried to bat his hands away, clearly not in the mood to be comforted, but he persisted. "I do not want your brother in danger any more than you do. But he is a grown man, Abby. I have no authority to gainsay him. What would you have me do?"

"Stop him." She stamped her little foot in emphasis.

"How?"

"I don't know. Do whatever it is you do. Work some demon magic or something. Heck, go ahead and kidnap him and lock him up in a stronghold somewhere. It seemed to work where I'm concerned."

Rule shook his head. "Your brother is not an innocent bystander, Abby. He's a trained soldier. If I tried to lock him in somewhere, he would try to escape. The only way for me to stop him from killing himself would be to do the job for him. I somehow doubt that is a solution of which you would approve."

"Rule, you can't let him do this. Please." Her voice went from brassy to begging, and her wide, mismatched eyes pleaded with him. "You have to stop him."

"He can't," Noah said.

The words came out harshly and Rule glared at him from over Abby's head. Rule would have snapped at the other man if he hadn't seen the haunted look in Noah's eyes. His brusque manner clearly served to hide just how difficult this was for him.

Abby turned in Rule's arms, aiming her miserable expression at her brother. "Why are you doing this? It's not your fight. Why put yourself on the line?"

"Because someone has to."

It was the same answer Rule had received when

he'd asked the same question. Rule suspected that kind of commitment to duty was what had inspired Noah to join the military in the first place. He had the strength and the skills to handle this kind of situation; therefore he was honor bound to do so. To Noah, it was that simple.

To Abby, it remained a mystery.

"*Someone* doesn't have to be you," she said, and pushed herself away from Rule's chest. He tried to pull her back, but she ducked out of reach. "I'm the reason you're in this situation, and Lou is already perfectly at home inside of me. There's no reason to drag someone else into this mess. If anyone is going to act as bait, it should be me."

CHAPTER TWENTY-FOUR

bsolutely not."

Rule's veto came immediately and unequivocally. Abby had expected that, but she didn't react. She just took a deep breath and went on with her alternate plan.

"Not only is Lou already inside me, *solus* spell and all, but that other fiend—Seth, Uzkiel's minion—knows where Lou is hiding. That's why Seth came after me in the first place. Why try to reinvent the wheel? The fiends know about me and they know I'm being protected by the Silverback Clan, so they must have some idea where I'm hiding. It's ridiculous to move Lou to Noah and then have to let the fiends find out about it before they can even come looking for him. I'm already set up and ready to go. We should move now. The sooner the better."

Tess pursed her lips. "Anyone else having déjà vu?"

Abby ignored that. She couldn't say her eagerness was all about the desire to see justice done. A lot of it had to do with the school of thought that decreed it was better to rip a bandage off quickly, so that the pain would be over with in the shortest amount of time possible.

"It's out of the question." Rule's features had settled into those harsh, granite lines again, the ones that said he was the demon and he made the rules. She realized he hadn't used that mask with her since before they'd made love, and she didn't like seeing it return, even if she understood the reasons.

"It's no more out of the question for me to be the bait than it was for my brother to be the bait. We're both human. We're both equally unequipped to do battle with an archfiend."

Rule glared at her. "Your brother happens to be equipped with an AK-47 and a kilogram of plastic explosive."

Okay, Rule had a point there. But still . . .

"Do you really think that when we take Uzkiel down, it's going to be with bombs or bullets?"

"When *I* take Uzkiel down, *you* are going to be nowhere in the vicinity."

She returned his glare with interest. "I already escaped one, Mr. Dictator. Want to see how fast I can repeat that if you try and wrap me in cotton balls and put me on a shelf until this is over?"

Rafe muttered under his breath and stepped forward again. "I swear I should be getting combat pay." He put a hand on Rule's shoulder to draw his attention. "If Noah were to act as bait, what would the rest of the plain entail?"

Abby opened her mouth to say the rest of the plan didn't matter, since her brother wasn't going to be involved in it, but Rafe sent her a look clearly designed to shut her up. What ended up being even more effective was the elbow Tess hurried over to plant in Abby's side. That knocked enough of the breath out of her that she actually couldn't protest for a few minutes.

"Since *Noah* is a well-trained and experienced soldier," Rule said, shooting Abby a pointed glare, "I have every confidence that he could hold his own in an emergency situation. We would spread the word that Lou had moved into a new human host, and then have him attract the fiend's attention with something suitably Lou-like. A fracas at a strip club would do nicely."

Mmm, just so long as I got to look for a while before the fracas.

"Shut up, Lou," Abby muttered under her breath. *You're such a fun-Nazi.*

"It would not take long for Uzkiel to put those pieces together and send his minions after Noah. We would allow Noah to lead them to a secured area, and once there, we would perform a binding spell and bring the fiend's imprisoned spirit back to the Below for the Parliament to deal with."

"And I'm sure it would all work out just that tidily." Abby crossed her arms over her chest and glared at Rule.

"That's why Rule pointed out he knows I can deal with emergency situations," Noah defended. "It wouldn't be the first mission I've been on that went straight into FUBAR, and I can sure as hell predict it won't be the last."

"It doesn't matter," Abby said, "because you won't

be on this mission. Like I said, if anyone here is going to put themselves in a situation like this, it's going to be me."

"Over my dead body," Rule snapped.

"Don't tempt me," Abby hissed.

"I am not certain anyone will be performing this mission," Rafe said. He was frowning, only this time Abby didn't think it was just because the bickering had resumed. He looked about as convinced of the feasibility of this grand plan as she felt. "It sounds like a very large risk with a very small chance of success. Do we even know if we have the capability to perform such a binding spell?" He glanced at his wife and arched an eyebrow.

"Maybe," she said, pursing her lips. "It wouldn't be easy. It would certainly be beyond my fiendish powers, but Rule is a demon. He's from the same plane as Uzkiel. That could give him an advantage. Plus, he told me he's got some kind of special grisgris or something that's been designed to hold archfiends like this one."

"It's a silver mirror," Rule informed them grudgingly. "Not a modern mirror, but a highly polished piece of silver with an accurately reflective surface."

"And that does what?" Samantha asked.

"Another piece of folklore attributed to the wrong place. Vampires have no fear of mirrors because they cast no reflections. One seldom fears an absence of something. But archfiends fear their own reflections. It is a reminder of how far they have strayed from what they once were. At one time, they were demons not so different from me. When they see proof of how evil has changed them, they can become bound to the reflective surface and trapped there."

Tess looked intrigued. "Really? I'll have to remember that little trick. I always carry a compact in my purse with me."

"I wouldn't advise using it," Rule cautioned. "The mirror I brought with me is silver and not glass for a reason. A mirror can bind an archfiend and even hold one temporarily, but mirrors are fragile. It doesn't take much force for the fiend to break free of one. They can also break accidentally, and when the mirror breaks, it releases the spirit of the fiend back out into the world. Usually, a much crankier fiend than the one you had originally captured."

"But the fiend will be unable to break free of the silver mirror?" Rafe asked.

"At least for long enough for me to return it Below."

"Right. That's a great plan," Samantha observed, her tone dripping sarcasm. "Totally foolproof. Except for the parts where you find the fiend that's currently hiding from you, let it track you to a secure location you haven't managed to locate, and do a spell even the witch isn't certain you can cast. What could possibly go wrong?"

"Anything could go wrong. Which is why it's going to be me acting as bait and not my defenseless baby sister." Noah smiled, an expression with a lot of teeth but no discernible humor.

"I agree. This is too dangerous to involve Abby in. Noah and I will handle it and return here when we've finished."

Abby turned on Rule, flashing a considerable number of her own teeth. So this was what the phase "her blood boiled" was referring to. "News flash, you arrogant putz, this is not 1942, I'm not the little woman, and I'm not going to stand on the dock and wave my handkerchief at you while you sail off to war. I'm part of this mess, and I'm going to see it finished."

Tess tilted her head to the side and looked Abby over from head to toe. "She looks pretty serious to me, guys."

"We outnumber her," Noah said. "The vote is two to one. Abby loses."

"Then Abby is going to cheat," she bit out. They had her talking about herself in the third person. It was another mark to add to their growing tally of sins. "You can plan whatever you want, and you can try to leave me behind, but the minute your backs are turned, I will start dogging your heels like the specter of a gruesome death."

The three of them faced one another in the center of the room, faces set, expressions grim, body language screaming with tension, anger, and determination.

The room fell eerily silent.

"I believe we have ourselves a stalemate." Rafe sighed the observation. "In situations like these, I have found the only workable solution tends to be something called a compromise. Have any of you heard the term?"

Abby supposed she should be glad at least someone could see the humor in the situation. "I have, but since it's got more than one syllable, I'd be surprised if the Neanderthal brothers over here had."

Rafe shot her a quelling glance. "I've had enough of the fighting, Miss Baker. It's time to move past our emotions and reason to a logical solution to our problem."

"That's what I've been trying to do. It's not logical to exorcise me, move Louamides into my brother, and then try to re-create a wheel that already exists. Lou is already inside me, and Uzkiel already knows he is. If we just use me as bait, we can skip all the preliminaries and go right to the trap. Noah and Rule are the ones who keep pointing out that we need to hurry. If we need to hurry, then we shouldn't be wasting time building a bunch of extra steps into the process."

Rafe looked at Rule. "She has a point."

Abby could see the muscle in the side of the demon's jaw pulsing and knew it took a considerable amount of self-control for him not to just roar out a denial, beat on his chest, and drag her out of the room by her hair. When it came right down to it, men were still ruled by primitive instincts.

"I will not deny there is a certain . . . efficiency to her proposal," Rule finally conceded. His reluctance came through loud and clear, considering he had to bite off every word through tightly clenched teeth. "But I have to balance efficiency with the possibility of something going wrong. If it does, I will not be able to protect her. Noah can protect himself. That gives him a distinct advantage in the event of a problem."

You might want to remind him that while you happen to be a girl—with terrific tits, I might add, even if you won't let me see 'em—I most definitely am not.

Hearing Lou's voice just then startled Abby out of her haze of anger. She had almost forgotten that it had been listening to the entire debate.

I mean, I can't say I'm thrilled with any plan that puts me in clawing distance of the big guy, but it looks like those two aren't gonna give me much choice. And even if I'm not up to taking him on, I at least make up for the differences between you and your brother. So I vote I stay put.

"Lou," Abby muttered under her breath, feeling herself start to smile. "If you had a body, I'd kiss you."

I'm gonna remember that next time I run into you, babe. Just remember, I like a lot of tongue.

Noah turned and frowned at her. "What did you say?"

Abby wiped the grin off her face. "I said, I think the two of you are missing something here. Sure, I'm not as big and strong as my macho older brother, but I'm far from defenseless."

He sighed. "Ab, a few rape prevention courses at the Y don't qualify you for potential hand-to-hand combat."

"Lou, help me out here," she whispered. She had never had trouble using the fiend's strength before when she needed it, but she figured that while they were on speaking terms, it would be polite to at least give him a heads-up. Then in her normal voice she said, "Maybe not. But this does."

Before her brother could guess her intentions, she

grabbed him by the arm, swept his feet out from under him, and tossed him over her shoulder like a feather pillow.

He landed like a ton of bricks.

"What the *fuck*?"

Relishing the gesture, Abby brushed her hands together and grinned smugly down at him. "Like I said, I'm not completely defenseless."

Thunderclouds rolled in across Noah's expression. Cursing a blue streak, he flipped himself to his feet and glowered down at her. "Mom and Dad should have beaten you regularly."

"A little late for that now."

"Oh, that was gorgeous," Tess laughed, wiping the tears from her face. "I think I may have pulled a muscle. I don't suppose you'd wait while I fetched the camcorder, then do it again, would you?"

"That proves nothing," Rule growled. And he had the nerve to call her stubborn.

"It proves that while I'm possessed, I'm at least as strong as Noah and more than capable of defending myself if it comes down to it. More capable, probably. From what I hear, I could probably bench press a Buick, and I doubt my oh-so-tough brother could make that kind of claim."

She saw Rule shaking his head, but she knew she'd found a chink in his logic.

"But if you can do that because you're possessed, think about what I'd be able to do if the fiend were inside me?" Noah glared at her and dusted off his fatigues. "Possessed, you may be stronger than me, but if I were possessed, I'd be nearly as strong as Rule."

"It's not just about strength," Rule chimed in. "Noah has had training. He has experience in combat situations—"

"And he'd be a nervous wreck when he saw me racing, alone and unpossessed, into the fray because you made the idiot decision to leave me behind while you two rode off into the enemy camp."

Rafe put a hand on Rule's shoulder and patted consolingly. "A true warrior," the Felix observed, "knows when the time comes to surrender."

CHAPTER TWENTY-FIVE

I really wish you'd let Tess grab a camera. I'd love to have a shot of the look on your brother's face."

Abby forced a smile she really didn't feel as she paced her way across the floor of her bedroom. Samantha lounged on the bed like a boneless puppy, but Abby couldn't make herself relax. She might have won the battle over participating in the plan to trap Uzkiel, but that didn't mean Rule and Noah had been gracious about it. They had immediately convened some kind of testosterone-laden powwow to adjust the mission parameters. At least, that's what they'd told her. She suspected they were drinking beer and playing pool and bitching about her stubbornness.

Samantha sighed. "Don't worry, Abby. They're not going to do this without you. You made them swear on their gonads. And anyway, Tess's spies are everywhere. If they so much as look toward an exit, trust me, we'll hear about it."

"I know." Abby halted near the foot of the bed and crossed her arms over her chest, hugging herself nervously. "I'm just . . . I guess I thought that once they announced the grand plan, we'd go ahead and actually do it. It's this waiting-around part that's going to give me a heart attack."

You know, a nice, hot bubble bath might be real soothing. . . .

"Oh, shut up, you little lech!"

"Huh?" Samantha frowned.

"Not you." Abby sighed. "What time is it?"

"About forty seconds later than when you last asked. You really have to relax, Abby. This isn't healthy."

"I know. I just want them to give me a time and a place and get moving already!"

"Okay, you know it's not that easy." Samantha spoke with the exaggerated patience you used on a three-year-old. Abby suspected that's what she most resembled at the moment. "First, they have to totally revise the whole strip club thing. I don't care if you were possessed by the spirit of Hugh Hefner, there's no way you'd be caught dead in a place like that."

"Hugh Hefner is still alive. He can't possess anyone."

"Propaganda," the Lupine dismissed with a wave. "He was replaced by a battery-powered cyborg years ago. But anyway, they need to think of another way to bring you to Uzkiel's attention without making it look like they're dangling you under his nose like fresh meat."

"Even if they are."

"Right. And secondly, finding a place in this city that's private, secure, and out of the way and that we don't mind having blown to smithereens, if it comes to that, is something like finding the Fountain of Youth. It's going to take a while."

Abby grumbled and resumed pacing. "Your logic has no power over me."

"Clearly. Come on, Ab, you're making me dizzy. Give it a rest."

"Shut your eyes."

A brief knock sounded on the door, but Tess didn't wait for an answer before she waltzed inside. "I come bearing popcorn and eye candy." She waved a DVD case in one hand. The other cradled an enormous stainless-steel mixing bowl overflowing with buttered popcorn. "I thought we might be reaching that scary stage of impatience where we start snapping at our friends for no reason."

Giving Abby a pointed look, Tess handed the popcorn to Samantha and opened the door on the wardrobe housing the TV. Tess popped the DVD in the player and dragged Abby back toward the bed.

"Pile in and get comfortable," Tess instructed, putting her own words into action. She climbed over Samantha, who had stretched lengthwise on the end of the bed and claimed it as her own, and settled back against the headboard. "We've got two hours of nature's glory just waiting to be drooled over."

Her glare managed to coax Abby into submission. Settling down next to Tess, she dipped into the popcorn and pulled out a salty handful. She could smell the rich scent of butter before she even lifted it to her mouth.

"Cardiologists everywhere must be cursing your name," she muttered.

"Without me, they'd be out of work. Now make yourself useful and go grab some drinks. There should be cans in the little fridge next to the closet."

Abby laughed. "Of course. I forgot all about the minibar. You do realize that this place is eerily well equipped for unexpected visitors?"

"It's a very exclusive club!" Tess called after her. "People come from all over to visit us. You expect Graham to send them to the Holiday Inn?"

Shaking her head, Abby grabbed three cans of soda from the miniature refrigerator and headed back into the bedroom. Samantha and Tess lounged on the bed, munching popcorn and commenting on the movie's opening credit sequence, looking like perfectly normal friends settling in for a quiet evening in good company. Abby blinked and faltered, stopping suddenly in the archway between the short hall into the bathroom and the open space of the bedroom area.

These were her friends.

It struck her, really struck her, in an instant and made her catch her breath. Tess De Santos, witch and mate to the shape-shifting werejaguar who headed the Council of Others, and Samantha Cartwright, werewolf secretary to the Alpha Lupine of the Silverback Clan, had managed in the last confusing, infuriating, surreal week of Abby's life to become two of the best friends she'd ever had. Her. Abby Baker, boring little girl next door. She'd gone from a perfectly ordinary, if unexciting, existence as an average human being to that of the kind of woman who had a witch and a werewolf as best friends and a demon as a lover.

She felt dizzy all of a sudden.

Tess looked away from the movie and frowned at her. "You okay, Ab?"

"Yeah," she said, shaking off the dazed feeling. "Fine."

Just having a little revelation over here, she thought. No big deal. I just suddenly realized that I kind of love you guys.

Why don't you go give them a hug? And maybe a kiss. You know, I hear communal nudity can be a real bonding experience. . . .

Trust Lou to turn a moment of emotional revelation into the setup for a bad porn film.

Abby didn't even bother to acknowledge it. "Did you know there're no diet sodas in there?"

Samantha looked at her as if she'd asked if they were aware there were no pygmy aardvarks in the refrigerator and took the can of root beer. "Of course not. Who drinks that stuff?"

"I do." Abby popped the tab on a ginger ale and sipped the sweet, spicy liquid. "It's the price I pay for what my grandmother so kindly refers to as my 'childbearing hips.'"

"I'm afraid Sam doesn't see the problem with childbearing hips," Tess said, explaining the confused look on the Lupine's face. "You see, most shifters find physical attributes like wide hips and a curvy figure to be turn-ons. I think it has something to do with the preservation of those primitive, animalistic instincts. Believe me when I say, you'll never meet a Lupine who's on a diet."

Abby blinked. "Are you serious?"

"Perfectly, but there's no need to look surprised. I mean, you can't tell me you've ever heard Rule objecting to your figure," Samantha teased.

"Well, no, but I thought that was just more evidence that a man that perfect couldn't possibly be human."

Tess snickered. "In a way, I suppose it is. Like I said, the Others tend to have different ideas of beauty than the human advertising industry. Haven't you taken a look around? I mean, Samantha has to be the skinniest woman you've met while you've been staying here. It's not like I don't have a curve or two."

Abby looked from one woman to the other and frowned. "Neither one of you needs to lose weight. You both look terrific."

"And so do you. If you don't take our word for it, take Rule's." Tess's expression turned wicked. "I'm sure if you're still having doubts, he'd be happy to demonstrate his satisfaction with your physical appearance."

Abby blushed. "I'm not having doubts that Rule finds me attractive."

Samantha grinned. "Well, at least he's doing something right."

"He's doing lots of things right, being thick-headed notwithstanding." Abby fiddled with the tab on her soda can, spinning it in little circles until the metal gave out and snapped off into her hand. Bracing herself, she took a deep breath. "I think . . . I'm afraid I'm completely in love with him."

Her declaration was met with utter silence.

Heart in her throat, she looked up and saw both women staring at her impassively. Neither said a word.

Abby started to squirm.

"And?" Samantha prompted.

"Were we supposed to respond to that?" Tess asked. "'Cause, I hate to break it to you, sweetheart, but . . . *DUH*!"

Laughing, Abby let her head thump back against the headboard. "Well, it may sound stupid to you, but this is a big thing for me. (A) I've never been in love before, and (B) this is the first time I've dated anyone outside my own species. This is a stretch for me."

Samantha patted Abby's leg. "It doesn't sound dumb that you're in love with Rule. What sounded dumb was that you were expecting us not to have noticed."

"Like I said, Ab, it's a really good thing you don't play poker." Tess swigged her own cola. "I understand the species gap, though. Trust me, I had problems with it, too, and at least I grew up knowing that other species existed. You've only had two months to assimilate it."

Abby sat forward and nodded. "Exactly! This is like a whole world shift for me. I mean, I've barely dated over the last couple of years, and now all of a sudden I'm falling in love with something that three months ago I would have said was an allegory for humanity's taboo impulses."

"Right. The thing you have to understand, though, and this is the most important part, so listen carefully,"

Tess leaned forward and put her hand on top of Abby's, "the thing to remember is . . . get over it."

"What?"

Tess laughed, which Abby wasn't entirely sure she appreciated. "Get over it. Listen, Ab, I love you. You're a great girl, but you're getting way too wrapped up inside your own head. Maybe it's that convent school upbringing of yours, but whatever. You need to move past it. I get that the idea of inter-species dating can put a little hitch in a girl's step, but you have to stop and realize that in the end, they're all just guys."

"Tess is right. Trust me, I've dated a lot of guys in my life," Samantha said, "and not all of the ones who were dogs happened to be Lupine. Men are men. No matter what species they come from, they all have the same impulses and the same incomprehensible way of looking at things."

"Take Rule and Rafe as an example." Setting her soda down on the bedside table, Tess resettled herself. Abby had already noticed that the witch tended to talk with her hands. "Two totally different species raised on two totally different planes. One a Felix, the other a demon. Sound pretty different, don't they?" She shook her head. "Uh-uh. The two of them took one look at each other, recognized themselves as long-lost blood brothers or something, and they've been thick as thieves ever since. I'm talking from day one. And it's not because their back-grounds are so similar. They're entirely different. But they're both men, and more than that, they're both Alpha men. Their main purpose in life is to claim and protect. It doesn't matter what bubble they fill in under the species column on the next census."

Samantha snorted. "And isn't that going to make for some interesting national statistics?"

"You've had a lot longer to come to that conclusion than I've had," Abby protested.

"Oh, screw that." Tess held up a hand and laughed. "No, hear me out. Yeah, I knew going into this that shape-shifters existed. I'd even met one or two, but it's not like I was pals with any of them. You wouldn't know this, since you didn't know about any of the Others up until the news broke, but until about five years ago the witches had absolutely nothing to do with the rest of the Others community. We kept entirely separate, had our own little council, our own laws, everything. So trust me when I tell you that it was nearly as big a leap for me to end up mated to a werejaguar as it's been for you to end up mated to a demon."

Abby shook her head. "No one said anything about mates."

"Right." Samantha rolled her eyes. "Of course not. We'll pretend that doesn't exist just like the whole love thing, shall we?"

"I'm serious. I'm having a hard enough time dealing with sex and love. Leave me a little breathing room, would you?" She turned back to Tess. "So how did you deal with it?"

The blonde snorted. "As little as humanly possible. I ignored it for a good long time, then I bitched about it for a while. Actually, I spent a lot of time bitching to Missy and the girls."

"The girls?"

"There's a whole group of us. The Benevolent and Protective Order of Women with Idiot Men on Their Hands. We'll discuss your induction later, when the others get back from their vacations. A lot of them managed to arrange to be out of town when the Unveiling broke." Tess waved a hand. "But that's not the point. In the end there was really only one thing that mattered. No matter how much the jerk got on my nerves or how many barriers stood between us, I was in love with him. Utterly and completely. And I still am. He's my husband and my friend and the father of my son and the person I want to wake up next to every morning for the rest of my life. He's my mate." She paused to stare at Abby. "Any of this ringing any bells?"

Abby just closed her eyes on a sigh.

"Look, I know it's inconvenient, Ab, but you're going to have to face the fact that love is rarely anything else."

She made a face. "That doesn't mean I have to be happy about it."

"Oh, Gods, no," Tess said, sounding completely taken aback. "Yell and scream and rant and rave. Trust me, the practice will come in handy. But when the dust settles, take a good look at Rule and try to imagine what your life would be like if he weren't in it anymore." She raised an eyebrow. "Is that something you're prepared to face?"

· · ·

*t*he movie, the popcorn, and the friends were long gone when Rule finally climbed into Abby's bed that night. He moved silently, but she had begun to recognize the feel of him in the room, the way the air seemed to shift and tighten when he was near. She turned immediately into his arms and burrowed her head against his shoulder.

"Is everything okay?" she whispered, her voice thick and foggy with sleep.

"Fine," he murmured, and brushed a kiss over her forehead. "Go back to sleep."

Abby grinned into the darkness. "Make me."

He hadn't needed to be told a second time.

She had reveled in his touch, not just because it felt so good, an aching excitement she was afraid had already become addictive, but because she needed the reassurance after their earlier argument that anger hadn't changed what was between them. By the time she had drifted, limp and boneless, into sleep, at least that worry had been thoroughly banished.

When she woke, though, a dozen others were clamoring to take its place.

Rule was gone, his side of the bed already cool to the touch. Abby hurried through a shower and yanked on the first clothes she found, surprised that she didn't even have to fight with Lou that morning. Maybe that was a good sign.

She hurried downstairs to the club's second floor and poked her head in the War Room. Empty. Frowning, she turned and headed down the hall to the media room. No one around here seemed to watch much TV, but maybe someone was catching up on the news?

That room was empty as well. Come to think of it, the entire floor sounded eerily quiet.

Hesitantly Abby walked down the steps to the club's main floor where most of the members and guests spent their visits. Even that seemed quiet. Of course, her watch told her it was only a few minutes after noon, and even the non-nocturnal members of the club tended to stop by only after nightfall.

She didn't open any of the closed doors, not wanting to interrupt a club member's private meeting, but she was starting to feel a little uneasy. Frowning, she turned toward the main entrance and the office Graham kept nearby.

A footman met her in the hall. "Miss Baker?"

Abby turned. "Yes?"

She still couldn't get used to the idea of the club *having* footmen, but calling them waiters didn't fit, considering they spent very little of their time serving food or drinks.

"Mr. Rule asked me to give you a message," the young man said. He had the look of a college student, someone studying the sciences or maybe engineering. "He said to tell you that Mrs. De Santos's informants had some information for him and he's gone to speak with them. He won't be long, and you are to stay in the club." At least the kid had the grace to look apologetic. "He, uh, he also told me to tell you that, uh, he's not trying to handle everything without you but that if you try to leave the club on your own to follow him, he'll . . ." He cleared his throat. "He'll, uh, paddle you so hard you won't sit for a week."

Abby just stared at him.

"I'm sorry, ma'am. He made me say it."

She gritted her teeth. "It's all right. Not your fault. I'd give you a message of my own to pass on to him, but I don't want to rob myself of the pleasure of kneeing him in the balls personally."

The footman just went pale and hurried into another room, presumably before it occurred to Abby to kill the messenger. Or demonstrate her own message. Plotting dire revenge, she turned to stalk back up the stairs but stopped when someone called her name.

"Hey, Abby!"

She turned and saw a woman standing in the hallway leading toward the club's rear entrance. "Carly?"

The Lupine nodded and grinned. She wore the same paramedic's jumpsuit Abby had first seen her in. "How've you been? I hear the warden in this joint can be pretty strict."

Abby laughed. "You have no idea. Are you on duty?"

"Of course," Carly ran a hand through habitually tousled hair. "I've been pulling doubles the entire week. That's why I haven't been able to stop by before now. At the moment, though, I'm on a lunch break. A long one."

"Cool. The chicken salad here is killer, if you're in the mood for something other than steak." She gestured to the stairs. "In fact, I'm ready for food myself.

Come upstairs and eat with me. One of the benefits of being under club arrest is I get great service."

Carly laughed. "Actually, Samantha and I thought you might want to go out for lunch. Just to the deli down the street," she said, grinning at Abby's look of shock. "We know better than to take you out of shouting distance, but the deli has killer Reubens, and we thought with a double werewolf escort you'd be safe enough. She's waiting out back. What do you say?"

Rule's threat, delivered in the stammering voice of a freshman physics major, made the decision for Abby. Threaten to spank her, would he?

"Wait right here. I'm just going to grab a jacket."

Abby bounced up the stairs and returned a minute later with the denim jacket she'd worn on her last, ill-fated excursion into the great outdoors. She was actually looking forward to fighting with Rule about this later, especially since his objections would be completely unreasonable given she would be under double guard the entire time she was away.

"Lead on," she instructed, waving Carly toward the back door. "I'm in the mood for extra sauerkraut."

"Ooh, you do like to live dangerously," Carly teased. "In fact, from what Sam told me earlier, it sounds like you're thinking of making the danger zone a permanent state of residence?"

Abby blushed and shrugged. "It's a little soon to be saying that."

"Oh? From what I hear, Sam and Tess are practically picking out their bridesmaids' dresses."

"That's *way* too soon." Abby reached for the handle

and yanked on the heavy metal door. Thankfully, she didn't need to disarm the security system to leave, since she didn't know the code. Samantha and Carly both did, though, so they could punch them back in after lunch. "First we need to deal with this whole fiend issue, then we can decide if we can keep from killing each other for the entirety of a long-term relationship."

Carly followed Abby outside and tugged the door shut behind them. The electronic lock beeped as it engaged. "I don't think that's something you need to worry about. After all, you'll be dead in just a few hours, so why borrow trouble?"

Aw, fuck.

Abby's reeling mind registered the empty alley, the change in Carly's tone of voice, and the shrieking of her self-preservation instincts all at the same time, about the time that Lou lapsed into profanity. Heart pounding, she turned just in time to see an unnatural glow burning behind the Lupine's brown eyes. Abby opened her mouth to scream, but the blow landed before she made a sound, and then all she registered was darkness.

CHAPTER TWENTY-SIX

Rule sat beside Tess in the back room of her shop, awkwardly cradling a steaming mug between his hands. He hadn't wanted the tea, but it had seemed rude to refuse it when she'd been passing out cups. Besides, having something in his hands seemed to set the older women in the room more at ease. When they'd first arrived and seen him, they had looked as if they expected him to pounce on them immediately and crunch their bones for his afternoon snack.

As if. All three were well past their prime, and two of them looked positively stringy.

He sighed. He should have let Tess handle this interview and gone with Noah to check out the scene of a recent fiend sighting.

"—tend to concentrate more on objects, you know. Wedding rings, wills, important legal documents, that kind of thing," one of the thin ones was saying. Rule thought her name was something like Daisy. "It was really Heather's suggestion that we branch out into missing persons. Children, mostly. It turned out to be a great success. And so rewarding, you know, to be able to see the little ones safely home."

The other two nodded. One of them, presumably, was Heather. Rule was going to go with the second stringy one. The plump one he thought had been introduced as Claire.

"Of course, those are the good days," Heather added. "Sometimes all we can provide is a sense of closure, and we have to be content with that."

Rule fought the urge to roll his eyes. If these were what witches were normally like, he needed to remind Rafe what a lucky man he was to have found a sane one to mate with.

"So, really, since then we've looked on branching out our services as something of a challenge," Daisy continued. "I have to admit, though, your request did strike us as a bit unusual."

Heather nodded and made a face. "Fairly unpleasant, too. I have to tell you, Tess, this isn't the sort of energy we would normally expose ourselves to. Very violent. Very unclean."

"The word you're looking for," Claire said from over the rim of her teacup just as Rule was beginning to wonder if she ever spoke, "is 'evil.'"

Heather glared at her. "You know I don't like that word, Claire. It's so . . . unforgiving."

Claire snorted. "Hard to be all that forgiving of something that wants to chew on your entrails."

Rule took back his uncharitable thoughts. Daisy and Heather might be fluffy-bunny idiot witches, but that Claire had a good head on her shoulders, even if it was long gone gray.

"In any event, we appreciate you helping us out," Tess said, almost as diplomatically as her husband. Had she been taking lessons? "We haven't had any luck finding it on our own, so of course I immediately thought of you three. You have such a gift with location spells."

Daisy preened. "We all have our talents, dear. Take your potions, for instance. Why, I couldn't brew a decent cup of willow bark if my life depended on it!"

Rule fought the urge to tell the woman that her life *did* depend on getting to the point and telling him what they had learned about Uzkiel.

"It's nothing." Tess waved away the compliment. "I'm fascinated by what you ladies do, though. Why don't you explain the process to me?"

Was she out of her mind? If they answered that question, it would take these three old biddies forever to get to the point. Rule glared at Tess, who pointedly ignored him.

"Well, of course, dear." Daisy set aside her teacup and folded her hands in her lap. "Usually we start with something that belonged to the missing soul. With children, we like stuffed animals. They absorb so much energy, and well, it's just pleasant to hold on to one for a couple of hours, isn't it?" She laughed.

Heather nodded. "We take it into our circle with us and call on the Goddess to open our minds to the child's mind. Once we've tapped into the little one's energy through the toy, it's much easier to locate that energy somewhere else. Wherever it's gone missing to."

"Of course, we didn't want to do that in this

case." Daisy frowned in distaste. "Not only did we not have a personal object from the fiend, but allowing its mind to join with ours . . ." She shuddered. "Well, that would have just been dangerous."

"Very. You did give us the fiend's proper name, though," Heather said. "And that meant a lot. Not that we normally dabble in summoning, you know—nasty work, that—but we do pride ourselves on knowing a little bit about most of the major forms of magic. And when it comes to summoning magic, the most important tool you can have is the name of the demon."

Rule growled. "The fiend."

Daisy and Heather jumped a little in their seats and eyed him suspiciously, as if they'd forgotten he was there and now that they remembered, he'd be feeling all noshy.

Tess sent him another glare and he subsided back into his chair. "So with its name, you were able to call on it?" she prompted the women.

"Oh no. That would be the equivalent of a summoning, and we certainly didn't want a creature like that popping up inside our temple room," Daisy said, aghast. "We'd never get the taint out."

Not to mention the bloodstains that would be left behind when Uzkiel tore the three of them limb from little old limb, Rule thought uncharitably.

"No, we wanted to sneak up on the creature, so to speak," Heather agreed. "To find out what it was up to without it doing the reverse. That type of snooping requires quite a bit of stealth."

Rule closed his eyes. In that case, his hopes for getting any useful information out of them were doomed.

"Oh, for the Lady's sake," Claire snapped, setting her cup down on the table with a thump. "These children don't want a blow-by-blow account of your highly innovative method for psychic spying, Heather. They want to know what we found out."

Rule could have kissed Claire. In fact, he'd talk to Abby about naming their first daughter after her.

She turned to face Rule and Tess and continued. "We can't give you an address. Our magic doesn't work that way. In fact, I can't think of a single kind that does. But we can tell you that it's some kind of old warehouse or factory and that it's located on the river."

His heart sank. Manhattan was surrounded by water on four sides, and most of the waterfront areas had been commercial property at one time or another. All this information had done was eliminate the interior of the island.

"Now don't look so stricken, boy," Claire said, shaking a finger at him. "That's not all we saw. If you look out straight over the water, you can see the sun going down behind the Statue of Liberty."

Tess looked at him. "It's got to be Battery Park City."

Claire nodded. "That's what I said. But there's one more piece of information you two should have. The building this fiend is hiding in, it's not just using it because it's abandoned. It's got a bigger reason than that. First off, the place has a basement. It's wet as a well-digger's arse down there, but it keeps out the light, and the fiend likes that."

Rule nodded, but he was already sorting through possibilities in his head. He didn't know Manhattan that well, but Tess had grown up here, and even if she couldn't name the building, they could probably get blueprints from the Planning Authority. Not many of the places on the water had full basements. Like Claire said, they tended to leak.

"You listen to me, boy." Claire grabbed Rule's hand, interrupting his thoughts and dragging him back to the present. "I wasn't finished with my story. The other reason that fiend has set up shop in this building is the energy in the place. It's as foul as he is. I don't know the history, and I tell you here, I don't care to. Not after feeling it for myself. But I'm telling you, something nasty happened in that place, and happened more than once, I can tell you. Enough misery and pain in that building that it's sunk into the brick, and that fiend is only adding to it. You ask me, when you're done, you should tear that place down to rubble and salt the land good. Maybe after the earth gets wiped clean, something decent can spring up in its place. But for now . . ." She shook her head. "If a place can be called evil, that one is. Mark my words."

Rule nodded and turned to Tess, trying to ignore the uneasy feeling the old witch's words had caused.

"The Council library will have records we can go through," Tess said. "It had to have been a pretty high-profile case to have been as bad as Claire says.

I'll call a friend on the Witches' Council and ask her to start digging." She grimaced. "I know it's not as fast as we would have liked, but at least now we have someplace to start."

Rule nodded.

"Thank you, ladies." He rose and pulled back his chair. "You've been very helpful."

Claire struggled to her feet, waving away the hand Tess offered to assist her. When she had steadied herself on the handle of a carved wooden cane, she lifted her pale blue eyes to Rule and pursed her lips. "I'm going to help you just a little more," she said, nodding as if to herself. "I'm going to tell you that if you move fast and trust her good sense, it will all work out in the end. Mark my words."

The jingle of the cheery little bell Tess had mounted over the door of the shop told them someone had entered, but it was the pounding of heavy footsteps that alerted Rule that something was wrong.

Noah shoved his way past Tess's assistant and into the back room. From the way he was sucking in air, it almost looked like he'd run all the way from the Upper East Side.

"Abby," he gasped, leaning over and bracing his hands on his thighs as he struggled for air.

Rule felt the world shift on its access and suddenly stop spinning. He shook his head, as if he could deny what he knew was coming. His heart froze in his chest, and his stomach clenched before he even heard Noah's next words.

"Abby's missing."

CHAPTER TWENTY-SEVEN

*H*ow Tess got Rule back to Vircolac, he never knew, but she managed it with almost frightening efficiency. Noah helped, too, primarily by restraining Rule from tearing the entire city apart brick by brick to find his missing woman. Between the two of them—ably assisted by Bette, Tess's shop manager, who herded the curious covenmates out the back door and out of the way—they got him into a cab and unloaded him into the front hall of the club in less than fifteen minutes.

If their cabbie didn't quit his job and join the NASCAR circuit, he was wasting his life.

Rafe was waiting for them in the hallway, along with a distinctly unhappy Tobias Walker, the head of Vircolac's security.

"What happened?" Rule demanded, almost before his feet hit the hallway tile. "What do you know?"

"We're working on it," the Felix said, holding up his hands in a useless calming gesture. "As far as we know, she is unharmed. There is no sign of a struggle, and we've already interviewed the last employee who spoke to her. According to him, she was alive and well, although a little miffed at you, at around noon."

Rule glanced at the ornate clock on the hall table. "That was almost an hour ago. No one has seen her since then?"

The Felix shook his head.

"No, but we have security cameras covering almost every inch of this club," Tobias said, stepping forward, his expression grim. "I've already pulled the tapes, and I have my entire staff combing through them. Trust me, Rule, we'll find her."

Rule had met Tobias the last time he'd been Above, and he knew the Lupine to be both reliable and very good at his job. But that didn't mean Rule didn't want to tear someone—anyone—into little bloody pieces just then.

"She was supposed to be under twenty-four-hour surveillance. She wasn't supposed to go near a *window* unsupervised! Who the hell fell down on the job?"

Tobias gritted his teeth. "No one fell down, Rule. The club is under twenty-four-hour surveillance, and it's completely inaccessible to anyone who isn't either a member or part of the staff. There were guards, footmen, and waitstaff on every floor. Abby wasn't left alone. We did our jobs. And we'll keep doing them until we find out what happened to her."

"Find out *now*."

Rafe stepped between the two men. Later Rule might be grateful for that, but now he just wanted to get his hands on someone, and Tobias was convenient. Plus, the Lupine was tough. He'd put up a nice bloody struggle.

"We are working on it," the Felix said. "Not just Tobias's staff, but mine as well. We will find her, I promise you. Even Fiona has gotten involved. She has called in some favors of her own and sent a small army of changelings out into the city to look for her. Abby will be all right."

"Tell them to concentrate on Battery Park City," Tess said, stepping forward and linking hands with her husband. "That's where the sisters think Uzkiel is hiding, and I have a bad feeling that if Abby is missing, that thing has something to do with it."

A shiver of pure fear ripped down Rule's spine. "If Uzkiel has her, we don't have a second to lose."

"Perhaps, but perhaps not," Rafe said. "We do have one thing going for us. It is the middle of the afternoon. Daylight. Even if one of Uzkiel's minions has captured Abby, the fiend will not be able to harm her until nightfall."

Tess winced. "The building they're in has a basement. Windowless. He'd be able to function down there."

Rule took a deep, steadying breath. As hard as the panic fought to overtake him, he knew he'd be no use to Abby unless he maintained control. "Function, yes, but not well. He would not be able to perform magic, and since the *solus* spell is what he wants, he will not be able to harm her until tonight. Fiends are not only affected by the light of the sun; they are weakened by its energy. Even if they cannot see the light, they are not at their full power until nightfall. So we have a little over four hours to find out where she's gone."

Tobias raised a hand to his ear and turned his head to the side, his expression intent. It took Rule a second to realize Tobias was listening to something in a wireless earphone.

"Still not sure where she's gone," he said after a long, tense moment, "but I think we know how she got there. Camera on the back entrance recorded Abby leaving at twelve-oh-seven this afternoon, and she wasn't alone."

"At least there's that," Tess said, sounding slightly relieved. "She had the sense not to go anywhere alone. Who did she take with her?"

"Carly," Tobias answered, "but it was Carly who did the taking. The alley camera shows her hitting Abby on the back of the head after they exited the building and knocking her unconscious. She carried her out of the alley and, we suspect, into a waiting vehicle."

Rule swore. "So you won't be able to track her then. Not if they drove away."

"Not by scent, but I have a very large staff and a very big grudge to settle. We'll start looking for treads and knocking on doors. If we have to interview every person in this city, we'll do it. Carly was pack. Her betrayal is a disgrace to us all."

Everybody turned when the front door slammed open and Samantha came skidding to a stop on the polished tile. "Oh, my God! Is it true?"

Tobias nodded shortly. "It looks like it is. What have you heard?"

Samantha shook her head and gulped in a deep breath. "Just the alarm. Since Graham and Missy are out of town, I was covering a meeting for him with one of our liquor distributors. I ran all the way back here. Scott told me about the tape just now. He was leaving when I came up the steps."

Rule looked past her businesslike skirt suit and down at her bare feet. Little shreds of nylon clung to the fair skin, the ragged remains of which had probably started the day as panty hose. The Lupine's shoes were nowhere to be seen.

"When was the last time you saw her?" Tobias demanded, all his attention focused on sniffing out any potential leads.

"Carly?" Samantha looked vaguely green as she said the name, as if the idea of her friend's involvement nauseated her. "I was hoping I'd heard wrong. I can't believe she would do something like this. I just talked to her the day before yesterday. On the phone. She was having a rough shift that night. A lot of people got hurt in the rioting in the Financial District."

"Did she say anything odd?"

"Not a word. She sounded completely normal. Tired, but normal."

"And she never gave the slightest indication she might be planning something like this? Never hinted that she had any reason she might want to hurt Abby?"

"Of course not, Tobe! Carly is a sweetheart. You know her. She's pack." Samantha looked hurt and confused, but no more so than any of them. "And even if she had said something like that, you know I would have told you. It would have set off every alarm in my head. I would have thought she needed serious help."

"Well, Abby is the one who needs our help now," Tobias said. He didn't look at all reassured by what Samantha had told them. "Do you know if Carly has a car?"

"She does. I always said she was crazy, but she said that once you've driven an ambulance through Manhattan at rush hour, a regular car seemed positively sane."

"What kind is it?"

Samantha frowned. "A little thing. Used. An old VW Rabbit, I think. Gray. It's almost more primer than paint. She said she didn't see the point in getting it repainted when it would just get scratched or dinged again inside of a week."

"You don't know her plate numbers, do you?"

"I'm her friend, Tobe, not a witness to her hit-and-run accident. That's not the kind of thing I pay attention to. Why would I?"

Just in case she got mixed up in a demonic plot for world domination?

Rule turned to Tobias. "Can you find out that kind of information?"

"I can try. I'll see if any of our people works at Motor Vehicles."

"I will contact her employer," Rafe offered, "and see if I can obtain copies of her logs to determine exactly where she's been working over the last few days. Maybe we will find something valuable in tracing her movements."

"You can get that stuff? Those call sheets are usually as confidential as hospital records." Tobias sounded impressed.

Tess snorted. "You'd be amazed at what Mr. Pussycat can get his hands on when he lays on the charm and waves around a big stack of money."

"We all have our little talents," the Felix demurred.

"Well, for the moment, mine is going to be good old-fashioned legwork." Tess grimaced. "I'm going to find out the name and address of that building the sisters pointed us to. If Uzkiel is involved in Abby's abduction—and I think her disappearance is too big a coincidence to discount the possibility—we're going to want to know where he might be hiding."

Rule nodded. At the moment, it was the biggest gesture he could manage, given that every muscle in his body had locked down in rage and fear. He turned blazing eyes on Tobias. "I want to see these security tapes. Then I want the best trackers you have to go over every last inch of the alley with me. If there's the slightest chance of picking up her scent, I'm going to find it." His hands clenched until the knuckles turned a stark, bloodless white. "And when I find her, there will be more than just hell to pay."

CHAPTER TWENTY-EIGHT

Abby woke with the feeling that a very large person had placed her head under the leg of his chair and then sat down. Hard. If her skull wasn't cracked straight through, it would be a miracle.

You can thank me for that later.

Abby didn't even try to lift her eyelids, let alone move her jaw. The most she could manage was a thought, and she couldn't even do that loudly. *Louamides?*

The one and only. How you feeling?

Like last week's moldy cat food. You?

Hey, all I can feel is you, but judging by that, I'd say that's a fairly accurate summary.

Where am I? Er, I mean, where are we?

Damned if I know. You're the one with the eyes. How about you open 'em and take a look around?

Abby groaned. *I was afraid you were going to say something like that.*

I would say take your time, but under the circumstances, I'm not going to be able to recommend that as a first-line strategy.

The only thing Abby could see when she first

opened her eyes was blackness, and considering even that felt like an ice pick to the retinas, she could only be grateful no one had thought to leave a light burning for her. After a moment the darkness began to take on depth and she found that if she held her hand about six inches from the end of her nose, she could just barely make out that there was something there.

She discovered simultaneously that any movement beyond shallow breathing sent nausea rolling through her like an invading army.

"Okay, that was so not worth it," she muttered, concentrating very hard on breathing very, very slowly through her nose.

Sheesh, this human thing is so limiting. Let me help with that.

Abby didn't know what the demon was talking about, and until the urge to vomit subsided, she didn't really care.

"I think I may have a concussion."

She did not get the world's most sympathetic feeling from Lou. *You're going to have worse if you don't take another look around and see if there's a way to get us out of here.*

"Why is that my job?"

You're the one with opposable thumbs. Actually, you're the one with any sort of corporeal being of any kind at the moment. You've been appointed.

"Swell."

It took Abby another minute or two to tamp down the nausea enough to open her eyes and take another look around. This time, she could actually see things.

It was a little like watching one of those TV shows on ghost hunting, where the people wandered through old houses with all the lights off, filming everything with night-vision cameras. She could see the walls and the doors of the small room around her, but everything had the appearance of black-and-white and grainy shades of gray.

"Is this really what the world looks like to you?" she asked. She couldn't imagine it. She'd go crazy in a world completely devoid of color.

At the moment it is. Normally, I'd see things in terms of their heat values, but your eyes aren't equipped for thermal imaging. Primitive, really.

Abby frowned and very slowly and very carefully turned her head to glance around the entire room. If she moved at a rate of approximately one millimeter per minute, she could keep her stomach from turning itself inside out.

The room she lay in was large and empty, not just of other living things but of other things in general. She saw no furniture, no boxes, no clutter, nothing to indicate anyone had ever been here before her, except for the fact that the walls were standing, so clearly someone had built it. She just couldn't tell if they'd ever been back since.

She saw no windows anywhere in the room, but two doors cut dark outlines into the cinder block walls, one at either end of the room. The walls themselves appeared bare except for a few streaky patches that looked like water damage. They didn't even sport the scrawl of graffiti to break the monochrome surface, which in itself was pretty creepy. In a city like Manhattan, pristine vertical surfaces rarely lasted an hour before someone left their mark on them. Either the building owners had a security system Fort Knox would have envied, or no one came down here. Ever.

"Um, I'm not thinking I'm real happy with this situation," Abby muttered, and carefully eased herself into a sitting position. The room swung a little around her, but everything stayed where it was supposed to. She wrinkled her nose at the musty smell.

You're not supposed to be. What? Did you think the werewolf bashed you upside the head because you forgot to mention you liked her new nail polish?

Lou's sarcasm brought the last few hours rushing back, in particular those few panicked seconds in the alley behind Vircolac when she'd realized something was horribly wrong.

Carly had invited her to lunch, and Abby had gone. It had never occurred to her not to trust the woman. After all, she was a member of the pack, was a friend of Samantha's. It wasn't like Abby had been taking candy from a stranger. There shouldn't have been a problem.

There wouldn't have been, she was sure, if it hadn't been for that glow in the back of Carly's eyes.

Abby shivered. "What was that?"

I don't know if it's got a true name. Some people call it hellfire; some call it the taint. Mostly you'll hear about people like that being demon-touched. Or fiend-touched. Either way, it spells trouble. It means Carly wasn't the only one home when she lured you out of the club. If you were Other, you would have been able to smell it. She didn't smell like she did last time.

"You're not human," Abby pointed out. "Why didn't you notice?"

Hey, what am I? Your babysitter?

"No, you're what's called my cross to bear," she grumbled, and slowly climbed to her feet.

For someone who'd been kidnapped twice in one week, Abby thought she didn't look too bad. Her clothes were wrinkled and dirty, but nothing a load of laundry wouldn't fix. She lifted a hand to her head and felt a sense of déjà vu when she reached the spot where Carly had hit her and didn't even find a lump, just a small tender patch.

Oh, good. Nothing's broken.

"Maybe not," Abby said, quickly taking inventory of any other injuries. "But it still can't be healthy. Things are going to get all scrambled in there if this keeps up."

She found no broken bones and no other serious injuries. She had a couple of minor scrapes and some very major bruising, but considering the alternatives, she figured she should count herself lucky.

You can buy a lottery ticket when we get out of here, but the getting-out part is the most pressing goal.

"It would help if I knew where 'here' was." She played a quick mental game of eeny-meeny-miney-moe and headed for the door to her right.

Wait! You're not going to just open *that, are you?*

"I thought you wanted to get out of here."

But you have no idea what might be on the other side!

Abby laid her palm against the door and raised an eyebrow. "It feels cool, so I think I can be pretty confident that the other side isn't a raging inferno. What else do you want to know?"

Who's out there? What do they want? What will they do to us if we try to escape?

"Well, the fire trick was the extent of my repertoire in these situations, so unless you plan to imbue me with some sort of psychic ability you've been hiding from me up until now, the only way to tell what's on the other side of that door is to open it."

You could at least try listening. You know, to hear if you can hear voices or anything.

"You mean just in case the villains are on the other side, outlining their plans for us in graphic detail?"

Or in case there's a chain saw–wielding psycho out there. You don't know. Don't you ever watch horror movies?

Abby snorted. "I hate to be the one to break it to you, Lou, but if we're in a horror movie, we are so already doomed. You're evil, I'm sleeping with the enemy, and we're trapped alone in the dark in what looks like a basement. By the laws of the horror genre, we should have died three scenes ago, at least."

Wow. Remind me next time I'm picking a human to hide in not to go with such a downer.

"Gladly."

Figuring it wouldn't kill her to humor him, Abby pressed her ear to the surface of the door for a moment and listened. The only thing she could hear was her own pounding heartbeat. It resembled the sound check for a speed metal band.

"Nothing," she muttered. "It looks like we're going to have to go downstairs to find out if the power going out in the middle of the thunderstorm while the escaped serial killer is on the loose had anything to do with that ear-piercing scream we heard coming from the basement of our supposedly empty house a few minutes ago."

Very funny. Do you see anything around here we can use as a weapon?

"Aside from my razor-sharp wit?" Abby shook her head. "We're going to have to take comfort in the fact that I'm not blond, stacked, or a cheerleader, and hope God doesn't hold grudges over the occasional crisis of faith." She took a deep breath and curled her fingers around the doorknob. "Here goes."

Holding her breath, Abby said a quick prayer and eased open the door as quietly as possible. She didn't even breathe as she cautiously poked her head out of the room and glanced around.

The door opened into a hallway, equally dark as the room, stretching in either direction for at least as far as Abby could see. She scowled.

Now, see, I don't like this, she thought to Lou, glad she was wearing sneakers, which at least minimized the sound of her footsteps on the bare concrete floor. *Who kidnaps someone, transports their unconscious body to a remote location, then goes away and leaves them all alone without even a token henchman to stand guard and make sure they don't run away?*

Carly?

No. I don't know what her damage was, but when

she was in her right mind, she seemed way too smart for that. Something weird is going on here.

Abby eased her way out into the hall and headed to the right. It seemed to have worked last time. The hall was as bare as the room she'd just left, nothing but walls and floor, though out here the distinct odor of dampness was even stronger. She had the feeling that if she reached out and touched the walls, she would feel the slime of accumulated mildew. Somehow, she stifled that urge.

Lou's enhanced night vision allowed her to walk through the hall without bumping into anything, but she still moved slowly, as if she didn't quite trust the unfamiliar perspective. An occasional door broke the solid line of the wall at her right, but after glancing in the first two and seeing bare rooms nearly identical to the one she'd just left, she ignored them and walked forward. Several minutes after she started, she reached another wall and realized she'd hit a dead end.

She swore under her breath.

Shhh!

Abby just gritted her teeth and turned around to retrace her steps. *I knew I should have taken that left turn at Albuquerque.*

Do you know what time it is?

Why?

Because I'm getting my nails done at six and I don't want to be late. Because I asked!

Abby raised her left arm almost to her face before she could make out the tiny lines on her watch face. *Four forty-six. Satisfied?*

Not hardly. It's nearly sundown.

So?

So the way people like Carly get fiend-touched is by consorting with fiends. And archfiends like Uzkiel do their best work in the dark.

Oh, bother. Abby hurried her steps, still trying to avoid making too much noise. *That makes me wonder, though. If fiends aren't supposed to be able to go out in the dark, how come I could? I mean, you're a fiend.*

Yeah, but I'm only a little evil. She could practically feel him shrug. *I'm a minor fiend. Don't tell anyone I said this, but I come from a long line of imps. We're less in the business of evil for the sake of evil than we are in the habit of picking the wrong side in any contest of wills. If I told you how much I've lost in the football pool over the years . . .*

So, because you're not bent on an existence of willful destruction and mayhem, I don't burst into flames?

Pretty much. If you stayed outside too long, you'd get a hell of a bad burn, but no, spontaneous combustion ain't in the cards for you.

Abby passed the room she'd exited a few minutes ago—at least, she was pretty sure it was the same room—and kept walking. She still couldn't see more than five feet ahead of her, but the hall seemed pretty straight, and since she'd only seen doors in the one side of it, she guessed she was walking along the outside wall of whatever building she was in. The lack of windows pretty much guaranteed that it was either a nuclear fallout shelter or a basement. Judging by the lack of canned goods and army surplus blankets, she'd put her money on the basement theory. And where there were basements, eventually there would be stairs.

"Ah-ha!" she breathed. There they were, at the end of the hallway, just three feet ahead. She'd been right. She should have turned left. "Ground floor. Coats, shoes, ladies' lingerie."

Placing one hand on the cold surface of a chipped metal handrail, Abby began to climb.

Wait! Did you hear that?

"Hear what?"

Would you keep your voice down! I thought I heard something.

Abby paused for a moment, then resumed climbing. *I didn't hear anything.*

I could have sworn I heard something.

Well, if you heard it, I should have, too, and I didn't hear anything.

You must be tone-deaf as well as night-blind. Listen. No, wait! Sniff!

Sniff? What do I look like, a bloodhound?

Don't tell me you can't smell that.

Smell what? Abby inhaled deeply and had to struggle against the urge to cough as her lungs flooded with probably toxic mold spores. *All I smell is a bad case of black lung waiting to happen.*

I smell sulfur.

She froze. *What?*

I smell sulfur, Lou repeated, *and it's getting stronger the higher we climb. There's a fiend up there. At least one. I think we should go back the way we came.*

Abby tried to steady her heartbeat. For one horrible instant, her mind had gone blank with panic, but panic wasn't going to get her out of there, let alone get her out of there with all her limbs and her soul intact.

There's no point in going back the way we came. It's a dead end. If we go back there, we're trapped.

There was another door in the room. Maybe it leads to a rear exit.

We're in a basement, Lou. In order to get out, we're going to have to go up. Personally, I'd rather not take the chance of getting lost in what looked like a maze of identical rooms.

And I'd rather not take the chance of getting my head ripped from my body and used as a Hacky Sack.

Abby swallowed hard and tried to grin. *What are you worried about? It's my head.*

Yeah, well, I'm using it at the moment.

She grew serious and leaned her weight on the handrail. *This is the way out, Lou. Either we can try it and see where it leads, or we can go back and sit in that little room until someone comes to strap us to the sacrificial altar. I don't know about you, but if I'm going to wind up dead, I'd rather meet the situation head-on, not wait for it to come get me like some kind of boogeyman.*

Trust me. The boogeyman is a pussycat compared to Uzkiel.

Dead is dead.

Yeah, but there's dead fast and painless and then there's dead at the hands of the cruelest fiend in the Underworld.

It still equals not breathing, right?

Lou fell silent, and Abby unclenched her fingers from the handrail. She might be all bluster and logic with the fiend inside her head, but she was all adrenaline and terror everywhere else.

You realize I can hear what you're thinking, right?

Keep your mind to yourself, she groused, and resumed the climb.

She counted twenty steps before she stopped. Maybe she was becoming hypersensitive, but she had begun to pick up the soft sound of the soles of her sneakers each time they landed on a stair tread. The steps might be concrete rather than creaky wood, but that didn't matter if whatever waited at the top could hear the pitter-patter of her little feet. Keeping one hand on the railing, she raised her right foot to the next step and leaned down.

What are you doing now?

My brother always said there was a reason Native American raiding parties didn't wear Nikes.

She untied the laces and removed the sneaker, shivering when her foot touched the cold surface of the floor. Even through her thick athletic socks, the concrete chilled her. She carefully repeated the process on the other foot, then tied the laces of the two shoes together and dangled them over her shoulder.

Now she just had to hope Noah's advice was enough to save her bacon.

Her brother was ten years older than her, so she barely remembered him before he'd left home to enlist. By the time she'd really gotten to know him, he was already a soldier, and some of her fondest memories were of times when he'd played "guerrilla fighter" with her, much to their mother's dismay.

Do whatever you can to make yourself quiet, he'd said, helping Abby pick her way through the woods behind their house and seeing how far she could go without scaring the rabbits. *Take off anything that jingles, like belts or jewelry, and go barefoot if you can. Feet make less noise than shoes. But once you've got your gear quiet, remember not to try too hard. No one makes more noise than a fellow who's trying to make none.*

All at once, she wished desperately that Noah were here with her. If her brother had been nearby, he would have taken care of her. She wouldn't have been half so frightened if she'd had Noah to lean on.

Or at least one of his really big guns.

Bullets don't do much good against the armies of darkness. Didn't anyone ever teach you that?

Maybe not, but even in this neighborhood, if I fired an AK-47, you could bet someone would call the cops. It never hurts to bring in reinforcements.

Cops don't do much good with demons, either.

Gee, thanks, Little Miss Mary Sunshine. And you called me a downer.

She continued to climb, wondering how long this stairway could possibly last. It seemed as if she'd climbed at least a flight, but she hadn't even reached a landing, let alone the next level.

Oh, by the way, Lou said, his tone suspiciously casual, *there's one thing I should probably mention.*

Abby scowled. *What thing?*

That spell I know . . . the one Uzkiel is after . . .

The one that will enable the destruction of all that's good and decent in the universe?

Yeah, that one.

What about it?

Well, I can't teach it to you, 'cause that would kill me, which seems really stupid considering all the trouble I've gone to not to die. But I've been thinking. . . .

That frightens me.

I've been thinking that if you knew the first part of it, like the first word, you'd be able to tell if it was coming.

Abby froze. *Why would I need to know if it's coming, Lou? If you recite the spell, you and I will both die, right? So why would it matter if I had five more seconds to prepare?*

Because. If we've gotta go, wouldn't you want to take Uzkiel with us?

That wasn't a question she wanted to answer. She wanted too much to live to care about who she took with her when she died.

The minute she thought that, she knew it was a lie. Yes, she wanted to stay alive, but she wanted Rule to stay alive, too. And Noah and Samantha and Tess and Rafe and Missy, and even Graham, even if she'd never met him, because Missy loved him and because her latest baby should grow up knowing its daddy.

Abby closed her eyes and gritted her teeth against

the impulse to cry. Now was not the time to break down. *We'll cross that bridge when we come to it, okay?*

Sure. Whatever.

Heart heavy in her chest, Abby resumed her climb. She had to keep going. Like she'd said, their chances of escape might be slim, but that didn't mean she could stop trying.

Abby?

Yeah?

It's "Spirits." If you follow along and say it with me, Uzkiel won't stand a chance.

And, she knew, neither would they.

She felt her throat knot up. *Yeah. Okay.*

CHAPTER TWENTY-NINE

Rule gritted his teeth and tried not to notice that the alley behind the club had already begun to fall into shadow. Dusk was less than an hour away, and he still hadn't managed to locate any sign of Abby's trail. He and Tobias and two seasoned Lupine trackers had combed the alley and the entire block around the club three times but had turned up nothing.

"If she hadn't used a car, maybe," one of the trackers had said, looking apologetic. "Or if she had a mechanical problem. But the car was clean. No leaks, no burnt rubber. A Lupine would know we could track those, so she made sure there weren't any. I'm sorry."

Rule didn't want an apology; he wanted blood. Not the tracker's, maybe, but Carly's definitely, and that of anyone else who stood between him and Abby.

"There's still a chance Rafe will be able to get those duty logs," Tobias murmured, coming to stand beside him in the diminishing light. "He should be back any minute. And every Other officer on the force is out looking for Carly's car. The minute they find it, we'll know. I swear."

Rule just nodded. He couldn't bring himself to speak. He'd lost the ability hours ago. Now he knew that if he opened his mouth, the only thing to emerge would be a primitive, earsplitting howl of rage.

The Lupine jerked his head toward the club's rear entrance. "Let's go inside. We're not finding anything out here, and Rafe and Tess should be back soon."

Reluctantly, Rule let himself be led inside. His helplessness maddened him. He commanded an army in the Below, planned strategy, and executed operations. Entire squadrons jumped at his faintest word, and no one dared to disobey his orders. He answered to the prime minister and the prime minister only. And yet here Rule could not even protect his own woman.

He felt Abby's absence like a raw, bleeding wound in his chest. A huge part of him had been torn away, a part so new he should barely have noticed the difference, yet here he was, struggling for his next breath. For the next beat of his heart. Their relationship was still new. Hell, it practically still had the dew on, yet if this was a sample of what his life would be like without her, he knew he wanted no part of it.

Never fall in love with a mortal.

The advice served as a mantra to his kind, as well as to others like him, the Fae, and even to vampires, to a certain extent. No one wanted to live forever and yet watch the one they loved age and die before their eyes. No heart, mortal or immortal, had been designed to withstand that kind of trauma. It had never occurred to Rule that he would one day have to face such a decision. There was no turning his back on this relationship now, but in forty or fifty or sixty years, when Abby's lifetime ended, he would have to decide whether or not he could go on without her.

He'd never imagined the decision would be so easy. He'd already made it.

Abby was his life. When hers ended, so would his. And since he planned on living a good long time to come, he was damned well going to get her back tonight.

Rule and Tobias stepped into the club's main hall and nearly bumped into Tess hurrying down it in their direction. The expression on her face made his heart flip inside his chest.

"What did you find?" he demanded, sprinting the last few steps toward her.

"The old Hudson Shipping and Mercantile Building." She grinned. "It's not right on the water, but Claire got in within a few blocks. It's one of the few old buildings left after the Battery Park City Authority got done with the neighborhood. Even they weren't willing to take the place on."

Rule grabbed her by the arm and spun her toward the front entrance. "You can tell me why not in the car. Tobias, get in touch with Rafe," Rule yelled over his shoulder. "Tell him where we're going and have him meet us there. Get the same message to Noah. Then gather whoever you can and follow us. Keep it quiet if you can and meet us one block east so we can set a plan. I want everyone there in twenty minutes."

"Done!"

Rule grabbed a coat from the closet and threw it

at her. He had no idea if it was actually hers, and he didn't care. Across the hall, he barged into Graham's office and grabbed his scabbard and sword and the small utility pack he'd stored there out of respect for Graham's policy of no weapons in the club.

"Rule," Tess protested, yanking the coat off her head where it had landed, "it's rush hour. It's going to take at least forty-five minutes to get down to that part of the city."

"Not if I have anything to say about it." He grabbed her again and dragged her out the door. She barely managed to grab her purse on the way out. "You're a witch. Get us a cab. Now."

Tess scowled at him. "Normally I'd tell you to shove it, because this is *so* against the rules. But these are extenuating circumstances." She furrowed her brow, closed her eyes, and chanted something under her breath. Five seconds later a very bewildered-looking cabbie pulled to a stop at the curb in front of them. "I'll try to get the traffic and the lights, too, but there's only so much you can do in this town, even with magic. If we fiddle with too many lights, we're going to get broadsided, and then we won't be any good to Abby anyway."

"Fine. Whatever." He shoved her into the cab and climbed in beside her. "Tell the driver where to go, make him do it fast, then fill me in on where we're headed."

"Wow, that debonair charm of yours makes it easy to see why Abby finds you irresistible," Tess grumbled, but she followed his orders, and just then that was all that mattered.

"The building," he prompted.

"Right." She settled back against the seat of the cab, half-turned to face him. "It was originally built in 1841 as warehouses and offices for the Hudson Shipping and Mercantile Company. The business belonged to a fellow named Isaiah Horner and his partner, Jonas Chapman. Apparently, these guys made their first fortune in the slave trade, but they saw which way the wind was blowing before the Civil War and tried to clean up their act by switching to coffee and cocoa. And a bit of opium."

"Much more respectable."

"Exactly. Anyway, they built the warehouse to store their goods, and rumors were that they dug a two-level basement under it to store some of their less legal imports. Including the last couple of cargoes of slaves they couldn't resist cashing in on."

"So there were deaths in the building?"

"Where slavers were involved, there were always deaths, but that was only the beginning of the building's shining history. Horner and Chapman went bankrupt just before the end of the Civil War. Apparently, they were convinced the South would remain independent and become a lucrative trading partner for them." Tess shook her head. "Not the brightest souls in the history books. When they had a little trouble unloading the property to pay off their creditors, they decided to pioneer that old classic scam, arson-for-the-insurance-payout."

Rule could see where this was headed, especially since Claire had made clear the place had more than its share of negative energy. "Let me guess. They didn't wait until it was empty, did they?"

"Not a chance. Torched the thing in the middle of a shift for the sailmakers they'd leased the space to. A hundred and thirteen people died, mostly immigrant women and kids."

"Dare I hope that was the extent of it?"

"Oh, you optimist, you. Just the beginning. Since that original fire, the building has gone up in flames three more times. Every time there have been fatalities, but strangely enough, the structure has never been damaged badly enough to warrant tearing the place down. It's also been the site of two suicides, both during the Great Depression, and at least one murder, in the early fifties. And in 1972 the police found evidence of a bunch of idiots playing at summoning using the old living-sacrifice trick."

He winced. "Human?"

"The police only ever found evidence of animal bones, but one of the cult members claimed they'd killed a woman. He was diagnosed schizophrenic and delusional, so they pretty much ignored him, but given the history . . ."

"Yes. Uzkiel should feel right at home."

CHAPTER THIRTY

By the time she reached the top of the stairway, Abby could smell the sulfur, too. It filled her nose with its rotting stench and made the task of breathing singularly unpleasant.

Okay, I can smell it now. Do you hear anything that I don't?

I'm not a guard dog, the fiend snapped.

Don't yell at me. I'm just trying to save our asses. Well, my ass and your whatever you call your noncorporeal backside.

Abby knew it was the tension making them snap at each other, and to tell the truth, she preferred it to being alone with only her own thoughts for company. At least the sniping gave her something else to focus on, other than the knot in her throat and the grinding in her stomach.

She pressed her back against the wall and peered into the darkness. The difference between her own night vision and Lou's had been startling at first, but now that she'd grown used to seeing with his acuity, she realized the pitch blackness of the building they were in looked dark even to him. She could see no more than about five feet in any direction, and the inky space beyond that point had taken on a sinister quality that made the hair on her arms stand on end.

That's not just the dark, Lou informed her grudgingly. *It's this place. There's some nasty energy here. Restless spirits and everything. Uzkiel must be in hog heaven.*

Are you telling me this place is haunted?

As Salem.

Great. Abby blew out a silent breath. *Just what I wanted to hear.*

Trust me, it's not the ghosts you have to worry about. At least, not much.

You're such a comfort to me.

Abby took a moment to steady her nerves, then gave up. She was as steady as she was going to get.

Which way do you think the smell is coming from? she thought.

Why?

So I can head in the opposite direction.

Right.

Good. We'll go left. Left worked last time.

Instinctively, Abby reached up to touch her gold and garnet cross. The action, the familiarity of it, gave her comfort. She just couldn't decide if the symbol itself still offered any.

I guess this is proof of that whole "demons aren't inherently evil" thing.

What is?

The fact that I can be possessed and still wear this. Sounds like proof to me.

It's proof that you can't drive one of us away with a symbol, Lou agreed, *but that doesn't make it proof of the absence of God.*

Abby did a double take in the darkness. *You believe in God?*

Well, I've never met him, if that's what you're asking. . . .

I'm asking if you believe.

The longer you live, the harder it gets to believe in anything, especially when you're living Below, he said. *I can tell you, though, that when you've been around as long as I have and seen as much as I have, you have to believe there's some kind of method to all this madness. I don't know if that's God, but it's something.*

Abby thought about that for a minute, then laughed silently. *I must be preparing to die,* she thought. *I'm standing in the dark debating philosophy with a fiend.*

Right. And what you should be doing is RUNNING!

Her instincts reached her feet before her brain, but that was okay with Abby. By the time she processed Lou's scream of panic, she'd already sprinted twenty feet down the hall and had no plans to stop.

Unfortunately, her plans changed when a hand reached out, caught a fistful of her hair, and yanked her to a stop.

Abby couldn't help it. She screamed. The force of the pull felt like it had taken half her scalp off with it, bringing tears to her eyes and making the corridor swim across her vision. She fell to her hands and knees and felt a new, stronger wave of nausea overtake her.

"Going somewhere, little human?" a voice rasped in the darkness. Abby couldn't turn her head to see who it had come from, but she didn't need to. She recognized the voice and the leg of the jumpsuit at the edge of her vision. The leg and the jumpsuit belonged to Carly, but the voice belonged to Seth.

"Tsk, tsk, tsk," the fiend clucked in a mockery of concern. "We can't have that, can we?" The hand in Abby's hair jerked back and forth in time to the tsk-ing, forcing her to shake her head in agreement. "After all, the party hasn't even begun, and you *are* the guest of honor."

Abby remained silent and concentrated on not passing out. *Do me a favor and let me stay for this, Lou. I won't shut you out, so don't you shut me out. If we're going to get through this, we're going to have to work together.*

We're not going to get through this.

Speak for yourself, she snapped. *I am* not *planning on dying tonight.*

"Come, little human," Seth hissed, and pulled Abby to her knees. She saw the inhuman voice coming from Carly's familiar, friendly face and shuddered. "I think it's time I took you to meet your host."

Every instinct Abby possessed screamed at her to *fight!*

Run!

Flee!

Away! Get Away!

—but she stomped on every one. She was in a

dark corridor in an unfamiliar building in the very physical clutches of an archfiend that was fully capable of bashing her head in just to hear it pop. Running would only hasten her death, and she wanted to put it off as long as possible.

"What? No begging? No screaming?" Seth-Carly pulled Abby along the hallway back past the stairs she'd climbed a few minutes before and down another short corridor. "By now, you humans are usually screaming like banshees. It's one of my favorite parts."

Abby kept her silence, at least partly because it seemed to annoy the fiend.

"Well, no matter," it chuckled. "You'll scream enough before the night is over, I assure you."

Wincing at the pain in her scalp, Abby put her hand on her cross and prayed, really fervently prayed, the fiend was wrong.

Faith doesn't need to be blind, she remembered, *and you can have it in more than one thing. I have it in God, and I have it in the guys in my squad, and I have it in the people who love me.*

And she, Abby realized, had it in Rule.

All at once, it was like a veil of calm settled over her. Oh, she was still afraid; she was scared shitless, to use one of Noah's expressions, but she realized right then that she wasn't alone. Rule was on his way, and he would move the Above and the Below if he had to in the attempt to save her. Sure, he might not succeed, but he was going to try. She knew that with the first unshakable faith she'd felt in a very long time.

That's all well and good, Lou said, sounding strained, *but please don't tell me you're going to turn into a damsel in distress and wilt like a delicate flower until your knight in shining armor comes charging to the rescue.*

Abby nearly grinned, because, as she had just discovered, where there was faith, there was hope. *I am a delicate flower. But even delicate flowers have thorns.*

She caught a glimpse of a crimson glow an instant before Seth-Carly gave a shove and sent her stumbling into another stone room, only this one was far from empty. She landed on the floor in an inelegant sprawl, but she had time to register a few details on the way down. The bloody light came from a series of torches mounted at shoulder height around the room, but the fire they burned with looked dim and unnatural. It also stirred a memory, a far from pleasant one. The light they gave off reminded her of the sickly crimson light in the vision Tess had shown her. The one in which Uzkiel had triumphed.

Abby beat back the surge of panic.

"Have you brought me a present, Set-halikel?"

The voice hissed from behind her, as if a great serpent had mastered the power of human speech, and just the sound was enough to feed Abby's fear.

It's magic. It's part of his magic, Lou whispered. *The fear. He generates it, like a toxic cloud. Try to fight it.*

Abby had no intention of giving in. She took her time getting her hands and knees under herself and pushing into an upright position. She used the time to prepare herself for what she would see when she turned to face the archfiend. Suddenly she was glad for Tess's scare tactics. At least Uzkiel's appearance wouldn't take her by surprise.

She still had to fight to keep from flinching. It looked as it had in the vision, an unnatural mishmash of incongruous parts. The bovine head, the serpentine torso, the misshapen satyric legs. Its hideousness was palpable, like a presence in the room, but Abby refused to let it cow her.

What's the point of faith, she thought, *if you don't test it?*

"Wow," she drawled, praying for strength to keep her knees from knocking, deliverance for her soul in case Rule came too late to help her, and speed to hurry that help along. "It's a little late for Halloween. You get a discount on the ugly freak costume?"

She moved too slowly. The fiend crossed the space between them faster than she could blink, and when its hand touched her, she fulfilled Seth's prediction and screamed.

Rule longed for nothing more than to burst into the building, sword swinging and guns blasting, destroying Uzkiel and saving Abby in one fell swoop. But the daring rescue, Rule knew, only worked that way in Faerie stories.

That was the reason that he skulked through the hallways of the Hudson Shipping building like a thief, following Noah's military hand signals and beating back his primitive impatience with every breath. Their extraction team, as Noah had labeled it, had assembled on the next block to arm themselves and review the rules of the operation before moving on the abandoned building that served as Uzkiel's headquarters on this plane.

Rafe had taken point, shifting into his wereform as soon as they stepped in the front doors, using his feline stealth to ease through the darkened corridors unseen and unheard. Behind him ranged a compact line of warriors, beginning with Rule and including Tobias and his two best soldiers, Silverbacks named Simon and Huck. Noah brought up the rear, the only one of them who needed to bother with night-vision goggles, carefully guarding their exit. He had his favorite assault rifle in his hands and a compact pack filled with enough plastic to level the lower half of Manhattan. "Just in case."

A small army of Lupines was stationed outside the building, covering the other entrances and waiting in case they received a call for backup. At least three of them, Rule knew, were also in Rafe's car with Tess, guarding her. It looked more like physically restraining her to Rule, but it wasn't his job to get involved in a marital spat.

His eyes had adjusted quickly to the darkness, and they tracked Rafe's movements as the Felix padded through the seemingly deserted building, following his nose, his keen night vision, and his instincts, toward Abby.

"I may not have the nose of a wolf," he'd said, "but my nose is sharp enough and my eyes sharper. I'll find her. The scent of sulfur is not easy to miss."

Rule hoped not, because he hadn't caught a whiff

of it yet. Rafe, though, moved through the empty halls as if he knew where he was going. He led the way to the back of the first floor and shifted back to human just long enough to raise the flat of his hand to signal the others to stop. He pointed toward the floor, and Rule looked past him to see the outline of a set of stairs leading downward. Gesturing to the others to follow single file, Rule gave Rafe the okay and moved forward.

The minute they broke below the ground floor, Rule felt the oppressive presence of evil. Much of it, he knew, came from Uzkiel, but not all of it. There was a subtler chill in the air, the kind that came from recorded misery and trapped spirits. No wonder the fiend had chosen this place.

When they reached the first basement level they paused while Rafe scented the air. Tobias, though, didn't see the need to wait. He tapped Rule on the back and gestured toward the right, down a hall that led into the center of the building. Before the demon could pass on the message, Rafe turned and indicated the same direction.

The hair on the back of Rule's neck stood up. He didn't bother to wonder if the others were right. Every sense he possessed told him they were getting close.

Single file, the men moved silently down the short corridor, passing like shadows through the darkness. Their plans were sound and their execution flawless, right up to the point when Abby's scream shattered the darkness.

CHAPTER THIRTY-ONE

afe tried to stop him, but Rule barreled past him like a freight train. Nothing existed in Rule's universe except Abby, and Abby was in pain. He had to get to her.

It took Tobias, Simon, and Huck to tackle Rule to the ground, while Rafe caught Noah when the human would have raced past the commotion. Still, even three of them couldn't hold Rule. He threw them off and burst through the door at the end of the hall with his sword blazing a trail ahead of him.

"ABBY!"

"How touching." It was Seth who greeted him, Seth in Carly's body. The evil smile on the sweet face looked doubly repulsive. Rule leaped forward, intent on slicing Carly's head from her body.

A small hand on his forearm stopped him.

It was Abby's hand, but when he looked at her face, he felt every cell in his body freeze with stony disbelief. Behind Abby's smiling mismatched eyes burned the evil of an archfiend.

"Now, don't hurt my servant," the thing inside Abigail purred, moving to stand beside a smirking

Seth. "Or I might feel inclined to exact revenge. And these human bodies are so very fragile. . . ." She/it swept one hand down over her torso, and her/its lips curved in a hideous smile.

"Madre de Dios!"

Through the buzzing in his ears, Rule heard the other men swarm into the room and registered Rafe's horrified exclamation, but he couldn't take his eyes off Abigail. Off what used to be Abigail.

She looked the way she always had, as ridiculously, beautifully plain as ever, her pale skin unmarred, her features as pure and perfect as ever. But behind her brown and blue eyes lurked an evil so pure and terrible it seemed as if the paradox of it would rend the fabric of the universe.

Uzkiel had possessed Abby. Her soul was imprisoned somewhere inside her while the fiend spoke with her tongue and moved with her body. Rule could think of no torture more vile. He felt his heart cracking into hundreds of tiny pieces.

"What's the matter, Rule?" she/it taunted. "Don't I please you anymore? Don't you love me anymore? Don't you want to touch me?"

She/it laid her/its hands on Rule's chest and leaned against him, letting her breasts press against him. He felt his skin crawl and fought against twin waves of fury and despair. He had come here to destroy Uzkiel, but how could he raise his hand against Abby? He could more easily slice through his own heart.

"What the fuck *have you done?"*

Noah's howl would have done any Lupine proud.

It tore from him in a choking agony, nearly shaking the walls of the room. Huck and Simon grabbed at Noah, but he spun out of their reach and charged toward the fiends. Rule reached out a hand to stop him, but he dodged and hit Seth-Carly at a dead run. The two figures flew halfway across the room and slammed against the opposite wall. Noah raised his weapon, but Seth slapped it away and flipped their bodies, pinning the human to the concrete floor.

"Ah, you must be the doting brother," the thing inside Abby said, amusement dripping from its tongue. "How quaint to think you would save her. But I'm afraid she's mine now. Well, mine and Louamides', but I'll fix that soon enough." It turned back toward Rule and smiled a hideous smile with the mouth he had loved to taste. "It's a little crowded in here with the three of us, but we must all make sacrifices in the pursuit of greatness. Louamides will just have to make a bigger sacrifice than the rest of us. Except maybe the human girl. Do you think she'll miss her sanity? The humans I possess never seem to keep it after I'm gone."

The rage and anguish that had paralyzed Rule suddenly loosened, like rock in an avalanche. He forced his mouth into a sneer and lowered the point of his sword to the ground. No matter what the fiend tried to tell Rule, he knew Abby was still inside her body, still somehow aware of what was happening. He just needed to find a way to reach her. A way to draw Uzkiel out and then spring the trap to imprison him.

"I think the girl is too strong for you, Uzkiel," Rule taunted, searching Abby's eyes for some sign of her presence. "I would be willing to wager you have never before possessed a human who was pure of heart like this one."

The fiend threw back Abby's head and laughed. "There is no such thing as a human with a pure heart," it derided. "Look at them." It waved toward Noah, who lay pinned to the floor beneath Carly, swearing the foulest forms of revenge Rule had ever heard. "They're so easily corrupted. A little rage, a little hatred, and look what happens. The evil comes to the surface. In the end, there's a little piece of me inside them all."

It smiled again, and Rule fought his revulsion. "But look at the source of that hatred," he said. "He hates you because of what you've done to his sister. Hate that powerful can only be born out of a love that's equally strong."

The fiend inside Abby shrugged. "What does it matter? In the end, it's the hatred that wins out, not the love."

"Are you certain of that?"

For a split second, Rule thought he saw something other than hellfire flicker in Abby's eyes. It happened so fast, his mind couldn't swear to it, but his heart soared.

"Of course," the fiend said, turning away and walking toward where Seth held Noah pinned. "I will even demonstrate for you. Set-halikel, release the human and stand."

Rule saw the look of displeasure on Seth's face, but it could not disobey, not when Uzkiel had used its full name. Reluctantly, the creature rose from its crouch on Noah's prone body and stood, its back against the cinder block wall.

"Now watch," Uzkiel said.

With a roar, Noah reached for his weapon and swung it around, squeezing off five rounds in rapid succession. The bullets sliced through the flesh below Seth-Carly's chin, severing the head from the neck and sending a lifeless corpse crumpling to the ground.

The fiend inside Abby grinned. "You see? Revenge, not love."

"I see both."

Rule jerked his head toward Rafe and the others. They swarmed Noah from behind, moving faster than his human reflexes could track, disarming him and knocking him unconscious.

"How noble you are," the fiend chuckled, "but it does you no good to spare him the consequences of attacking me next. You will all be dead soon enough."

"No." Rule looked deep into the eyes that had once belonged to Abby, the eyes he'd fallen in love with, and prayed that the woman he adored could hear his voice. "I do not believe we will be."

"Oh?" The fiend's amusement seemed to deepen. "And what makes you so certain, Watchman? The cavalry stationed outside? Do you really believe they can save you? Do you have a secret plan to defeat me?"

"No," Rule repeated, and he reached out to the essence of Abigail. His love. His heart. His mate. "I have faith."

Uzkiel laughed, a horrible grating sound that

threatened to crumble the mortar in the walls until it ended as abruptly as it had begun.

With his breath in his throat, Rule watched the strange flickering appear again in Abby's eyes, saw it linger this time. Saw her lips form silent words.

"Spirits."

The first word came so softly, Rule wasn't sure he heard it. By the time she'd spoken the third, he wished he hadn't.

"I pass this spell to Arulnagal, and forfeit all remaining years."

"Abby, no!"

He reached for her, but she struck out, the strength of both fiends within her combining to send him slamming to the ground.

In the background, Simon hissed, "What the hell is going on?"

Rafe just shook his head. "She's teaching him the spell."

"Spirits dark and powers light, sun in day and moon in night."

"Abby!"

But the strength of her voice only increased. Rule could see the power crawling beneath her skin, making it ripple and writhe as it had in the library at Vircolac when he had first made contact with Lou. Only this time, the effect had increased tenfold. This time her skin moved and bulged as Uzkiel fought to free himself from the body that had suddenly gone from being his toy to being his prison.

Rule reached for her again, but this time he never even got close. A bright silvery-golden glow began to radiate from her skin, forming a halo around her entire body. It acted like a shield around her, keeping him from touching her. Keeping him helplessly distant as he watched her destroy herself.

"A spell I cast to bind your power, subject unto me this hour." She spoke faster now, and louder still, the last traces of Uzkiel fading from her voice until she sounded only like Abby. Like herself. Like the woman willing to sacrifice her own life to save everyone else. "Fade with every spoken word, hide until my voice is heard, to call you back from prison cold and restore you to your places old. The spell is cast, the magic spun; in this place my will be done!"

She ended on a shout. Vaguely, Rule realized he had expected a flash of light or a sudden explosion, something to mark the end of the destructive spell. Instead, the light surrounding her blinked out and there was an instant of terrible silence before Abby crumpled, lifeless, to the floor.

Rule was on her in an instant, scooping her off the cold concrete to cradle her against his chest. From a distance, he heard a terrible roaring sound, but it took a moment to register that the noise was coming from him. He crushed Abby to him, as if he could will the life back into her, as if the faith he'd claimed to have just a few minutes before could somehow restore her to him. If it couldn't, his life had ended as surely as hers.

"Ow."

He drew in a shuddering breath and bent his head. His eyes burned, and his throat felt as if a fist had clenched around it and squeezed with all its might. He felt the sting of hot liquid against his cheeks and realized they were tears.

"Ow! Leggo!"

It took a moment for the noise to register and another moment for Rule's heart to resume beating.

"Too tight!"

Afraid to breathe, afraid to hope for even a second that his ears weren't deceiving him, Rule lifted his head and stared at Abby's petulant frown.

"Loosen up," she complained. "I think you're cracking a rib."

"Abby!"

Rafe's shout reflected the joy Rule felt but couldn't utter because his lips were otherwise occupied. They were currently covering every inch of Abby's face with kisses of joy and relief and love.

With a laugh, Abby reached up and grabbed him by the ears, yanking his mouth down to hers. She gave him a real kiss that reciprocated every single one of those feelings with interest.

"How is it possible?" Rafe marveled, hurrying to their sides. "Tess was certain that when someone passed the spell on to another, the spell would kill the one who taught it."

That made the smile on Abby's face fade. "It did. But the spell wasn't designed to take into account possession, let alone multiple possessions. It killed indiscriminately, but it wasn't designed to kill three entities at once."

"It killed only Uzkiel."

She shook her head. "Uzkiel and Louamides. They're both gone."

"It does not matter." Rule stroked his hands reverently over her face. "You are alive. Everything is perfect."

"Everything is good," Abby qualified, "but I was starting to get used to hearing that little perv in my head. I think I'm actually going to miss him."

Rule did a double take. "You cannot mean that."

"No, I do. You know it was his idea. In the end, he was willing to sacrifice himself to make sure Uzkiel didn't get his hands on that spell." She laid her head against Rule's shoulder. "It seems to me, Lou might have been a little less fiendish than we all imagined."

Rule bent his head and rested his cheek against her baby-fine hair. "I will inform the Parliament. At least we can ensure that he is remembered properly."

"Good." Abby sighed and raised a hand to cover her yawn. "Um, do you think we can go home now?"

Rafe laughed. "Certainly."

He offered a hand to help Rule to his feet, but the demon refused to take either of his own from Abby long enough to accept it. He simply shifted her higher against his chest and used his powerful leg muscles to lever himself to his feet.

"First, though, we should wake your brother," the Felix said. "I'm certain he would like to . . . shall we say . . . leave his mark on this place."

EPILOGUE

*t*he story of the explosion in the old Hudson
Shipping and Mercantile Building led the
news the next morning on all the New York
stations. The blasts that had brought the structure
down had been perfectly placed to make the old
building collapse in on itself without damaging any
of the adjacent properties. The best explanation the
authorities could come up with was that a professional demolition crew had gotten the wrong building. Even though there was nothing scheduled for
demolition within fifty blocks of the Hudson within
the next six months.

Abby flipped off the TV with a grin and settled
back against the pillows. Beside her, a very warm
and still sleepy demon stretched and curled a heavy
arm over her waist.

"I thought you were never going to wake up," she
murmured, turning her head to smile and press a
kiss to his sleep-warmed skin.

"It was entirely your fault," he rumbled, "keeping
me up half the night with your insatiable appetites."

Abby rolled her eyes. "Sure. It was all my appetites. Absolutely. You played no part in it whatsoever."

He winked at her. "Exactly."

That earned him a kiss, and several minutes passed before he spoke again.

"How are you feeling?" He stroked the hair away from her face, his black eyes warm and tender as they gazed into hers.

"Surprisingly okay," she answered, her mouth curving. "I was expecting to feel like I needed a psychic shower or seven, but you seem to have washed all that away most effectively."

"Glad to be of service."

"I still have a moment here or there where a stray thought hits me, and I realize I can't blame it on Lou, but I'm adjusting."

He pressed a kiss to her forehead. "I know."

They lay cuddled together beneath the covers for a few minutes, just savoring the feel of being together and of knowing no one's life hung in the balance that day. It made for a refreshing change of pace.

Finally, Rule shifted and stretched again, rolling onto his back and dragging her against his side. "If we stay in bed too much longer, I would not put it past the others to come looking for us."

"You're right." Abby made a face. "So, what do you want to do today? I mean, we don't have a fiend to catch, so . . ."

Rule turned to look at her, his expression serious. "Actually, there is something I need to do."

"What?"

She saw him hesitate and draw in a deep breath. "I am going to ask Tobias if he can find me a place in his private security firm. I think I would be a very good bodyguard."

Abby pulled back to stare at him. "But you already have a job."

He shook his head. "Not for long. I'm resigning from the Watch."

"But why?"

"Because the Watch is Below and you are here."

And just like that, Abby felt her heart melt all over again. When she spoke, her voice was soft and choked with tears. "You mean that? You would leave your home, your career, and your position in your society just to be with me?"

"I would leave my soul to be with you, Abigail."

Her smile, though watery, was radiant. "I love you, Arulnagal."

"And I love you, Abby Baker."

Their kiss, soft and sweet and lingering, tasted of forever and felt like a benediction.

When she pulled back, Abby was smiling brightly enough to light up the city. "So, what do you think? Can a demon really wind up living happily ever after?"

Rule wrapped his arms around her, and Abby nestled against him like the other half of his being. "This one will."